W9-BYX-687

DIRTY
ROTTEN
Liar

Also by Noire

Natural Born Liar

Sexy Little Liar

Lifestyles of the Rich and Shameless
(with Kiki Swinson)

Maneater
(with Mary B. Morrison)

DIRTY ROTTEN *Liar*

NOIRE

Kensington Publishing Corp.
www.kensingtonbooks.com

DAFINA BOOKS are published by

Kensington Publishing Corp.
119 West 40th Street
New York, NY 10018

All Kensington Titles, Imprints, and Distributed Lines are available at special quantity discounts for bulk purchases for sales promotions, premiums, fund-raising, and educational or institutional use. Special book excerpts or customized printings can also be created to fit specific needs. For details, write or phone the office of the Kensington special sales manager: Kensington Publishing Corp., 119 West 40th Street, New York, NY 10018, attn: Special Sales Department, Phone: 1-800-221-2647.

ISBN-13: 978-0-7582-6610-1
ISBN-10: 0-7582-6610-3
First Kensington trade paperback printing: July 2013

eISBN-13: 978-0-7582-8924-7
eISBN-10: 0-7582-8924-3
First Kensington Electronic Edition: July 2013

10 9 8 7 6 5 4 3 2 1

Printed in the United States of America

This misadventure is dedicated to my boo.
Thank you for your lub. I get it now. I finally get it.

Acknowledgments

Thank you to the Father above for super-charging my pen and blessing me with a creative mind. Big thanks go out to Black, Reem, Missy, Jay, Ree, Man, and my entire crew for keeping the train running smoothly on the tracks. Much lub to my UETBC fam and all my loyal readers and friends for riding the train every time it rolls into the station. Lub y'all! Muahhhh!

Noire

WARNING!

This here ain't no romance;
It's an urban erotic tale
Mink is out for moolah
And she's straight-up raising hell
But Dy-Nasty's greedy ass is throwing salt up in the game,
Double-crossin' tricksters like she just don't have no shame!
Sneaky little tongues,
Forked and slithering like a snake
Puttin' in mad work as they try to get that cake!
Someone's telling lies
Knowing damn well they ain't true
Is it low-down dirty Dy-Nasty?
Or rotten Mink LaRue?

CHAPTER 1

Watching your mama take her last breath was a hurtin'-ass thang.

Especially when you had a mannish hater flappin' her gums in your ear and talking trash right over her dead body!

It had all happened so fast. One minute I was chillin' down in Texas tryna pull off the flimflam of a lifetime with Uncle Suge, Bunni, and a skanky chickenhead from Philly named Dy-Nasty, and the next thing I knew, Bunni's brother Peaches was on the phone telling me my mama was about to die!

"The nursing home called and said your mama had a stroke," Peaches had said. "I'm sorry, sweetie, but they don't think she's gonna make it."

With those words swirling around in my head I busted straight up in the Dominion mansion and lied my ass off! I told them rich fools that my boss had just caught a stray bullet in a kick-door robbery, and then I hopped my ass on the first thing smoking back to New York City to see about my sick mama!

I made it up to the hospital just in time to catch the last few minutes of Jude Jackson's life, and I almost blacked out from grief as I stood beside her bed feeling helpless as hell as Mama pursed her twisted lips and reached out to me with her crooked hands like she was tryna tell me her deepest, darkest secret. "*Shhhlll . . . Shhhlll . . . Shhhlll . . .*" she had squinted up at me and gasped. "*Shhhlll . . . Shhhlll . . . Shhhlll . . .*"

I tried my best to make out what she was tryna say, but Mama died before she could spit it out. And now, as I stood next to her body shaking with grief, my bald-headed aunt Bibby clocked me with some wild shit that dropped me right down to my knees!

"There was two of y'all, you know. Somewhere out there in the world you got yourself a sister, Mink, 'cause you was a twin."

My head jerked up in surprise as I squatted down with my ass touching the floor.

"C-c-come again?"

"You heard me," Aunt Bibby snapped. "Ain't nobody stutter! Your mama shoulda been woman enough to tell you the truth straight from the jump!"

"You dirty bitch!" I spit real softly as tears ran from my eyes. Mama's spirit hadn't even left the room yet and this box-shaped bitch was already hatin'! "How the hell you sound talking bad about my mama?"

"How the hell I said it?"

My aunt put her hands on her stud hips and stared me down. She was grilling me with a killer look, but I could tell she wasn't really tryna cut me with no slick talk the way she was known for doing bitches out on the street.

"You're a twin, Mink. You can believe it baby, because it's true."

I wiped my eyes and then smirked at her real shitty-like. Uh-huh. I knew what time it was. Aunt Bibby used to fuck with duji real bad back in the day, and her ass musta been playing with the needle again.

"See there," I told her. "You need to stop shootin' that dog food in ya veins, cause with all that bullshit you talking you *must* be high."

"Ain't nobody getting high and ain't nobody bullshittin' neither, Mink! My brother Moe had *two* daughters, baby. And like I said, you got you a twin!"

I stared down at my mother's still body.

Me? A *twin*?

That shit was impossible!

But then . . .

Dy-Nasty!

That guttersnipe's name exploded in my brain and my heart skipped about five beats! I looked at Aunt Bibby again and all of a sudden the room got real hot and my head started buzzing. I couldn't hardly get no air in my lungs. I tried to say something but it felt like glass splinters were sticking me all in my throat.

All I could think was, *What if that Philly heffa was my god-damn sister?*

I could feel the possibility of it all down in my bones, but I damn sure didn't wanna believe it. *That trifling trick could actually be my fuckin' sister!*

"Uh-uh." I shook my head and slung snot everywhere. "You's a liar, Aunt Bibby!" I moaned as I keeled forward and hit my knees, ready to deny that shit with my last breath. "You ain't nothing but a big-ass bald-headed *liar*!"

"Mink!" Aunt Bibby barked in her jailhouse voice. "Why don't you stand up and face the truth for once in ya life! Everybody in this *room* is a goddamn liar! But the biggest liar of us all"—Aunt Bibby pointed down at the body in the bed—"was your *mama*! Jude Jackson wasn't nothin' but a *lying sack a' shit*!"

Her eyes flashed and Aunt Bibby crossed her muscled-up sailor-looking arms over her tatted-up titties and grilled me. "Now, there! I done said what the fuck I had to say, and I ain't taking none of it back neither!"

I stared at her mannish ass with my nostrils flaring like a racehorse. I wanted to *bite* that bitch! I wanted to shove my fist down her throat and make her choke on her lying-ass tongue!

But instead I stayed right there crouched down on my knees as my aunt continued to lay the cold, naked truth on me.

"Now, don't get me wrong," Aunt Bibby said quietly. "I loved me some Jude, but that heffa didn't have a truth-bone in her whole damn body! Why you think she drove her car into that goddamn river with you sitting right there in the front seat next to her, Mink? Huh? Why you *think*, stupid girl? Not even the lowest, raggediest, black-hearted *trash-ass* mama does no crazy shit like that!"

I grilled Aunt Bibby through a watery haze of tears. Oh for true, for true, I was 'bout to clock this big beefy bitch! Just wear her ass *out* for calling my dead mama outta her name! But before I could come up off my knees Aunt Bibby nailed me with another gut shot when she opened her big mouth and said, "And while ya bullshittin', Jude didn't even give birth to y'all right there in Harlem Hospital like she said, neither."

"What?" I squeaked. "How you know? How the hell you know something like that?"

" 'Cause Jude *told* me!" Aunt Bibby barked. And then she glanced over at my scandalous-ass, welfare-queen grandmother, who sat in the corner styling her stolen Gucci gear with her long pretty legs crossed all proper.

"Tell her, Mama. Tell Mink the goddamn truth!"

My grandmother wagged her leg and nodded. She twisted up her lips like she was still twenty-five and fine and said, "Bibby's tellin' it right, Mink. You got a twin sister, baby. You was about three years old when Jude first brought you around here. She told everybody she went down south and had twins and put one up for adoption. So I guess you do got yourself a sister out there somewhere in the world, baby. I just wish Jude woulda told you how to find her before she drove off in all that cold water and fucked herself up!"

★ ★ ★

Cold water. Cold water. Cold water.

I was freezing inside. All the way down to my trembling bones. All I wanted to do was go somewhere where I could get warm and block out the pain and the noise, but no matter how hard I igged her, my best friend Bunni Baines just wouldn't leave me the hell alone.

Instead of flossin' fly and fancy in a big mansion down in Dallas, Texas, me and Bunni were right back home in the gritty town of Harlem. I was laying on my little cot in her bedroom with my face turned toward the wall and my eyelids squeezed tight. I was sniffling into a boogered-up snot rag I had pressed up against my stuffy nose, and the top of my head was banging like a drum. My breath felt hot and stank as I breathed through my mouth, and my bottom lip trembled as I slobbered and cried into my pillow.

"C'mon now, Mink," Bunni begged me for the two millionth time. "You gots to get up outta this bed, boo! You gotta get your ass *up*."

I shrugged her off, wishing she would just leave me the hell alone. Bunni was barking about how I needed to get my shit together and get back on my game, but I kept tryna tell her I didn't have no fight left in me. It was gone. All the grime, all the hustle, and every drop of my love for the con game. *Poof.* It was all gone.

"Madame Mink," Peaches jumped in with his deep, baritone voice. "Me and Bunni know what you going through right now, baby. But the funeral is gonna be starting in an hour, darling! Now, I'ma need you to get up out that bed and get yourself dressed, sugar, and ready to roll!"

I laid there and igged the hell outta Peaches too.

Shoot, I wasn't thinkin' about him, and I wasn't thinkin' about Bunni, and I damn sure wasn't thinkin' about going to Mama's funeral neither!

Bunni sighed real loud, then crawled underneath my blanket and snuggled up behind me like she used to do when we was kids. She wrapped her arms around me and spooned me, rocking me back and forth as she tried her best to convince me that I needed to stand up on my feet and face what was left of my shitty little life.

And it was definitely shitty too. Just when I thought I was at the top of my game and everything flowing through my hood was damn good, I'd been blasted with a major shot to the gut that took my feet out from under me and sat me right down on my plump apple ass.

"It's been a whole damn week, Mink," Bunni said from behind me, "and, girlfriend, you ain't put enough food in your stomach to feed a fly! Hmph. You ain't combed your hair or brushed your teef." She backed off of me a lil bit. "And you ain't took a damn bath neither!"

I still didn't say shit. I just laid there in igg mode.

"I don't know why you be listening to that old crazy-ass Bibby *anyway*." Peaches jumped back in with a whole lotta bass in his voice this time. "Jude was your *mama*. And no matter *what* the hell she did, or how she did it, she was still your *mama*!"

"Jude was a *liar*!" I screamed into my pillow. My whole chest ached from Mama's lies and her low-down betrayal. "She was a goddamn *liar*!"

"Ermmm herrrm," Peaches said agreeably, and even without looking at him I could tell his lips was twisted.

"Yeah, that's right. She was a liar. But so are *you*, Madame Mink! Lying is what schemers like us *do*! So get your ass up outta that bed so we can get down to that funeral home and make sure they send your lying-ass mama off right!"

Deep in my heart I knew I had to go pay my last respects to the woman who had given birth to me but I still didn't wanna move.

So I laid there on my shaky lil cot in Bunni's junky room and thought about the next moves I was gonna make in my life. I had always been the type of slick, carefree diva who flounced around flossin' like everything in my life was all Hennessy and weed, but for the first time in a real long time I was forced to take a real good look down the gutter road that I had traveled. I *made* myself remember all the shit I had tried to erase from my mind. All the shit that I had been running from for so many years. The kind of shit that had been way too painful for a thirteen-year-old girl to live with, so she had fought like hell to forget it.

CHAPTER 2

My daddy was a woman killer. He was a big-time street slanga they called Big Moe LaRue. He was tricky and underhanded, and that's why the hustling game ran so thick in my blood. He was second in command to one of the top drug kingpins in Harlem, but he also gambled, pimped hoes, and ran game anywhere and anyhow he could.

Moe came from a real big family. They had dipped up outta Louisiana right after he was born and came up north to set Harlem straight on fire. He was the youngest boy outta twelve rotten kids, and he was the finest too. Back then my Granny ran a number joint and took in boarders on the side, and my daddy had learned the ways of the streets from a very early age. And with all of them older sisters he had adoring his fine ass, he learned the ways of women too.

When I was a little girl my daddy had me spoiled rotten. I was the shit in Big Moe's eyes, and while he didn't give my mother no kind of ends on the regular, all I had to do was act like I wanted something and the whole damn world was mine.

It was never no secret that my daddy kept a string of bitches munching on his jock, and right after my mother died

Aunt Bibby laid a hush-hush story on me that everybody in my family had kept on the low.

Aunt Bibby said my daddy used to be married to some fine, crazy chick named Valentina, who got pregnant by him and then ran off and disappeared on his ass. She said Tina knew Daddy was in the hustling life when she met him, but Big Moe had promised her he was gonna quit all that dick slangin' and cut all his other bitches loose.

Aunt Bibby said Tina was kinda off in the head. All that drinkin' and partying Daddy was doing, not to mention the boo-coo chasers out on the streets just'a throwing that ass on him left and right, just wore her out. Tina was about four months knocked when she walked out on Daddy and left him a note promising that she was gonna hurt him the same way that he had hurt her. And if you let Granny and Aunt Bibby tell it, that's exactly what went down. Tina had her baby and signed it over to the state, and then she took her crazy ass up on the roof of her building and jumped right off the ledge.

By the time Daddy found out about all that their baby was long gone, somewhere deep in the system, and for a hustler who was so big on the streets and wild with his game, the loss of his only child had cut Moe real deep, and he never again let another chick get too close to him after that.

And then Mama busted up on the scene. Finer than fine and acting just like Tina. Crazy as hell over Moe. Granny and them couldn't stand her because they claimed she drank a lot and was always whining about something. My aunts swore Mama wasn't nothing but a jump-off to Big Moe, and they said she knew from the gate what kinda playa my daddy was.

But that ain't stop her from getting strung out on Big Moe's sweet-ass game, though. By this time Daddy was selling mad dope and tricking off more bitches than ever before, and even though Mama was real cute in the face and had a stacked, killer body, she was just another complaining-ass chick to Big

Moe. They fought like cats and dogs. Mostly about him staying out till all times of the night and running the streets and trickin' off loot on his other hoes. It didn't take long for my daddy to get tired of all that clingy shit. He cut Jude loose and moved on to the next fine bitch, and never looked back.

Mama was so broke down behind him leaving her that she pulled up outta Harlem for a little while, and when she came back a few years later she had something for my daddy that none of his other bitches had ever been able to give him, no matter how hard they rode his dick.

She had *me.*

According to Granny, I was three when Mama brought me back to Harlem, and I was the spitting image of Moe LaRue. Granny said I was such a pretty baby that he ate my ass up on sight, and he wouldn't let nobody else touch me or even hold me. Over the years there wasn't nothing I couldn't get my daddy to do for me, and there were plenty of times when the only way Mama could make him come around the house was to send me up on Lenox Avenue to get him from one of his spots and bring him home.

But the year I turned thirteen all them desperation moves finally got to my moms. I was starting to smell my own ass by then, and I didn't have time to be runnin' behind my daddy tryna drag him away from none of his other bitches. *Sheiit,* I was Moe LaRue's daughter to the tee. The streets turned me on like a muthafucka, and I was attracted to all the grimy shit that went on when the sun went down.

On the real, I loved my mama, but I loved me some of Daddy's on-the-side hoes too. Them was some bad-ass chicks, and most of them were slick and beautiful and had side-hustles of their own. And I looked so much like my daddy that they took right to me and spoiled the hell outta me. I used to play hooky from school and hang out with them up on the avenue, and they would sneak me cigarettes and weed and as much liquor as my lil young throat could swallow.

And by that time I had some brand-new titties poppin' out on my chest, and my hips and booty had poofed out and spread deliciously wide too. My daddy would give me money to buy food and shit, but instead of taking it home to Mama I would trick it up on Kush and Coronas, and it wasn't long before I started dressing like his most butter hoes and flaunting my firm young body on the streets just like they did too.

But my father peeped my game when he overheard some little corner slanga talking about how he was gonna get at my cherry, and Daddy put the brakes on all that ill shit. He busted up in Mama's crib screamin' on her for not watching me and dogging her out for letting my hot ass run wild and loose on the streets.

I felt so bad when I saw how hard my mama cried!

Sniffling and hollering, she broke down and confessed that she had liver disease from all that drinking she used to do when she was younger. She told Daddy she was sick and she couldn't be running up and down the streets behind my fast ass no more! Mama got on her knees and pressed her face to Big Moe's shiny shoes, hugging his ankles as she begged my daddy to come back home so they could get back together and raise me together as a real family. But as bad as I felt for Mama, I wanted to slap the hell outta her for getting down on the floor and begging a man like that! As young as I was, I knew it didn't matter to a playa if a chick had his kid or not! When a nigga didn't want you no more, he didn't want your black ass no more! I was only thirteen years old, but I knew damn well that Moe LaRue was *never* coming back home, and I would never forget the look on my daddy's face when he told Mama that.

"*We* ain't no goddamn family, Jude!" he spit at her. "*Mink* is my baby, and me and her is gonna *always* be blood. But me and you?" He kicked her off his foot like a dirty Kotex had dropped outta the sky and landed on his shoe. "Bitch you ain't shit to me. You never was and you never will be."

It seemed like something just broke in Mama's spirit after

that. All them years of hoping and praying and running the streets behind that man just fell down on her head and she couldn't take it no damn more.

"I'ma kill your ass, you yellow muthafucka!" Mama rolled over on the floor and screamed as Daddy kissed me then headed toward the front door.

"Just fuckin' watch!" she hollered. "You think Valentina fucked you up? Well you just watch, you piss-colored muthafucka, you! I'ma *kill* your ass!"

Mama didn't sleep a wink that night. I heard her walking a hole in the floor in our small apartment just'a crying and muttering nonsense under her breath.

She was standing right by my bed the next morning when I woke up.

"Get up, Mink. I need you to come with me to my appointment," she told me as I slid out the bed and got ready for school. Mama was already dressed, and her hair was done real nice. She had on makeup and all that. Perfume too.

Mama said there wasn't enough time for me to fix breakfast, so she handed me a Pop-Tart and a cup of sink water with two ice cubes floating in it. We went downstairs and climbed in our car, but instead of driving me to her doctor's appointment like she said she was, that fool went and drove both of us off a loading dock and straight into the Hudson River.

My mama fucked up three lives that day.

When Daddy got word that she had driven me into all that cold water he jumped straight in his whip and jetted toward the west side of Manhattan tryna get to me.

But Big Moe never made it. Less than a mile from the pier he had a heart attack and crashed into a light pole. One of his girlfriends was riding with him, and she said the last words to come outta his mouth were *My baby. My baby. Mink, my baby.*

And then he died.

I don't know how I got outta that sinking car, but I did. It was dark as hell as I scrambled outta my open window and clawed my way up to the surface, and then I coughed and choked on all that cold water until some white man jogging on the pier jumped in the river and dragged me out.

They pulled Mama out too, but not in time. She was still alive when the ambulance got her to the hospital, but she had brain damage from being under that water for so long, and even though her body was still here, her mind was way gone.

Daddy's family wasn't shit after that. They blamed my mother for killing Big Moe, and whatever money and jewelry his hoes didn't pocket when they found out he was dead, them trifling-ass sisters of his stole and I didn't get not one penny.

The state made me go see all kinds of counselors and psychologists so I could get my head right, but it didn't matter what nobody said because it still added up to the same thing: My own damn *mama* had tried to kill me. Now tell me, what kid would wanna remember, let alone live, with *that*?

CHAPTER 3

"Ummm, hold up. Say that shit again?" Pilar Ducane batted her fake eyelashes at her cousin Barron as he sat across from her with the two-hump-chump look on his fine chocolate face.

"You heard me. The board met. I signed the papers Suge got drawn up and they voted to open Daddy's trust fund and kick out the first cash payment. To everybody."

Pilar blinked. They were kicked back and chilling on Barron's king-sized bed, drinking expensive wine and eating some gourmet Chinese food.

"What do you mean to *everybody*? Including Mink and Dy-Nasty?"

Barron frowned and nodded. "Well, yeah. Whichever one of them ends up being Sable is gonna get three hundred grand every year."

"Uh-uh, B!" Pilar exploded. Her blood boiled at the thought of those ghetto bandits digging their grimy fingers around in the Dominion's multi-billion-dollar cookie jar. "Your black ass has *got* to be bullshitting!"

She held her slim, manicured hand in the air.

"*Please, please, PLEASE* tell me you didn't go do no stupid shit like that!"

"Yo, it wasn't *stupid*," he grilled her and frowned.

"But you were supposed to *stall* them, dammit! You were supposed to submit a request for a vote delay!"

Barron's broad shoulders slumped forward and his eyes searched the bedspread as he tried to figure out how the hell he was gonna tell Pilar the rest of his fucked-up story.

"It ain't like I *wanted* to sign that shit. I just didn't have no other choice," he said quietly.

"What the hell do you mean you didn't have no other choice?" Pilar dropped her chopsticks and hissed through her clenched teeth. "You fuckin'-a-right you had another choice!" Her pretty face was twisted up in rage and a thunderstorm was crackling in her gray eyes.

"Oh I did? Then what the fuck was it?" Barron sat straight up and barked. "Yo! That ol' slick nigga Suge had my back against the wall! He had me bent over kissing my own nuts! What the hell was I supposed to do?"

Pilar narrowed her gray eyes. "You were *supposed* to tell him you weren't gonna sign a *goddamn* thing! We needed the board to name you the CEO of Dominion Oil *before* those thirsty hood bitches got their DNA results back, remember? I don't understand why you just gave up and wimped out on all our plans just like"—she snapped her manicured fingers—"that!"

Barron bit down hard on his lip as he felt his control slipping. Pilar was about to go too damned far. It was bad enough that Suge had ass-fucked him with no Vaseline. He didn't need Pilar digging up in his guts too.

"Yo, I'm telling you. I did what I had to do. Uncle Suge got crafty on me. He paid some chick to go on camera and say I was the father of her baby and that she wasn't getting no child support. That nigga had me by the balls so I had to tap out."

"A baby?" Pilar shrieked. *The only coochie you better be shoot-*

ing a goddamn baby up in is mine! "Are you telling me some skeezer went on camera and said she had a baby by you?"

Barron grilled her as he nodded. "Yeah. But I also told you it was a setup, didn't I? Yo, I ain't nobody's baby daddy, and you can believe that shit. Besides, I ain't never seen that white girl in my life. And I definitely never boned her ass."

"Aw, *damn*!" Pilar jumped off the bed and marched around in an exasperated circle, throwing up her hands and stomping her feet on the shiny hardwood in disgust. "You and your goddamn *white* girls! When are you gonna get over that dumb shit, Bump?"

"Yo, hold up!" Barron said, getting real swole. He jabbed his pointer finger toward Pilar as rage bubbled up out of him. "What the hell are you talking about? I had one white girl, Pilar! *One.* She was the only woman I ever asked to be my wife, and I dropped her ass for *you*! So I *am* over that shit! I don't know *where* he got that young chick on the film from, but she's probably just a stray piece of ass that Uncle Suge laid a buck on to put the squeeze on me. The only reason I went along with that shit is because I can't be having no kind of negative light shining on me right now."

"But still"—Pilar crossed her arms over her breasts—"why in the world would you fall for that kind of hustle anyway? Even if Suge *did* pay somebody to run that baby-daddy bullshit all over the local news, you're an attorney, Barron! You've built yourself a solid rep in this city! There's no way in hell those kind of bogus charges would stick to you! A quick paternity test would bury that tired-ass scam deep in the dirt real quick. I can't believe you let Suge twist your arm up like that!"

Barron took a deep breath. This chick was always pushing. Digging. Probing. She didn't even know how to chill. But if he was ever gonna shut her up then he was gonna have to give up the goods and come clean.

"There's a little bit more to it than that though, Pilar," he said quietly. "Matter fact, this shit gets a whole lot worse. See, I ran up on some trouble when I went to that frat party the other week, you feel me? One of them hatin' niggas must have dropped a bomb in my drink because I passed out. I don't really remember a whole lot, but I guess I woke up at some point because I tried to get out of there and drive home. But"—he swallowed hard—"I fucked around and crashed my ride and I . . ." Barron's face turned to stone as he lowered his eyes and frowned. "I ran over a little kid."

"Oh my God!" Pilar shrieked. "Barron, *no*!" She jetted over to his side and wrapped her arms protectively around him. "You hit somebody's *kid*?" She pulled his face deep into her juicy breasts. "Oh, damn! I'm so sorry! Why didn't you tell me this from the jump? Is the child okay?"

Barron nodded as he closed his eyes and sucked up her titty fumes. He snuggled his nose into her warm cleavage as his hands circled her tiny waist.

"That damn kid is fine," he muttered. "His ankle is broken, but other than that he's okay."

Barron didn't tell her the little bastard's father was trying to shake him down for five hundred grand, but he *was* gonna have to tell her about those X-rated pictures that somebody had snapped of him before he left the frat party.

Shame flashed through Barron's body and he pulled out of Pilar's embrace. His hands shot up to his face as his fingers skimmed over the brittle stubble of his growing eyebrows. One of them frat fools had slipped him some knockout dust and shaved his brows until they were damn-near bald. And then some idiot had drawn some new ones on him with a thick black pencil.

Barron thought about that ugly-ass rose-colored miniskirt they had dressed him up in and that skimpy little push-up bra. It was bad enough that he'd had to stand up there and take a mug shot wearing that shit, but it fucked him up that his moms had seen his dick hanging outta that skirt, and she'd seen him with mascara on his eyes and some clown-ass lipstick colored all around his mouth too.

And them fuckin' pictures!

His boy Animal had called and told him all about the photo shoot that he had starred in while he was fucked up, and even now bitter tears of rage sprang to Barron's eyes as he remembered going to that Web site and seeing some strange nigga's meat pressed up against his painted lips. That shit had fucked him up so bad that the only thing on his mind had been to get him some get-back. He was about two seconds away from calling his gutta peeps down in Houston and flying a posse up to Dallas so they could bust the door down on that frat house and blast it up with a couple of fuckin' Uzis, but the thought of having to explain them pictures to *any* fuckin' body was simply more than his manhood could handle.

But still, Barron bit down on his shame and told Pilar everything. Trembling in fury, he laid it all out and ran the whole shit down to her, because if she was gonna be fighting on his team then she needed to know exactly what kind of shit they were going up against.

By the time Barron finished running it down Pilar's ass was on fire. She crossed her arms over her plump breasts and grilled her cousin like he was an idiot for real.

"You can't be fucking serious!" she spit. "I know damn well you're smarter than that! You're a *lawyer,* Barron. Criminals pay you big dollars to lie and scheme under oath, baby! I can't believe you let yourself get caught in a trick bag like that!"

Barron grimaced. If he'd been expecting a little sympathy from her cold-hearted ass he was shit out of luck.

"I know I'm an attorney, Pilar. And that's why I hooked up with a top judge who's gonna handle all this shit for me. But I still couldn't let Suge toss me under the bus while all this other bullshit was still going on!" He threw up his hands. "So I signed the fuckin' papers, man. Suge was out to burn me, and I ain't got enough skin left on my black ass to take that type of heat!"

Pilar stared her cousin down as she fought the urge to knock the shit out of him. After everything they had worked for. After all of her scheming and conniving. They had gotten *this* damn close to cutting that stank bitch Mink out of the family trust and Barron had almost thrown it all away.

"So what now?" she asked, turning her lip up as she eyeballed him in disgust.

Barron felt like a piece of shit as he shrugged.

"Now we wait. The next step is getting the final documents signed and notarized. Once that's done, we get those DNA results in our hands, and if they come back saying what I think they're gonna say, then we still come out on top."

Pilar smirked. "And how's that?"

"Easy. Mink's results are gonna be negative, so we just expose her ass as a fraud, and then make an official declaration that Dy-Nasty is Sable. And then after that we pull out Dy-Nasty's arrest records and get her ass disqualified from the trust fund real quick."

Barron reached out and patted Pilar on her firm booty. "And once that's over, me and you can go back to doing what we always do, baby. And everything will still be everything."

"Yeah, but that's your Plan A," Pilar whined. "What if it doesn't go down like that, Bump?" She saw her potential piece of the Dominion pie shrinking, and shrinking fast. "What if the DNA results don't come back on time and the board signs off and finalizes the vote before we know which one of those skanks is really Sable?"

Barron shrugged. He was feeling Pilar's pain because tearing off three large bills to that scandalous trick Mink LaRue every year would be the greatest fuckin' failure of his life.

"I don't know, P," he sighed. "If the DNA results ain't back before the cash is kicked out then we gotta find another way to stick their asses." Barron shook his head miserably. "We'll just have to dig around in our trick bag and come up with a Plan B."

CHAPTER 4

There were plenty of "Bad News LaRues" stirring shit up on the streets of Harlem, but only a handful of the half-hungover ones had come out to the Three Brothers Funeral Home to see my mama put in the ground.

I was sitting in the front pew between Granny and one of my half-blind uncles, and the skinny black preacher who had come with the one-price-fits-all funeral package was standing up front talking about Mama like they went way back and had been tight runnin' buddies from the cradle.

"Jude Jackson was a *saintly* woman . . ." He stood up there and lied like a muthafucka as everybody looked around to make sure they was at the right funeral. "A woman who lived her life like she knew *God*!"

I ignored all that bullshit yang coming outta his mouth as I sat there staring at my mama's stiff-looking body while some spooky-ass organ music played over the speakers. The lil chapel where they had laid Mama out was so empty it felt like the chill coming off of her body was keeping the whole room cool.

Even though only a few people were sitting around slumped in the pews today, almost the whole damn family had shown up last night when Granny threw a card party and big-ass fish fry and called it a wake for Mama.

Granny had charged five dollars a head for a plate of fried porgies and a scoop of potato salad, and she tacked on three dollars if you wanted a shot of cheap liquor to go along with it. All the money she raked in was supposed to come to me so I could finish paying the funeral home and square up with the car service for the limousine I had rented for the close family. Aunt Bibby had passed around her pimped-out Kangol and told everybody to dig deep down in their bras, socks, and drawers and be sure to come out with a couple of dollars to help me send my mama off right.

Sheeeiit. That sweaty-ass hat had gone around the room about three damn times, and I coulda sworn I saw mad slick-fisted LaRues drop a dollar bill in and then skim out a couple of fives. By the time Aunt Bibby's Kangol got back across the room where I was sitting there wasn't but sixteen one-dollar bills left in that sucker and three gooey, stuck-together pennies.

I still had me a little pocket change because Uncle Suge had torn me off ten g's before I left Texas, but it cost a real big gwap to bury somebody in New York! You had to pay for the grave, pay them to dig the damn thing open, and then pay them to throw that same damn dirt back down once they dropped the coffin in the hole too. You had to pay the funeral home *and* the mortician, and I won't even talk about how much them lil cheap-ass cardboard caskets cost!

The whole setup was a racket for real, and by the time the Three Brothers Funeral Home finished gankin' me for every dime they could squeeze me for and call it a one-price-fits-all deal, I barely had five grand left in my pocket.

I looked toward the front of the room at Mama's body again. Even dead and stiff, Jude Jackson still looked damn good. The funeral parlor had a beautician named Mrs. Freeman, and she had whipped up Mama's hair so tight it laid down on her shoulders like a silky Asian weave. Mama's makeup had been done up perfectly too, and some Chinese chick had given her a killer manicure.

Laying up there in that pretty blue box my mama was the flyest dead person I had ever seen, but as I stared at her from across the room, a big part of me felt like I was looking at a stranger.

There was so much stuff about Mama that I just hadn't known and would never know. So much shit about her life that she had hidden from me, so many lies that she had told me, so many doubts that she had left me with, and now that she was gone, all the skeleton bones rattling around in her closet were about to bust right out through the goddamn door.

Mr. Hired Preacher was still up there talking about Mama like he had dunked his cookies in her milk way back in kindergarten. The old lady who was playing the organ and singing at the top of her lungs had tears running down her face like Mama was her favorite dead daughter laying up there in that box.

As I sat there choking on the big ball of grief that was clogging up my throat, tears fell from my eyes and I had to admit that Peaches had been right about at least one thing: No matter *what* the hell Jude Jackson had done, or why the hell she had did it, she was still my *mama*!

I don't know how I made it through Mama's home-going service, and if it wasn't for Peaches and Bunni half-carrying me outta that funeral parlor I woulda crawled out on my hands and knees.

I was still crying and sniffling as they led me over to the black limo that was waiting outside at the curb. A tall driver dressed in a dark shirt and a pair of dark pants was standing there holding the door open for us. Peaches fell back to let me go in front of him, and I had just leaned forward and stepped one foot inside the whip when all holy hell broke loose on the sidewalk behind me.

"*Yayyy*!!! She's dead! She's dead! That fuckin' bitch Jude is finally *dead*!"

Halfway in the limo, I paused in the middle of a sniffle.

Then I turned around and peeped some old crazy chick in high heels and a bright red dress. That fool was screaming and hollering at the top of her lungs as she waved her arms over her head and hauled ass straight toward us. Grinning real big, she darted over to the back of the hearse where they had just swung the door closed on Mama's casket and started banging on that shit like she had lost her damn mind.

"Open this shit up and lemme see her dead ass for myself!" she screamed, jumping up and down as she slapped her hands all over the glass window. "Open it up! Lemme see that bitch! Lemme see Jude's old dead funky ass one more time!"

I pulled my shades off so I could get a good look at the chick who was calling my dead mama a bitch and then—

"Get ya ass in there!" the limo driver barked as he clamped one thick hand around the back of my neck and thrust his other hand up my skirt and between my legs. That nigga lifted me in the air by my neck and my crotch, and chucked me face-first down on the floor of that limo and slammed the door shut!

I hit the floor hard and bit down on a mouthful of carpet, and by the time I scrambled up on my knees and started beating on the window, all I saw was a cold, deadly gat gripped in the driver's hand and a look of shock and fear on Bunni's face that told me my shit was a wrap.

"Help!" I screamed as that fool jumped in the front seat and slammed the door. I grabbed at the door handle and tried to twist it but that shit was locked up tight, and the last thing I saw before his tires screeched and he jetted out into traffic was Peaches and Bunni and them Bad News LaRues, standing on the curb with their mouths wide open as they watched us speed away.

"Yo what the fuck is you *doing*?" I screamed as that big fool unlocked the limo door and came around back to drag me outta the whip. He had driven me all the way downtown. We were somewhere in the Garment District, and it was practically deserted at this time on a Sunday morning.

I was balled up in the corner so tight that dude had to dig up in the backseat to get my ass outta there. I screeched and went up on my tippy-toes as he yanked me outta the ride, then he twisted my wrist real hard and jerked my hand up behind my back.

"*Owww*! You got the wrong chick!" I hollered as he manhandled me down a narrow, dirty alley and pushed me through the rickety doorway of some abandoned-looking warehouse. "I didn't do nothin', nigga! You got it all wrong! You got the *wrong* chick!"

I stumbled into the darkness with my heart beating on a thousand. I couldn't think. My whole body was covered in sweat, and my ankles kept wobbling left and right in the six-inch heels that I had boosted from Neiman Marcus.

"Where the fuck is you takin' me?" I whined and bitched as he muscled me through a big room with twined bundles of old fabric and moldy-looking clothes stacked everywhere. "What the fuck is you doin'?"

Dude wasn't in the question-answering bizz because he didn't answer a single one of minez! But a few seconds later, after he opened a set of double doors and chucked me down on the cold floor inside a small damp room that smelled like gasoline and firecrackers, all my questions got answered at one time.

"Well, well, well. It's con-mami Mink LaRue."

I fell sideways into the small room and tripped over my

own feet. I reached out to catch myself on the edge of a metal desk, but I missed and I felt my lil funeral dress split up the back as I landed hard on my ass.

I looked up at the muscle-bound beast who had just spit my name off his tongue, and my mouth dried up as a cold chill trickled all the way down my spine.

He sat behind the desk looking fine as hell. Long dreads, boulder shoulders, cold eyes, and a devious, killer smile.

I stared into them jailhouse eyes and I knew my shit was done for. I could hear every last one of my chickens just a' clucking as they came home to roost. And since I knew there wasn't a damn thing I could do to save my ass, I just sat there with my dress hiked up and my legs all crooked, looking stupid as hell as I coughed and said, "Gutta!"

His name came rollin' outta my mouth sounding just like a frog croak, and then I swallowed extra-hard and cooed up at him and smiled. "Hey there, boo! I missed the shit outta you, boo! When you hit the bricks, Papi? How long you been back home?"

CHAPTER 5

"Good evening, Mrs. Dominion. What are you wearing for Daddy tonight?"

Selah Dominion blushed as she lay spread-eagle on her chaise lounge wearing nothing but a sex jones and a midnight-colored thong.

"Black," she whispered breathlessly. "I'm wearing black."

Ruddman might have been a round-belly toad of a man, but with all his money, power, and status, he had confidence, swagger, and sex appeal oozing out of his pores. It had taken quite a few late-night erotic phone calls and endless promises to return her ultra-expensive diamond engagement ring, but right now he had Selah melting like butter in a hot frying pan.

He had taken that little public slap she had laid on him like a soldier. Instead of fighting back, he had gotten even by seducing her with constant late-night phone calls and endless little love notes that kept her on a string until he got her right where he wanted her.

In his bed.

It had been eighteen years since Ruddman had pounded his foot-long love muscle up in Viceroy Dominion's wife, and he had never gotten as much satisfaction from fucking an enemy since. Using her engagement ring as a pawn, he had lured Selah back to his penthouse suite and stripped her naked in his outdoor Jacuzzi and then fucked her so good that she broke down and cried.

And even though Selah was well aware of where her dangerous indiscretions could lead her, she had willingly followed Ruddman down a road of sexual sport that had her squirming in her master suite, stretched out on her sofa with her door tightly locked and her desperate fingers greedily massaging that hot spot between her legs.

Selah may have looked real sweet and innocent on the outside, but her woman jones ran high and she had always been a firecracker between the sheets. The truth be told, she had been in a sexual slump for years, even before Viceroy had his oil-rig accident. Her husband's little "problem" had started twenty years ago, and it had robbed them of a normal marriage and led to both of them doing things they would never want to admit.

But right now, with Rodney talking that nasty talk in her ear, Selah didn't give a damn about any of that. It had been a long, long time since her body had been sexed so sweetly, and she had to admit that no man, not even Viceroy in his *best* damn days, had ever come close to knocking her back out the way froggish little Rodney Ruddman did.

Twenty years of missing out on the good wood. Twenty fuckin' years! And where the hell had all those years gone? What had started out as a giving up a little revenge pussy to pay Viceroy back for screwing her sister had turned into a sexual addiction that Selah had been jonesing like crazy for and wished she could forget. But no matter how hard she'd tried, she had *never* gotten the taste of Rodney out of her mouth, and she had never forgotten the way he had worn her out in his bed.

Sure, she had forgiven Viceroy for causing her so much pain, and over the years they had moved on to a comfortable place in their marriage. His little "problem" came and went without rhyme or reason, and even though Selah had been able to get pregnant with Jock and Fallon, sometimes they had dry, no-nookie spells that lasted for months. Over time they had learned to sexually satisfy each other in different ways, but there was only so much pleasuring that a fist full of fingers or a dildo could do.

And now, not long after hauling off and slapping the shit out of Rodney Ruddman in broad daylight, excitement crawled down Selah's spine as they played his favorite game of phone sex. She was scheduled to hook up with him the next morning for a brunch-time quickie in his penthouse suite, but Rodney couldn't wait and he had called her so they could get started on a little sexual foreplay.

"Tell me where you want me to touch you, Mrs. *Dominion*," he demanded. Ruddman hardly ever called her by her first name. Instead he got a perverse shot of power and pleasure every time he reminded himself that he was fucking the wife of the great Viceroy Dominion.

"Everywhere," Selah panted as her hands kneaded the flesh on her smooth, supple body. "I want you to touch me everywhere."

Ruddman let out a low, wicked laugh.

"Tell me exactly where," he urged. "Tell me exactly how."

The sound of Selah sucking in her breath, then licking her lips came through the phone.

"I want you to spank my nipples," she whispered, squinching her eyes closed tight as her hands moved feverishly.

"Spank your nipples?" he taunted.

Selah nodded and then breathed, "Yes. With your . . . dick."

"What was that, Mrs. Dominion? You want me to spank your nipples with my hard dick?"

"Yes," Selah panted as she pinched her two rigid peaks until waves of electricity shot through her body. Ruddman had awakened the sleeping freak in her. Truth be told, Selah wanted her nipples *and* her ass-cheeks spanked. She wanted her hair pulled and her tongue sucked. She wanted a hard dick to fuck her in every hole on her body. And she wanted it now!

Ruddman growled a string of sexual obscenities in her ear as he described exactly how he was going to dig her out. With just the excitement in his voice and the threat of his words, Selah climbed a sexual cliff and free-fell over the side as her pelvis pulsed and she shot sweet cum into her own palm.

Viceroy had never made her feel like this. Even before the mysterious breakdown between them that made him become impotent. Not a single doctor could find anything physically wrong with him either. There was absolutely no medical reason why he couldn't get it up and be a real man for his wife, but no matter how sexy she dressed, or how much foreplay they shared, Viceroy just couldn't get an erection for his wife.

Her husband was a proud man, but he had submitted to his doctors and exhausted every sexual enhancement drug on the market. He had popped the purple pills, the yellow ones, and the blue ones too. He'd smoked weed, dipped his rod in liquid cocaine, and even tried ancient Chinese acupuncture.

Viceroy's inability to get his dick hard for Selah had taken a toll on both of them. He was still young and in his prime, and as bad as he wanted to fuck his wife he just couldn't make a muscle for her. It was like his manhood had decided to take a really long nap, and Selah wasn't woman enough to wake it up.

Selah was a highly sexual woman, so early on she had been frustrated and crushed. But she had been proud of herself, though. As much as she loved sex, and as frustrating as their lives had become, she had never once considered stepping outside of her marriage or cheating on her man.

Until that fateful afternoon in New York City when she walked into her husband's office to find him gripping a rock-hard dick that looked like it had been packed with cement as he pushed it down her baby sister's throat!

That trifling little bitch! Selah thought. But guess who was being trifling now?

With her legs gapped open wide, she was wheezing from the effects of her third over-the-phone orgasm, and she almost jumped through the roof when somebody banged hard on her door.

"Who's there?" she called out with the phone still cradled between her shoulder and her ear.

"It's Dy-Nasty, Mama Selah! I came to watch one of your shows and I brought us a lil snacky-snack too!"

"I gotta go," Selah whispered into the phone.

"Wait," Rodney panted. He was about a mile behind her and Selah could hear him still stroking and beating his meat. "I didn't get it yet, baby. Wait."

"I can't!" she whispered, cupping her hand around her mouth. "My daughter is at the door! I'll make it up to you tomorrow. I really have to go now."

Ruddman sighed heavily. "It's always about you," he growled, but Selah didn't hear him.

She'd already hung up the phone so she could pull herself together and open the door for Dy-Nasty.

CHAPTER 6

Gutta was digging all up in my ass. I mean he was getting beastly with it. I was begging for mercy like he was Jesus in the flesh, and to say that nigga was stomping a mudhole in my yellow behind wouldn'ta been saying enough.

That fool was straight up *punishing* me as he slapped me from wall to wall in that lil-ass office. He didn't have a damn bit of mercy on me neither, 'cause I had fucked with his paper and he was teaching my ass a lesson!

"Gutta please!" I mumbled as I staggered back and forth between his front hand slaps and his back hand whaps. The room was heating up and it stank like gas fumes and fried Glama-Glo wig up in that bitch. "I swear to *God* I was gonna pay you back! I was gonna *pay* you!"

"Nah," he said, steady swinging. "No you wasn't, Mink. You wasn't gonna pay me shit 'cause you just slick like that, baby!"

The face I used to think was so damn gorgeous, and that sexy Haitian accent that used to keep me moist between the legs, was looking like a gigantic nightmare right about now.

Gutta threw a hard left that caught me dead in my chest.

"Omph!"

I sucked my breath in and farted, and I just knew he had cracked my chest bone.

He capped me with a right on my jaw after that, and his next blow was an overhand punch that slammed into my back as I was on my way down to the floor.

And that's when the Haitian in his ass came out.

Gutta kicked me all up in my guts and ribs like he was playing soccer for the national team. It was stomp-the-thief time up in the house, and all I could do was roll and dodge as he punted me all over that room until he was breathing hard and sweating like crazy.

"You's a nasty liar, Mink," he drawled in his singsong accent.

I didn't even tryta dispute that shit. I couldn't. I was too busy hugging that floor in pain and fear.

Gutta bent over me and I heard a click. I froze and then peeked out the corner of my eye and saw a shiny foot-long switchblade glinting in his hand. I almost peed as he pressed the tip of that big-ass knife under my left ear and drew a smiley face across my throat and all the way over to my right ear.

"You thought you was out-hustling me, didn't you?"

I didn't answer him. I couldn't. I was trembling like a muthafucka when he pressed the point down so deep I felt a sudden burn, and then he scratched the tip of the knife from my ear all the way over to the corner of my mouth.

"The whole time I was locked up you was out here spending my money and lying your ass off, Mink. Just wait. When I get through fuckin' you up I'ma cut that little pink snake right outta your mouth. And then I'ma wrap some cement around ya big head and plant your greedy ass in the bottom of the East River."

For true, for true, Gutta *meant* that shit, and I was wheezing in fear when he stood up and turned to the limo driver, who had been standing in the corner all this time and said, "Put your foot on her neck until I get back, Petro." He passed dude his bear-skinning knife. "And if the bitch gets stupid or makes a slick move, buck-fifth her grimy ass."

My entire body was throbbing in agony as I laid sprawled out on that damp concrete floor. The salt from my tears rolled down and stung the shit outta my busted lip. I reached out to lick it and that baby was swollen like I had a big fat grape stuck up underneath my split skin.

For the first time I was able to take a look around, and what I saw shocked the shit outta me. There were mad hundred-dollar-bills laid out everywhere, like a big green load of laundry that had been spread out to dry. The scent of Tide laundry detergent was all over the place, but the smell of gasoline was strong in the air too. I thought about some crazy shit that I had seen on the news.

A car full of money had blown up in Harlem a couple of days ago. They said some white nigga had been driving around with damn near a million dollars in his whip when a crowd of hoes jumped on him and beat his ass down to the ground. Ol' boy had scrambled behind the wheel and tried to jet, but his gas tank blew up and mad dough rained down on the streets of Harlem like a gift from the ghosts of every drug kingpin who had passed.

The TV cameras had been on that shit. Niggas had swarmed all over that whip, damn near killing each other tryna scoop up all that half-burnt cheese. And now, stretched out on the cold floor and sniffing gas fumes, I didn't have to be a genius to figure out that Gutta had washed him some of that loot and stashed it away in this warehouse.

My brain was steady calculating the sum of all that dirty money when somebody banged real hard on the door. The dude who was standing watch over me looked up and frowned.

"What up?" he barked.

"It's me!" some chick said all happy-like. "Open up dammit!"

"Me *who*?"

"Stop playin', nigga," she giggled, "and let me in!"

Dude got right up on the door as he unlocked that shit. He opened it just a crack, and even with all them gas fumes in the air the sweet smell of Pure Poison by Dior at a hundred smacks a bottle still rushed into the small room.

I tried to peer through the door crack, but from where I was laying the only thing I could see was a big foot and a long, sexy calf. The foot was perched in a hot-pink open-toe stiletto, and I heard bracelets and jewelry tinkling out the ass.

"What the fuck—" was all dude got out, and then I heard a smashing sound and the door busted open wide.

"Fool!" I heard a grown man growl, and the next thing I knew Peaches' big gorilla ass was up in the room. He swung his muscular arm and bashed dude in the face with his gat, and when dude stumbled and reached for his busted grill, Peaches kneed him in the mug and slammed his burner down on the back of dude's head hard enough to crack his skull.

Ol' boy hit that concrete floor like a dropped rock, and I was already up on my knees by the time Peaches scurried over and reached for me.

"Get up, Madame Mink!" he growled as he stepped over dude and yanked me to my feet. "We gotta get the fuck outta here!"

He had that shit right! I forgot all about the pain in my bones as I held on to P's strong arm and he half-carried my broke-down tail outta that warehouse and back through the alley as we hauled ass toward freedom.

CHAPTER 7

Die, Viceroy, Die! Dy-Nasty thought wickedly as she fantasized about all the fly shit she was gonna buy when that trust fund paid out and she got her three hunnerd large!

She had been laid up in the crisp king-sized bed with her fake mama watching reruns and eating Ritz crackers outta the box when a call from the hospital down in Houston came in and messed every damn thing up.

Selah had sounded shook right off the bat, and Dy-Nasty was all ears as her fake mama hit the PAUSE button on the remote and clutched the blanket up to her chest.

"Oh my *God*!" Selah's voice was screechy and high-pitched. "What do you mean my husband's condition has changed drastically? Did something go wrong with one of your new procedures? Please, just tell me. Are you trying to say his life is in danger? Okay. Okay, yes! I understand. Yes! Yes, of course! I can get there right away. Just let me alert my pilot and I'll be there in an hour."

Selah slammed the phone down and jumped straight outta the bed.

"We have to get to Houston," she told Dy-Nasty breathlessly as she scurried toward her huge closet filled with endless shoes, jewelry, and designer clothing. "Something's happened to your father. It must be pretty bad, because they won't tell me anything over the phone."

Dy-Nasty rolled her eyes behind Selah's back and checked herself before she could suck her teeth out loud.

We gotta get to Houston? She thought, twisting her lips up real stank. *We?*

Fuck a damn Viceroy!

Why in the hell did she have to go? That old rich gangsta didn't need her to be there so he could die! Besides, she hated flying on that scary-ass jet, and she wasn't *even* tryna get up outta his big old comfy bed!

Dy-Nasty was scandalous and greedy but she wasn't no fool. She had been performing like a muthafucka up in that mansion while Mink's stupid ass was gone to New York, and she wasn't about to fuck herself up now that she was just days away from hitting the jackpot of her gutter life!

Maids, drivers, credit cards, every luxury in the world had been at Dy-Nasty's grimy little fingertips ever since the moment she'd kicked Barron in the face at that strip club in Harlem. And now that the board at Dominion Oil had finally met, and her tight-nut "big brother" Barron had gone to get the final paperwork signed, she was ready to collect her three hunnerd bills and get the fuck up outta Texas!

She pushed the plush blanket back and poked her lip out. Instead of actin' funky like she really wanted to, she made all the right noises and said all the comforting shit that Selah needed to hear as she jumped her frauding ass outta that bed and threw on her gear like she was rushing into a bank to throw a bucket of water on a burning stack of cash!

Since Jock was at football practice, Fallon was at the beauty parlor, and Dane was prolly somewhere getting high and digging up in some college girl's twat, Dy-Nasty went ahead and played her role as the dutiful daughter and held Selah's hand as they flew down to Houston in the Dominion's private jet.

They landed at a local heliport and then hopped in a limo for the short trip over to the hospital. A team of doctors rushed out to meet them as they pulled into the private parking area, and their faces looked so stone-cold serious that Dy-Nasty figured Viceroy's black ass had already kicked the bucket.

The doctors whisked them inside the building without saying a word, and after dropping Dy-Nasty off in the waiting room, they escorted Selah down the hall to the intensive care unit.

"Die, you old muthafucka, die!" Dy-Nasty whispered under her breath as she plopped down sideways in a chair and propped her feet up in the seat next to her. She sat there twirling a few curly strands of her brand-new weave around her grubby little fingers as she fantasized about the three hundred thousand big ones these fools was about to deposit in an account for her. She giggled inside as she thought about that meeting they'd had at Uncle Suge's house and the fifty-fifty deal that she had cut with Mink.

Sheiit! Dy-Nasty laughed her ass off. Fifty-fifty *hell*! If that dumb Harlem broad was counting on getting half of that moolah when she got back to Texas, then that bitch's big head was sho'nuff *bumped*!

Dy-Nasty pulled out her phone and started texting back and forth with plottin'-ass Pat back in Philly. Pat was a master fraudster, and Dy-Nasty loved that chick with all her heart! Between the two of them they was gonna blow the City of Brotherly Love right off the map when she rolled back in town with all that Dominion cash!

Dy-Nasty couldn't wait to get her ass back home and get out there on the hot Philadelphia streets. Her name was gonna ring some real big liberty bells when she switched her booty up on the block with cream oozing all outta her pores, but first she had a sweet lil Dallas hustle she needed to handle and a few more Texas two-steps she needed to make!

* * *

Selah felt frozen inside as she walked down the hallway flanked by the stern-faced crew of doctors who were about to lay some real heavy news on her about her husband.

"I must tell you that your husband's mental status has changed drastically, and so has his appearance," Viceroy's chief neurosurgeon said as he led her down the long hall toward her husband's private ICU room.

"We wanted to call you sooner," Viceroy's chief internist added, "but we had to be sure his condition was permanent and that there were no other treatment options left."

"Please don't be alarmed," the neurologist soothed her, "but as you might recall, you granted us permission to proceed with any treatment we deemed necessary in Mr. Dominion's care and recuperation."

Selah nodded as she listened to the doctor trying to cover his wide-open ass. She knew the deal. They had fucked up. After all those experimental treatments with stem cells and placentas and monkey brains and whatnot, the doctors had fucked up, and now they were trying to prepare her for the hot human mess she was about to see when she stepped inside that room.

She took a deep breath.

Twenty-five years. She had been with Viceroy for over twenty-five long years. A few of them had been pretty good, and a whole lot of them had been pretty damn bad. But none of that mattered right now. After living with a man for twenty-five years the thought of losing him forever was hard as hell. In the back of her mind Selah had been prepping herself for life as a single woman ever since she got the news of Viceroy's accident and found out the extent of his injuries. For months he'd been hanging on by a thread, with every slight improvement countered by several backward steps. Selah had thought she was ready for the inevitability of losing him, but now that the time was here, maybe she wasn't.

The closer they got to his room the shorter her breaths became. Her throat felt like it was closing up and her heart felt swollen in her chest.

Selah gripped the surgeon's hand tightly as they pushed through the door of her husband's room. And the sight that greeted her as she stepped inside was enough to buckle her knees and send a small scream tearing from her throat.

"Hey, baby," Viceroy croaked in a voice that sounded like it came out of a cold, gravelly grave.

Her man was sitting up in bed, with a slew of pillows propping his frail body in place. "Damn. What the hell took you so long to get here?"

CHAPTER 8

Barron Dominion walked down the long executive corridor at Dominion Oil's headquarters, kicking himself up the ass all the way.

The DNA results on Mink and Dy-Nasty still hadn't come back yet. Pilar had jumped all in his shit for signing the papers that gave the board permission to hold a voting session without having those results in their hands, but there wasn't shit that Barron could have done about that.

And now, once the board signed off on the final documents today, there wouldn't be a damn thing he could do to stop that sexy Harlem scam-artist from getting her paws on three hundred hunks of sweet Dominion dough each and every year, either.

The last paragraph of that fucked-up letter that Suge had made him sign flashed like a strobe light in Barron's head.

And in conclusion, I hereby request that the board's vote not be delayed, but held on the original date as scheduled. Lastly, I swear and affirm that all parties to the Dominion Family Trust have been properly investigated and deemed qualified to receive their proper annual disbursements.

Fuck!

The board members his father had appointed to watch over his stash were a crew of oil-grubbin' gangsters who robbed the country blind with one hand and thumped the Bible with the other one. Barron knew them old jackers would've chewed his black ass down to the bone if they ever got some dirt on him.

His gut got tight again as he mentally replayed Suge's blackmail videotape of that skank-ass white chick claiming he was her baby daddy!

Channel Seven Keep Them Honest! I'm only seventeen and DNA doesn't lie! Can you make Barron Dominion take care of his son and pay me my child support?

Barron had been telling the God's honest truth when he swore to Pilar that he had never even met the bitch, and he had damn sure never fucked the girl, but Viceroy Dominion hadn't raised no fool. When it came to money, Barron knew the truth didn't matter, especially in the eyes of a board like the one his father had set up. If they'd found out about him running over a kid and getting a DUI they would've kicked his ass out of the trust fund in two seconds flat.

And those pictures?

Barron's gut clenched again and he turned off his cell phone as he approached the door to the conference room. He would've been *ass-fucked* if the board members had peeped those shots of his nuts hanging out of a skirt and his lips all over some random dude's dick!

He was sweating all underneath his five-thousand-dollar suit by the time he opened the door and stepped into the huge room where a group of powerful businessmen were seated around a large, oblong table. The body of rich white men, some old enough to be his granddaddy, rose to their feet out of respect for Barron's title as he approached the biggest chair at the head of the table.

Barron paused for a few moments as the men all stood up

and clapped as they beamed and smiled at him. He knew it was all fake love, but on the real tip it didn't matter how torn-out his asshole was—he was *still* the acting CEO of one of the largest and most profitable oil companies in the country, and every last one of these old bastards better recognize that shit too.

"Gentlemen," he said in a deep, commanding voice, motioning for them to take their seats so he could get down to business. "I trust everyone is in good business spirits today. The last time we met we voted to have my father, Viceroy Dominion, declared incompetent to make sound legal decisions and to carry out his primary business responsibilities here at Dominion Oil."

Barron cleared his throat and extracted a folder from his briefcase, and then he took a few sheets of paper off the top.

"Today's meeting will serve as a finalization of that vote. We have our staff notary public standing by to record your votes and notarize your signatures, and Hank"—Barron passed the document to a middle-aged man on his left whose family owned the biggest law firm in Texas—"if you could review the top document quickly and then sign it and pass it around the table, we can conclude this order of business and get on with the rest of our day."

Barron felt small as shit. His father had clawed his way up out of the trenches of the ghetto and built his business from the dirt up. Barron wanted to smash the shit out of something as he sat there watching the piece of paper that would end Viceroy's reign of power get passed around the table from greedy old white hand to greedy old white hand.

The oil rig accident had been bad enough, but all the shit that had gone down afterwards had been Barron's fault. Sitting there in his father's chair, he couldn't help feeling like a total fuckin' failure.

And he *had* failed too. Big fuckin' time. Viceroy had trusted him with billions of dollars in cash and assets, and all it had taken was two dirty rotten liars, Mink LaRue and her crusty-toe look-alike Dy-Nasty Jenkins, to run up in the Dominions' lives and fuck everything up.

Barron's chest felt tight as he thought about those two scandalous bitches. The one from Philly was gonna be easy to get rid of. His boy Frankie Gaines had dug up enough shit on her to bury her out in a cow pasture. And the other one, the one who came to Barron's bed every night and sexed the dog shit outta him in his dreams, well, she had run back to Harlem to see about her so-called boss.

Boss hell. Barron allowed himself a small chuckle inside as he thought about the hunk of cash he had wired to New York. He wasn't gonna have to worry about Mink much longer, though. Because if Gutta was good to his criminal word and he gave Barron his money's worth, then Mink was gonna get real wet when her ex-convict boo tied a cement block around that greedy bitch's neck and sent her floating to the bottom of the East River.

"Viceroy! Oh my *God*!" Selah rushed over to her husband's bedside as tears fell from her eyes. "I thought you were . . . I thought . . . Thank God you're awake!"

She squeezed him tight and planted kisses all over his face, and then she perched her slim body on the edge of the bed and cried into his shoulder as Viceroy stroked her back and tried to soothe her.

"I'm okay, baby," he murmured over and over. "It's all right. I'm okay."

"But I was so scared," Selah moaned as she cried. "I prayed for you every minute of every day, and I tried so hard to keep the faith, but the doctors said . . . they made me think . . . they said you might not be able to talk or walk or even *think* for yourself again!"

"Well them fools were wrong." Viceroy soothed her and leaned over to kiss her forehead. He had been pretty busted up in the explosion and had lost a lot of weight, but when he smiled at Selah, she saw the same old devilish dude who had knocked her off her feet all those years ago.

Fresh tears ran from Selah's eyes, but they damn sure weren't for her husband.

"Don't cry, Selah," Viceroy said in a deep voice. He lifted a shaky hand to wipe her tears away. "The time for crying is over now, baby. I'm back and I'm about to be better than ever. It's gonna take a helluva lot more than a little rig blast to stick a cat like me in a goddamn coffin."

Selah nodded and pressed a big wad of tissue to her eyes, but the truth be told, Viceroy had picked a real bad time to decide to wake his ass up! It was almost like he had gotten some kind of vibe while he was knocked out. Like somehow he'd peeped the love jones that was going down between her and his arch-enemy Rodney Ruddman and had woken up to throw some ice-cold water on their red-hot flames.

Selah suddenly felt stupid as hell for slapping Ruddman in the face in downtown Dallas. They had been right out on the street, and she never would have done something like that if she thought Viceroy had the chance of a snowball in hell of waking up and being in his right mind. Selah knew she was a high-profile figure in an elitist oil town. She was gonna have to be way more careful. Any Joe Blow with a cell phone camera could have filmed her little dust-up with Rodney and posted it on YouTube for the whole world to see.

But foolish wasn't the only thing Selah was feeling as a male nurse came to get her husband and take him downstairs for a therapy session. Rodney Ruddman had released her inner freak, and now, watching her husband get helped into a wheelchair but knowing damn well she was dying to get back to Dallas so she could see her overweight lover, had tears of frustration running from her eyes and a knot of shame eating its way through her stomach.

Selah walked toward the door with Viceroy as he was

being wheeled out. Clutching her soggy tissues, she bent down to kiss him good-bye. He took her guilt for grief and reached out and wiped at her eyes.

"C'mon, now, sugar. I'm okay, baby. I'm straight. Just gimme a minute to get back on my feet and everything is gonna be just the way it used to be. I can promise you that."

Again, Selah nodded, but behind her wet ball of tissues a hot streak of attitude flashed in her eyes. Viceroy had her twisted! Who the hell said she wanted things to go back to the way they used to be? She thought about his limp, shriveled up dick and poked out her lip. With all that good wood Rodney had been putting down on her she'd been digging her life just fine the way it was!

"Mr. Barron?"

Barron jumped and blinked his eyes real quick as his father's personal assistant handed him the small stack of documents. He glanced around the boardroom and then looked up at the elderly assistant.

"The only signature left to record is yours," she said gently, and placed her wrinkled hand on his shoulder. Sallie Kendall had been working for his father since before Barron was born. She loved Viceroy and had been steadfast in her prayers for his recovery. Right now her eyes were full of sadness and sympathy as she patted Barron's shoulder again and gave him a small smile.

Barron glanced down at the documents and then pulled out his favorite fountain pen. He had just bent forward to sign his name on the dotted line when suddenly the door burst open and Viceroy's lead secretary rushed in waving a big message pad.

"Wait, Mr. Barron!" she pleaded, waving a notepad in the air. "Wait just a second! I'm not sure you want to sign that just yet!"

Barron paused with his pen in the air.

"Why? What's the problem?" he asked, his eyes narrowed in confusion. "Is something wrong?"

"Your mother called," the old lady panted, blinking rapidly. "I was in the restroom and I missed the phone. But she left a message. She's in Houston. At the hospital. She asked me to tell you that your father is *out of his coma*! She said he's sitting up and talking! Praise the Lord, can you believe it? I guess y'all can tear up those papers and freeze the vote now because Mr. Viceroy just woke up!"

CHAPTER 9

Pilar Ducane walked into the kitchen of the Ducane manor and poured herself a small glass of orange juice. She took a sip of the chilled liquid, then shot a nasty look at her father as he sat at the table eating breakfast.

Digger Ducane might have landed himself a job at Ruddman Energy that paid decent money, but Pilar was still salty with his ass. Every last one of her credit cards was still canceled, and her father had put a restriction on the amount of money she could withdraw from her debit account each day.

Living on a tight string wasn't something a bad bitch like Pilar was accustomed to doing, and she blamed her father for causing her social status to tumble into the gutter right along with her bank account balance. She didn't give a damn about that little regular paycheck he brought in every two weeks because she wasn't interested in that kind of temporary cash.

No, Pilar wanted that perpetual shit. The type of money that rolled in generationally on the regular, year in and year out, whether you worked for it or not.

She wanted the type of dough that her relatives the Dominions had stashed away in nooks and crannies, under the floorboards and deep in the crevices of all their pockets. The kind of money that Barron's dumb ass had practically thrown away when he signed those papers letting the board give that ghetto bitch Mink and her street-slime Dy-Nasty access to the Dominion family trust fund!

Just the thought of those two bitches rolling around in that type of free cash every year while she struggled to get her luxury shopping on and her nails done and flounce her fine, cultured ass around in the best finery that money could buy, burned Pilar up.

She had done a damn good job of luring Barron between her sheets and wiping so much good pussy on him that she had his chocolate ass stuttering and strung out, but no matter how good she fucked him and no matter how much she hinted around, dude still hadn't popped that big question yet.

Pilar just didn't understand it. Everything about her was prime and she knew it. Barron should have been hopping at the chance to marry a prize piece of ass like her so he could jump her bones every night. And hell, with Viceroy on his deathbed and about to slide into his grave, it was only right that a new generation of Dominions added some fruit to the family tree and stepped up to take over the throne.

And that's why Pilar had chucked her birth control pills in the trash and started lifting her skirt and letting Barron dig her out raw as much as possible. Because the way she saw it, the best thing that could happen would be for her to miss her next period and pop up pregnant. With Barron taking over as the CEO of Dominion Oil, Pilar and her baby would be laced for life. And unless Barron wanted her to bust up in front of that board with her lip and her belly poked out like that white girl he said was on Suge's tape, his ass wouldn't have no other choice but to put a ring on her finger and put a Mrs. in front of her name.

Finishing her juice, Pilar giggled her ass off inside. She was about to pull a gold-digging extraordinaire move on Lil Bump, but she didn't feel bad about it at all. She was gonna love Barron up, and she would work her ass off to be a damn good Dominion wife.

Now, how the rest of the family was going to feel about her and Barron getting married? She glanced at her father as he slobbed down a stack of blueberry pancakes and about a pound of curled up, crunchy pork bacon. Well, that wasn't her damn problem. Pilar was on a mission to set herself up lovely as the new queen of the Dominion castle, and whoever the hell didn't like it could just kiss her ass!

She was sashaying out of the kitchen with much pep in her step when her phone vibrated and a text message came through. Clicking on her phone, Pilar's heart fluttered in her chest when she saw the message was from Barron.

Her heart damn near stopped beating when she read what was staring at her from her screen. The message read, *The board's vote has been canceled. My pops just woke up.*

Digger Ducane set his fork down on his plate when he saw the shocked expression on his daughter's face. Pilar had been walking around giving him the shit treatment for weeks, but right now his baby girl looked like somebody had slapped the taste out of her mouth.

"He woke the hell up?" she shrieked, and then started punching numbers into her cell phone as she dashed from the kitchen.

"Pilar!" Digger called out behind her. "Who woke up, Pilar? *Who* woke up?"

But his daughter ran up the stairs without answering and Digger's heart skipped a beat as he stared down at the half-eaten stack of blueberry pancakes on his plate.

Oh shit, he thought as his mouth went dry. *He woke the hell up?*

He grunted. There was only one damn person Pilar could have been talking about and he knew exactly who that was: his brother-in-law, Viceroy Dominion.

A wave of guilt washed over Digger and turned his bacon sour in his stomach. Viceroy had been his runnin' dog for over thirty years. He'd gotten Digger started in the logistics business and had even financed his very first business loan. His brother-in-law was a ruthless businessman and he wasn't the type to take betrayal lightly.

Especially the kind of betrayal that Digger had pulled on him when he jumped across the tracks and switched over to Rodney Ruddman's team.

Digger pushed his plate away and wiped his mouth on the sleeve of his shirt. His sister Selah was barely speaking to him behind that shit. She had been mad as hell when she found out he was leaving Dominion Oil while Viceroy was down and out. But Selah wasn't half as pissed as Viceroy was gonna be when he got wind of that shit, and Digger knew there was sho'nuff gonna be some hell to pay when that little bit of news landed in Viceroy's lap.

Which didn't make his current fucked-up situation at Ruddman Energy any easier either. After just a short time at his new job, Digger had managed to step on his own dick and get caught up with the wrong people.

When the economy tanked and his contracts started drying up at Dominion Oil, Digger had sworn on his dead wife's grave that he would never again get so damn broke that his credit cards melted in a roadside steak house and his baby girl couldn't afford to buy herself a new pair of shoes.

He knew the only person who could guarantee that Pilar's future was secure was *him,* so after taking the job at Ruddman Energy and scoping out what he thought was a wide-open deal, Digger had jumped under the covers with an outside trucking firm and made a back-alley deal to undercut a few of Rodney Ruddman's shipping products.

It wasn't a whole lot, just some extra shit that he had leftover from his days at Dominion Oil. But Digger had hooked up a deal to sell his products to a local trucking firm at half the price that Ruddman charged them, and he stood to make a solid hunk of change under the table.

But for some damn reason, at the last minute, just as the money exchange was scheduled to go down, the local company had backed out of the deal and left him hanging.

Digger didn't know what was up at the time, but the Texas oil bizz was a real small industry and rich people talked. And to make shit worse, for the last week or so that shrewd bastard of a boss of his, Rodney Ruddman, had started playing him real close. Digger's invoices and sales documents had recently been sent up to their financial team for a so-called routine audit, and no matter how many times his co-workers told him this was standard procedure for new partners, he had a feeling his days with the big-time oil conglomerate were about to be over damn near before they had begun.

And that meant Digger was going to be financially fucked any which way he looked at it, and he was going to be super-fucked when Viceroy found out that his old running dog didn't have a loyal bone in his body.

He woke the hell up?

Pilar's words echoed in his head like alarm bells and Digger could actually feel his ass frying. Because after the stunt he'd pulled, there was no going back to Viceroy and Dominion Oil. And if Rodney Ruddman found out that he'd been playing a little side ball with his customers, there'd be no future with Ruddman Energy either.

Digger stabbed his fork into the last of his pancakes and shoveled the syrup-soggy mess into his mouth.

Yeah, he thought as he chewed the sweet wad of dough. He was fucked all right.

Ass fucked.

CHAPTER 10

The first thing Selah had done when she left Viceroy's hospital room was to place a call to Barron. He was at Dominion Oil headquarters finalizing some paperwork and Selah knew she had to stop him.

His cell phone rang until it went straight to voice mail, and the only thing Selah could do at that point was call her husband's secretary. She started getting nervous when nobody answered at the office either, and the best she could do was leave a frantic voice mail for her son and pray he would get it in time.

Selah walked down to the waiting room and pushed open the door. Crazy excitement danced in Dy-Nasty's eyes and Selah frowned as she beckoned to the girl.

"Wha' happened? Is it over? He dead yet?"

"Excuse me?" Selah said sharply as she paused in the doorway. Dy-Nasty was kicked back and lounging with her legs swung to the side and her crusty feet up in a chair. A faded corner-store toe ring complete with a fake plastic jewel was on her big toe.

"I mean," Dy-Nasty caught herself and sat up straight, "what's up with Daddy Viceroy? Is the old fella doin' a'ight?"

"He's fine," Selah said shortly, motioning for the girl to get up and follow her down the hall. "I've got some business to take care of," she told Dy-Nasty as they headed out the exit where the limousine waited.

Selah nodded as the driver jumped out and opened the back door.

"Go ahead and get in." She waved Dy-Nasty off. "The driver will take you to the heliport and put you on the jet. My pilot's going to drop you off at home, and then he'll pick up Barron and Dane and bring them down here to meet me."

Dy-Nasty bucked. "Drop me off at home? *Whut?* So I came all the way down here with you and now you gonna be a flat-leaver and make me ride back by myself?"

Selah smirked, nodded, and shooed her toward the limo. "That's right. You'll be fine, Dy-Nasty. It's a very short ride. Take a nap or something, and by the time you wake up you'll be there."

Dy-Nasty was pissed off about getting the boot, but there wasn't a damn thing she could do except poke her lip out and shoot Selah some eye-daggers as she climbed her booty in the back of the sleek, shiny whip and headed for the house.

"Uh-uh, I ain't going," I said and stared out the window. "I ain't fuckin' going."

"Umm . . ." Peaches twisted his lips and lit into me as we sped toward the airport in his boyfriend's whip. "I hate to be the one to tell you, boo-boo, but you ain't got no other choice!"

I pressed a cold can of Pepsi to my dotted eye and winced. It was like the Wild, Wild West in Harlem. The bullets was flying and Peaches was tryna sneak me outta Dodge. He had jetted outta Lower Manhattan and was zipping my ass straight over the bridge to the airport.

"I can't just up and leave like that, Peaches," I protested into a tissue filled with the blood that Gutta had punched outta my nose. "It ain't that simple, dude."

"Don't be stupid! It ain't that hard neither unless you wanna die! You gots ta get up outta here and take your ass back to Texas, Mink. Ta-*day*!"

I was grateful as hell that Peaches had tracked me down and rescued me from Gutta's crazy ass, but I wasn't feeling this plan of his *at all*!

I shook my head and got dizzy as shit.

"Boy you know I can't go back down there to them Dominions! Their *real* daughter rolled up in the joint, remember? They ain't gonna let me stay there no more. Especially after they get them damn DNA results back and find out I was gankin' them the whole time!"

Peaches smirked, dismissing my excuse. "You's a con-mami, Madame Mink. A grifter. Your life is one big game of chance. Cross all them other bridges when you get to 'em. You can lie your way around that DNA test when the time comes, but right now you gots ta *go*!"

"B-b-but"—I glanced down at my black and white funeral dress that was covered in big red splotches of blood—"I can't get on no airplane looking like no stabbed-up penguin!" I protested. "As soon as some nosy-ass square peeps me walking around looking like a crime victim they gonna call the police. And besides, I ain't got no ends on me. I hid my last little bit of money at the crib. I taped it way up inside the toilet bowl plunger!"

Peaches smirked and waved me off. "I gives not a damn about none of that. You gots to get up outta here, Mink. Gutta is gonna *execute* your yellow ass if you step foot back in Harlem, baby. Don't worry. All we gotta do is call Bunni and tell her where your money is. She can get that shit and grab you some clothes and whatnot, and then she can catch a cab and meet us at the airport 'cause both of y'all heffas gotta disappear."

"But what about *you*?" I moaned, scared as shit and trembling in my thong. "We can't leave you here by yourself! What's gonna happen if Gutta comes after *you*?"

Peaches sucked his teeth and tried to sound all brave.

"Just let that fool come fuckin' with me if he wanna! I'ma run right up in his tight ass, okay? He probably got his lil chocolate cherry took while he was upstate in the bing, but if he didn't and he brings it over here, it's gonna be *minez*!"

I stared at Peaches as silent tears rolled from my eyes. I owed this dude my life in so many damn ways that I couldn't even count them all. He was like a mama, a daddy, a big brother, and a best friend all rolled up in one. He had done more for me than anybody else in the whole damn world, and I woulda never forgave myself if Gutta or somebody went at his throat just because *I* had fucked up.

"P, please." I waved him off. "I don't believe nothin' you saying right now, boo. You talkin' all that gangsta shit about drillin' Gutta's hole when that ain't even your role. You's a bottom bitch, remember? You ain't no top, so don't go out there tryna pop nobody's cherry and don't be playing Superman no more tryna save my ass neither, okay?"

He twisted his lips and cut his eyes at me as he drove.

"You don't know *everything* about me, Madam Mink! Yeah I look damn good in a hot-pink dress but I ain't nobody's faggot! Besides"—he pursed his extra-glossy lips and batted his eyelashes—"when I feel like being on the bottom, I'm a bottom. And when a fool gets too fly and I need to be on top, then I gets my ass up on top! Now call Bunni," he demanded, and reached into his bra and passed me his cell phone. "Call her," Peaches said. "And tell her to meet us at JFK."

A chill went through me as I thought about that killer look I'd seen in Gutta's eyes. And then I grabbed that phone and did exactly what the hell Peaches said.

With Dy-Nasty out of her hair, Selah headed back to the visitor's lounge and got down to business. Seeing Viceroy wide awake and sitting up in bed like that had shocked the shit out of her, but now that he was alert she wanted to make sure her husband was as comfortable as possible. The male nurse had said Viceroy would be downstairs in therapy for quite a bit, and it was going to take at least two hours for the jet to get Dy-Nasty to Dallas and then fly back with Barron and Dane, so there were a couple of key things Selah could do while she waited.

She relaxed in an armchair and took her cell phone out of her purse and got to punching in some numbers. She knew her husband, and she knew what he liked. No matter how far they'd crawled away from the ghetto or how much money they had stacked over the years, there were certain things about Viceroy that would never change. He still got his hair cut by Harvey, the slick-talking Houston barber who'd been edging him up since he was a kid.

Selah called Harvey real quick and told him she was going to send a car to pick him up so he could come to the hospital and give Viceroy a nice trim, and then she arranged to have a professional manicurist brought over from an exclusive Houston spa to give her husband a much-needed hot eyebrow wax and a professional shave.

An hour and a half later, Viceroy's fingernails had been cut and cleaned up, and his feet had been soaked, buffed, oiled, and massaged. A shopping service had delivered a bag filled with a rich man's luxury items. It contained his favorite cologne and all of his expensive personal hygiene items, along with copies of every top business magazine in the country.

Selah put in a few more calls and had several pairs of satin pajamas and smoking jackets sent to Viceroy's private room, and while he was downstairs in therapy the plain cotton hospital sheets had been switched out with a brand-new set that had two-thousand-count Egyptian fibers.

Selah was mentally exhausted when a nurse poked her head in the waiting room and said the doctors wanted to talk to her. She was led to a small conference room where Viceroy's doctors were waiting for her.

"How was your visit with your husband?" the internist wanted to know.

Selah shook her head in disbelief. "It was amazing. Simply amazing. You guys are miracle workers. You brought Viceroy back from the grave!"

"Well," the neurologist cautioned, "Mr. Dominion has come a long way but he's not completely out of the woods yet. The brain is a very delicate organ and it can take quite a long time to heal. I advise you and your family to take it slow and be very patient as your husband recovers. Try not to bombard him with complex issues or overtire him with anything that might pose a challenge to his memory or his emotions."

The doctor placed his hand on Selah's arm and lowered his voice. "I would also strongly advise you against placing any heavy demands on Mr. Dominion right now, such as leading a global enterprise like Dominion Oil. Give him time. It's likely that his cognitive functioning will return to normal rather quickly, but his emotional centers were badly damaged, and that kind of healing may take a little longer."

The worried look on Selah's face prompted the doctor to go into reassurance mode.

"Don't worry, Mrs. Dominion. Your husband is a very strong-willed man and his prognosis is excellent. We've conducted an extensive battery of tests on him, and after being conscious for just twenty-four short hours, he's already alert and showing signs of a strong personality. Any residual effects from his brain injury will probably be short-term, and given enough time your husband could very well make a remarkable recovery. But don't be surprised if his mood swings erratically or if he's easily confused and forgets things. Brain trauma can have a really tough effect on a patient's emotions."

Selah's head was spinning as she was taken back to the

waiting area to wait for Barron and Dane to arrive. And when they finally showed up she cautioned them and gave them the same run-down that the doctors had given her, and then she kissed and hugged them and escorted them down the long hallway to their father's bedside.

Selah couldn't help feeling some kind of way inside. She was a realist from the streets of Brooklyn, and she knew her marriage wasn't going to catch a brand-new spark just because Viceroy had come back from the dead. But for the sake of her kids Selah was glad her husband was back in the world, and no matter how low she had been creeping while he was knocked out, deep in her heart she was happy that Viceroy had pulled through too.

But all those happy feelings went flying right out the window as soon as the three of them stepped inside his hospital room.

Viceroy was sitting up in a plush leather recliner that had been brought down from the hospital's executive suite. A copy of *Forbes* magazine was open on his lap, and the stock pages from the *New York Times* were folded up neatly at his feet.

"Ay, tell me something," he barked, ignoring Selah and grilling his sons with ice chips in his eyes as they approached his bed. "Which one of y'all is the fuckin' idiot and which one is the goddamn fool?"

Selah's smile hit the floor as she froze in her tracks.

Barron and Dane shot each other a quick, puzzled glance and then Barron automatically stepped up to the plate.

"It's good to see you too, Pop! Hey, we missed you, man!"

"Oh yeah?" Viceroy looked like a snake on a hunt as he nodded. "Well I missed you too. Matter fact, I missed you so much I checked up on your asses! Lemme ask y'all something." He leaned forward in his chair like a predator who was about to pounce. "Did anything go down while I was knocked out that y'all wanna tell me about?"

Barron glanced at Selah, then frowned and shook his head. "Nope. No, sir. Not that I can think of, Pops. Everything's been pretty chill, actually."

Viceroy leaned forward even more. "You sure about that? I mean, nobody got fucked up, ain't nobody pregnant, nobody's on drugs or in jail?"

"Nah, everybody's pretty stable, Pops. Why? Everything is good with you, right?"

"Hell naw, everything ain't good!" Viceroy exploded as he sat up straighter and tossed his magazine to the floor. "Matter fact, shit is wrong as all hell when I gotta find out from somebody outside my family that my own *sons*"—he spit, and then turned his icy gaze on Selah—"and my own damn *wife*, are out there trying to steal my fuckin' *company* away from me!"

Selah backpedaled from the killer heat burning in her husband's eyes as Barron held up his hands and tried to calm shit down.

"Whoa, whoa, *whoa*! Hold up, now! Nobody tried to steal nothing from you, Pops!" Barron glanced at Selah and Dane with a look of pure-dee panic on his face. "I don't know what's going on, but you got some bad info, man. Some real bad info!"

Viceroy might have looked weak and frail, but the ghetto streets were still running deep in his blood, and underneath his tailored smoking pajamas his nuts were just as big and hairy as they had always been.

"Bad info? You call this here shit bad info?" he said, glaring at Barron as he held a sheet of paper in the air. "I just got faxed a copy of the minutes from the board meeting that *you* called last week!"

Barron's eyes got big as shit.

"Boy"—Viceroy was so pissed off that his hands shook and spit flew outta his mouth—"you called *my* fuckin' officers together so they could vote me outta *my* position and knock me off *my* fuckin' block?"

Barron shook his head real fast.

"You think you doggish enough to snatch a bone away from me, Barron? You think you *hard enough* to go head-up against a hustler like me and try to put your paws on something that's *mine*?"

Barron felt a chill run down his spine. "No, Pops! No!"

"You mean *hell* naw!" Viceroy barked from between his clenched teeth. "I'ma tell you right now, you don't even wanna *think* that shit, Lil Bump! I *bite* pups like you for lunch, baby boy! Trust what I'm saying. You don't even wanna try it!"

The raging anger that was radiating off his father was so hot and out of the blue that Barron was having a hard time catching his breath.

"Yo, nobody tried to take nothing from you, Pop!" he insisted. "We worked our asses off trying to do everything the way we thought *you* would have wanted us to do it!"

"And how the hell did y'all do that? By sitting around in a goddamn Holy Roller circle praying for my black ass to *die*?"

Barron raised his hands slightly in the air.

"Hold up. Now calm down, Pops—"

"Fool, is you crazy?" Viceroy exploded, and tried to come up out of his chair. "Don't you tell *me* to calm the fuck down, Bump! You wanna tell me something?" he demanded as he reached behind his back and grabbed a small stack of papers from the cushions of his chair. He held them up high in the air. "Then tell me what the hell you was gonna do with *this*?"

"I . . . I . . . I . . . ," Barron gasped and stuttered like a little kid when he recognized the copies of Mink and Dy-Nasty's test results from Exclusively DNA.

"Since when do you hide shit from me," Viceroy blasted, "especially when it comes down to *my* family and *my* fuckin' money?"

Barron's eyes got big as hell.

"We wasn't tryna hide nothing from you, Pop! I swear to God we wasn't! You was knocked out, man! I was gonna run the whole thing down to you right off the bat but the doctors said not to put too much on your plate at one time!"

Viceroy's eyes got narrow as he cupped his hand behind his ear and wigged out on his son. "Excuse me? What was that? You didn't wanna put too much on my plate? Fuck them doctors! Who the fuck are you trying to *handle*, Barron? Don't you know I'm from the *hood,* son? I came up out there in them goddamn *gutters*! Didn't nobody give me *nothing*! I hustled for mine in the trenches! Scrapped for it, fought for it, and scrambled for it! Don't you know a nigga like me been grubbin' off a big plate *all my life*?"

Barron threw up his hands and stood there with his mouth wide open. He glanced at his mother for help but Selah couldn't call it either. She was stunned by the words that were rolling out of her husband's mouth. He sounded gritty as hell. Just like he used to sound thirty years ago. Like he had never left the streets of Houston and was still living the thug life in the projects and scratching his way out of the crab barrel just to survive.

Even the look on Viceroy's face was pure hood. It was like that bump on his head had reverted him right back to the old hooligan he used to be, and that smooth, polished front he had worn to keep up his high-class image was now a wrap. No, Selah hadn't heard her man get down this gutter in a very long time, and he had never, *ever,* blasted on their sons like this before.

Never.

But Viceroy was still burning on fire as he clenched his lips and grilled all three of them at the same time.

"See, I know what I gotta do now," he muttered, his eyes darting from one of them to the other. "Yeah, I know *exactly* what the hell I gotta do! I'm about to switch up my will and restructure that trust fund! I'm about to kick all y'all out from under my nuts! Y'all fools damn-near ran my business into a black hole while I was laying up in here. Goddamn profits are way down and expenses are way up!"

Viceroy glanced down at the DNA results he still clenched in his fist.

"And this right here." He shook the papers in the air again. "This bullshit *right here*? Man, I spent thirty fuckin' years keeping my hands clean and my shoes shined! And the minute I close my eyes y'all let these two . . . *cash cows* get up in my house and shit all over my good name!"

"Daddy, I *swear*," Barron pleaded. "All I was tryna do was figure out which one of them was really Sable," he explained. "We knew one of them was lying but we didn't know which one!"

"Fool! Both of them are lying!" Viceroy exploded, and then he keeled over and grabbed his temples and squeezed his eyes closed as he clutched his head between his trembling palms.

"Pops!" Barron shrieked, and jetted to his father's chair. But Dane had already beat him to the spot, and all Barron could do was stand there and watch as Dane eased their frail father into a sitting position and wiped a few furious flecks of drool from his lips.

Selah grabbed a glass of cold water from the nightstand and tried to get him to drink some, but Viceroy shook his head and shoved it away.

"Let's get one thing straight right now dammit," he said, going hard again as he caught his breath. His sunken eyes swept over his wife and sons in a rage. "Both of these goddamn scam artists are frauds! *Both of their asses!* There *is no* DNA match for Sable out there because Sable is *dead*!"

Selah shrieked and clapped her hand over her mouth.

"She's dead, dammit! She is DEAD!"

"B-b-but those are the original DNA results," Barron insisted, pointing at Mink's and Dy-Nasty's papers, which were still clutched in his father's hand. "Both of them came back a match for Sable so we made 'em both take the test again and—"

"You's a goddamn *idiot*!" Viceroy spit. "Do you know how many pieces of that paper money can buy? I can get a DNA test to say *any damn thing* I want it to say!" Viceroy stared Barron down and there was no hiding the hood contempt that was in his eyes. "I'm disappointed in you, son. I'm damned disappointed 'cause I *know* I schooled you better than that!"

"But, Pops—"

"They suckered you, Barron! They ran a scheme on you and you folded under the pressure, son! You let them two trifling gold diggers grab hold of your nuts and twist you up! But I know one thing. By the time I get outta this hospital you better have both of them greedy bitches outta my goddamn house or I'ma—"

"Viceroy!" Selah barked. "That's enough, goddammit! What the hell is wrong with you? *Bitches*? You wanna call *me* a bitch? Do you wanna call Fallon one? Hell no! And those girls aren't *bitches* either! Now, one of them is Sable. Our daughter. Our *baby*! And I don't give a damn what you say, I'm not gonna stop until I find out which one it is!"

The look Viceroy gave Selah should have knocked her to her knees.

But instead it brought the Brooklyn out of her and pissed her the fuck off.

"*Muthafucka* . . . ," Selah spat with her jaw clenched tight. "Who the hell are you looking at like that? Yeah, you heard what I said, and I damn sure didn't stutter! I'm gonna find Sable. I'm gonna *find* my child! And if you hadn't been out there fucking around with that jailbait piece of ass then we probably wouldn't have lost her in the first damn place!"

Barron and Dane turned toward their mother with a stunned look of complete shock on their faces. Selah had *never* gone off on Viceroy in front of them. Never. They were used to seeing her cry and beat herself up over Sable all the time, but they had never, *ever*, heard her put the blame on their father before. But Selah wasn't bullshitting. All traces of her lady-like cool had disappeared, and the hard streets of Brooklyn glinted in her eyes.

Looking like a shamefaced old dog, Viceroy held up his hand and pulled back on some of that beef he was spitting.

"Uh-uh, Selah," he told her. "Don't even go there. This ain't the time and it damn sure ain't the place. Let's leave the past in the *past*, a'ight? I'm tryna deal with what's going on right *now* and find out why the hell Barron let those two slum bunnies take him for a ride! No son of mine could be that damn stupid. No damn son of mine!"

His words cut across the room and slashed Barron like a knife, and Selah felt her son jerk like his nuts had been sliced off.

"Oh, is that right?" Selah stepped forward and put her hands on her hips and asked her husband coldly. "Well, I thought no damn *sister* of mine could be that stupid either." She smirked. "But after that little head-on-heels party y'all fuckers had going on in your office the day Sable was kidnapped, I guess I was wrong. *Remember*?"

Selah locked eyes with Viceroy and dared him to get brand-new. She'd tear a hole in his damn throat, fuckin' with her Barron like that! Shit, bumped damn head or not, it was time for this fool to get shut *down*!

Viceroy's lips trembled like he wanted to spray off at the mouth again, but Selah eyeballed him a warning and dared him to pounce. She would fuck him straight up!

After a second or two she saw the fight go out of his eyes and she pulled back a little bit too. Oh, it was still going to go down between them, but Selah knew Viceroy was right, and with their sons standing there looking shell-shocked this was neither the time nor the place.

Besides, she knew exactly how nasty Viceroy could be and how deep his sharp tongue could cut. And no matter what those damn doctors had said, she wasn't about to blame everything on his head injury either, because underneath all that smooth, glossy shine her husband wore when he was in public, Viceroy was a cutthroat, ruthless snake right down to his ghetto bones! Hell, you didn't steal a profitable oil company out of the back pocket of your best friend and swindle your way into a billion dollars and not have some hoodlum in you!

When it was time for them to leave, Viceroy waited until Barron and Dane were almost out the door and then he called Selah back.

"Hey baby," he said softly, and waved her over to his chair.

Selah stared at him cautiously. She didn't know what bag her husband was about to come out of, but the doctors had warned that his moods might swing, and besides, the look in his eyes had changed. They looked calm and serious. Sensuous and intense.

Selah took the hand he had extended her and let herself be pulled close to his chair.

"Look, I'm sorry, baby," Viceroy said, gazing up at her with an apology in his eyes. He reached for her waist and pulled her down into his lap. "I don't know what got into me. I didn't mean to go off on you like that."

"V-Viceroy," Selah stuttered as her fluffy ass sank down into his groin. He was so skinny she could feel his thigh-bones poking through his flesh. "It's okay, dear," she said, shifting her weight so that she was turned halfway toward him. She stared into his dark, handsome face and reached up and ran her hand over his smooth, freshly-shaved jawline.

"You've been through a lot, Viceroy," she soothed him. "It's all right. The doctors warned us that it was going to take a little time for things to go back to normal. Let's just take everything slowly, okay?"

Viceroy nodded and Selah saw something else creep into his eyes.

"I think some things are already back to normal," he whispered thickly.

His hands slid down her shoulders and gripped her hips and he thrust his pelvis upward in an obscene humping motion.

Selah stiffened.

"Viceroy," she said sharply. She went to pull away and he grabbed her hips and gripped her even tighter as he pumped his bony hips up at her. "I'm not sure this is a good idea. I'm pretty heavy. I put on a couple of pounds after your accident, and it's too soon for you to be doing this type of thing anyway. Let me get up, baby. I don't want to hurt you."

"What? You still don't think I can handle you, huh Selah? Come on, baby," he whispered as he slow-grinded his hips and nuzzled his nose into her cleavage. His hands roamed over her breasts and hips like he was a horny teenager. "I'm a man, baby, and we both have needs. It's been a real long time, Selah. You feel this shit? I'm back in business now!"

Selah paused in place as he dry fucked her and squeezed on her titties. She reached between their bodies and felt for his crotch. And just as she expected, his bone was soft and limp.

"That's enough," she said, jumping out of his lap as she tried to hide her disgust. Selah had the type of pussy that craved power, and it was power that had attracted her to Viceroy from the start. His loose, flaccid penis didn't do a thing for her. It just made him seem weak.

"Damn," she said, smoothing her clothes down. "You just survived a horrible accident and woke up from an extended coma, Viceroy. The last thing you should be thinking about right now is *fucking*."

Her husband grinned as he shot her a cold look.

"That's right. And it's the last thing *you* better be thinking about too. Remember that!"

CHAPTER 11

We landed at DFW airport and I got off that plane walking like a trauma victim and looking like a stomped rat. I had fidgeted and twitched in my seat the whole damn time we was flying, and every time I dozed off and started to get a little sleep I'd get hit with a flashback and wake up crying in a cold panic.

"You're safe, Mink. You're gonna be okay," Bunni told me over and over again, shhh'ing me and stroking my hair like I was her pet poodle. She had gotten the yardage I'd stashed outta that nasty toilet bowl plunger and met me at the airport with a couple of stuffed suitcases, and then we had jumped our asses on the first thing smoking down to Dallas.

"Just hold on, girlfriend," she said. "We about to get you straight, Minkie-boo, and ere'thang is gonna be okay."

I didn't know where the hell Bunni was getting that lie from but I could understand why she was telling it. My ass was all the way on the ground. I hadn't felt this low since the day when I was thirteen and that jogger had pulled me wet and screaming outta Mama's car as it sank to the bottom of the cold Hudson River.

Right now my heart was all twisted up and my emotions

were all over the map. I kept going back and forth between grieving over Mama's death and being scared shitless that Gutta was gonna hunt me down and kill my yellow ass.

"You prolly depressed or some shit, Mink," Doctor Bunni called herself diagnosing me, and the bad thing was, I kinda felt like she was calling it right.

"Losing your mama and finding out about all her lies, then having that big gorilla fool jumpin' all over you like that . . . hell, my ass would be depressed too."

Getting my behind kicked in by Gutta had been a hurtin' thang, but it was definitely a beat-down that I'd had coming. As a certified con-mami of the highest order, I was well versed in the code of the streets, and by all rights that crazy nigga coulda *killed* me for fucking over his moolah like that. And sadly, there was something inside of me that wished he had just taken me out and gotten my miserable life over and done with!

"I know it's gonna be hard for you to go right back to work," Bunni warned me as we inched our way outta the terminal step by little tiny step. Gutta had tried his best to stomp my tailbone into itsy-bitsy pieces, and I could still feel his boot hammering on me back there with every step I took. "But we back in Texas now, Mink. You gonna hafta pull yourself together boo-boo so we can get back on this grind, *okay*?"

Bunni could go 'head with all that. I couldn't answer her and I couldn't even look at her. The only thing I could do was keep my eyes on the floor dead in front of me and concentrate on swinging my right leg around in a way that didn't make the bones in my lower back crunch together and scream bloody murder.

"Mink, did you hear what I said?" Bunni asked as she gripped my arm to steady me.

I felt kinda bad for iggin' her. My girl was already lugging all the shit she had packed for us in two bags, and here she was tryna hold my busted ass up too.

"I heard you," I muttered. "I just don't know what more you want me to do, Bunni. I'm done. Can't you see I'm done?"

For once the God's honest truth was coming outta my mouth.

And I was dead serious about that shit too. I knew I had a role to play if I was gonna keep ganking these rich Texas folks and get my hands on that three hundred grand every year, but it seemed like all the greed and all the gusto for the game had gone right outta me. My mama's lies had put my hustle on a block of cold ice. My heart wasn't in scheme mode like it usually was, and I could understand why Bunni was worrying so hard about me.

"C'mon," she said, stopping dead in the middle of the terminal so she could fix my hair and straighten up my clothes. She had brought me a pair of tight jeans and a red low-cut shirt to change into at the airport, then made me throw my jacked-up funeral dress in the trash.

She frowned and grilled me for a hot second, then dug around in her purse and came out with a balled up piece of tissue.

"Here," Bunni said. She licked the tissue and got it wet, then held it out to me with her lip all turned up. "Hit that right nostril real quick, why don't ya. Uncle Suge is outside waiting for us and you gonna be lookin' real stupid walking out that door with all them crusty boogers stuck up in ya nose."

Uncle Suge was waiting right outside where Bunni said he was gonna be, and the minute I saw him posted up like a big black stallion standing next to his silver-bullet monster truck, I felt some kinda way inside.

I had missed me some of him, but for once I didn't give a damn whether I looked delicious or not. Suge could take me or leave me just like I was, but since I knew Barron was gonna toss my orphan-ass outta the mansion just as soon as them

DNA results came back, I reached out for Suge like he was a chocolate-covered homeless shelter.

"Hey sexy," my Texas dude growled hungrily. He pulled me into his big strong arms and started attacking my lips like he was starving for me.

I winced and moaned out loud as he squeezed me tight and my sore bones got to crackin'. He pulled back a lil bit and stared down into my eyes.

"You okay?" he asked, eyeballing my swollen lip and all my bruises. "What the hell happened, baby?"

"I . . . umm . . . our taxicab got into a little bumper bender on the way to the airport," I lied. "It wasn't that bad, but I was sitting up front and forgot to put on my seat belt and did a face-plant into the dashboard. Bunni and the cabdriver didn't get not one scratch. But I'm good, baby. I'm good."

Suge gave me a doubtful look. "You want me to swing you by the hospital so you can get checked out?"

I shook my head too quick and almost cracked my neck.

"Umm, no. I'm okay. For real. I just need a hot bath and a double shot of yak-daddy and I'll be okay."

He nodded and pulled me closer to him. "Did everything go okay with ya boss?"

That's when I lost it. I just couldn't help myself when I hiccupped and two fat tears slid from my eyes.

"Hey, hey, hey!" Suge rubbed my back gently. He sounded real surprised to see me crying.

I pressed my face into his chest and wiped my two little tears on his shirt, and then I looked back up at him and tried to smile a lil bit.

"Nah, my boss didn't make it. She passed," I said, shaking my head sadly. "She was almost gone by the time I got there, but at least I got home to see her in time."

I sniveled again, then glanced at Bunni and she had an evil look plastered on her grill that said, *Get a grip, dammit! Ya shit is slippin'!*

I wiped my eyes and shrugged. "I guess me and her was kinda close for her to just be my boss, but that's a long story. I'll tell you about it one day."

Suge used his big ol' thumbs to wipe my eyes, and I sniffed as he leaned forward and pressed his lips lightly to my nose.

"I'm sorry to hear that, baby," he said as he opened the front and back passenger doors so me and Bunni could hop in his truck, "but I got a story to tell you too. Actually, I've got some news for you."

I paused with my foot up on the running board. "Oh really?"

He gave me the "hold up" sign as his phone sounded off on his belt. He took it off the clip and glanced at the screen, and then put it right back on the clip without answering it.

"That was Barron. I'll get back with him later."

"So what's your news?"

"Well what do you want first? The good news or the bad news?"

My shot-out ass only hesitated for a real quick second.

"Gimme the good news."

"A'ight, well, the good news is, Barron signed the letter I drafted up for him, and the board had their meeting. They agreed to open up the trust fund and activate our annual payments, and Barron is up at Dominion Oil headquarters right now getting the final paperwork signed."

Bunni screamed real loud and started holding her belly and winding her hips and singing, "Buh-buh-buh! *Baby*, I'm a rich bitch! Yah-yah-yah, *baby,* I'm a rich bitch! A rich bitch!"

I rolled my eyes and shook my head. "The damn money ain't in our hands yet, Bunni! Barron is just taking care of the paperwork, girl, dag!"

I turned back to Uncle Suge. Uh-huh. My dumb ass just had to go 'head and ask.

"So what's the bad news?"

Uncle Suge's grin fell right off his face.

"The bad news is, the DNA tests still ain't back yet. Yours or Dy-Nasty's."

I shrugged. "So what? The board already voted, though, right? That means we're in there and me and Dy-Nasty already agreed to split the money fifty-fifty, so what's the problem?"

Suge sighed and shook his head. "The problem is, I dreamt your results came back a positive match and Dy-Nasty's came back negative."

"*And*?" me and Bunni both spit at the same time. "What's so bad about that?"

Uncle Suge looked grim. "Well, I got with my bookie and put a little cash on that dream. I bet fifty grand on you to win and Dy-Nasty to lose."

"Yeah, and what happened?" my dumb ass asked.

He stared at me for a quick second and then said, "Your horse stumbled right out the gate and broke his damn leg. They had to put him down right there on the track."

"Well damn! So what about Dy-Nasty? What happened to her horse?"

Uncle Suge shrugged and patted my arm.

"Sorry, baby. Her horse won. That sucker came in first place."

Soaring high in the sky on the short flight from Houston to Dallas, Barron listened to his uncle's phone roll to voice mail, and then he stretched out in a corner lounge seat feeling shook like fuck.

The rage his father had displayed when Barron walked into his hospital room had hit him right in his heart and he didn't know if he was ever gonna get over that shit. Barron couldn't stop hearing the gutter noise rolling off Pop's tongue as dude barked on him like he was just some little stray nigga he had run into on the streets.

As tight as him and Viceroy were, and with all their closeness, their respect for each other, and that special bond of father-son love they used to share, it had all been shaken in just one fucked-up conversation. And no matter how many medical excuses Selah came up with to justify what Viceroy had said, the grimy level of disrespect in his father's words had knocked Barron off his feet and it hurt.

"Blame it on his head and not his heart," Selah had begged her son over and over as they rode in the limo on the way back to the heliport.

"Nah," Barron had mumbled. "Pop knew what he was saying. He just spoke his true mind, that's all."

"Your father has a *brain* injury, Barron. It's not like he just walked past a rock and stubbed his damn toe, you know. The brain is a very fragile organ. The doctors warned us that his mood might be off and his personality might not be the same as it used to be. They expected this and we should have expected it too. Don't take it personal, baby. The doctors say it might take a little time, but they believe your father will be himself again one day. We just have to do like they said. Be patient and take it slow."

Barron understood where Selah and the doctors were coming from, but it didn't make it any easier for him to stomach that shit, though. He had distanced himself from Dane and Selah and grabbed a blanket and went to sit in the way back of the jet. He'd tried to take a nap, but that shit wasn't happening and all he could do was lay back and stare at the ceiling and second-guess the hell outta his every move.

On the real, Barron had never really expected his father to come up outta that coma in the first place, and now every single thing that he had done, every single decision that he had made since the day Viceroy got hurt, was being examined under a magnifying glass in his mind.

He mentally replayed his actions over and over, searching for any fucked-up steps he mighta taken that his pops could zero in on and then smash him over the head with.

Yeah, the messed-up night that he'd gotten drugged in that frat house was gonna be a problem, and the DUI he'd been slapped with and the little kid he'd run over was going to be a real bitch to explain too. But the biggest issue fucking with Barron's head right now was the twisted-up sex thang he had going on with Pilar.

He would've been better off sticking with his white girlfriend, Carla, because there was no way in fuck his father was gonna be cool with him splashing his dick around in family coochie and mashing it up with Pilar.

No way in hell! Barron could see it now. Viceroy would lunge at his throat like a pit bull on a kitten if he found out his son was tapping his first cousin's ass! All that "adopted" shit didn't mean a damn thing in the Dominion house. Family was family, *period*, and the Dominions weren't the type of black people who played that kissing-cousin shit.

It was gonna be hard getting Pilar off his dick, and Barron knew she was gonna buck and bitch and act a real live fool, but he didn't have no other choice. He had to clean his shit up and clean it up fast.

Yeah, Barron sighed. He reached under the blanket and gripped his balls and gave them a squeeze through his pants. That pussy was good and he was gonna miss it like a muthafucka. But Pilar had to *go*.

CHAPTER 12

We rode back to the mansion with me sweating Uncle Suge's crazy dream and them damn DNA results all the way. I could tell he was kinda pressed out over how me and him was gonna be if my results really did come in positive, and I wished I could just tell him we wasn't related so he could stop worrying about that shit.

"Maybe you really are Sable." He reached over and touched my hair as we sat outside the mansion in his truck. Bunni had already gone inside, and it was just me and him, the truth and the lie, sitting out there in the driveway.

"I don't really know," I lied. "I mean, shit's been real shady since I first came down here, Suge. Y'all rich gangstas got the kinda pull to make a piece of paper say any damn thing you want it to say, right? So who's to say what the DNA results are gonna be? Who's to say that I'm Sable and Dy-Nasty's not? Or who's to say that she's Sable and I'm not?"

I was talking a real smoove game, but deep inside my heart I knew exactly what time it was. That damned Dy-Nasty really *was* Sable. I'd known the truth about her for a while now, and as much as I hated to admit it, that donkey-ass trick was also my *sister*. Why in the world Mama had decided to keep me with her and give Dy-Nasty away was an unsolved mystery, but that shit *had* to have happened because it was the only damn thing that made any sense.

"Listen up," Suge growled as he leaned over and pressed his lips to my cheek. "I don't give a damn who you be, lil mama." He rubbed his nose over my earlobe and whispered in a deep, husky voice, "I just don't want you to leave me no more, you feel me?"

Oh, I'm feeling your ass all right!

I turned my head and looked into his dark eyes and then I swallowed real hard and nodded.

"I'm glad you don't want me to leave," I said softly, and then thought, *'cause my black ass ain't got no place else to go!*

Bunni's way of thinking could be way, way, outta the box, but this time my girl was on point and she had at least one damn thing right: If I was gonna walk away from this hustle with more than two nickels in my pocket, then I was gonna hafta forget all the bad shit Mama had done to me and get back on my game.

Climbing outta Uncle Suge's truck, I ignored the waves of pain that pulsated down my spine and shot up and down my legs. Taking a deep breath, I nodded what's up at the security dude named Durant and then I switched my gangsta booty through the front door of that mansion like I was a Dominion diva on the grind.

And wouldn't you know it, the first damn person I ran into was that horse-tail, weave-wackin', scandalous-lookin' slouch, *Dy-Nasty*!

That two-dollar Philly stripper had a nasty hood scent rollin' offa her that made my stomach turn sour, and the look in her hazel eyes told me she had sniffed the same damn scent on me.

We stood in the front parlor grilling each other like two alley cats with our tails up in the air. She put her grubby hands with the bit-back nails on her thick ghetto hips, and I put my slick gel manicured hands on minez. I twisted my lips up like she was foul and grimy, and she shot me the same damn look right back.

"Where's Mama Selah?" I demanded. The mansion seemed real quiet. Like the only energy in the whole house was rolling off of me and Dy-Nasty.

"She ain't here!"

"Stop playing." I shot her a funky look. "Where is she?"

"In my bra, stupid ass! Where you think?"

"Oh, you funny as hell. Funny-lookin'!"

"Your ass is funny-lookin' too. And don't be eyeballin' me all stank, Mink," Dy-Nasty giggled like she was up on something slick as she cut her amber cat-eyes at me. " 'Cause when them DNA results get back ere'body up *in* here is gonna know who is really who!"

"Oh you damn right they gonna know!" I said, bluffing my ass off.

"Yep, 'cause minez is gonna be a match."

"And minez is gonna be a match too!"

"Bitch, *please*!" we both said at the same time.

"You ain't even slick. I already know who yo ass is!" I said like I was a detective on a case.

"And I know who yo ass *ain't*!" she spit back.

"Yeah, whatever."

"Yeah, whatever-whatever! That's why I'm the one Mama Selah took with her to Houston to visit my daddy today and you *wasn't*!"

"What damn *daddy*?" I smirked. "A trick like you wouldn't know your goddamn daddy if he reached down in his pants and smacked you in the forehead with his big fat—"

"Y'all two cut that shit out," Uncle Suge growled as he walked up carrying me and Bunni's suitcases. He shook his head and shot us both a shitty look.

"How many times I gotta run this game down on y'all?

Both of y'all is greedy and hardheaded as hell, but neither one of y'all is gonna get a dime around here unless y'all learn how to cooperate."

"Cooperate, *hell*," Dy-Nasty muttered under her breath as she rolled her eyes and folded her arms over her bulging titties. She hit me with a look that was so full of trickery that I felt bitch-smacked, and then she poked her lip out and whirled around and flounced her big booty off down the hall.

Uncle Suge carried my suitcase up to my room, and while I unpacked my few pieces of gear he ran me a hot bubble bath and called downstairs to have one of the servants fix me a cup of hot tea. He started making noise when I told him to get his butt outta the bathroom so I could get undressed in peace, but I didn't care. I knew it turned him on to watch me step outta my panties and slide underneath some hot bubbles, but with all those hundreds of black and blue bruises that Gutta had kicked up on my body I was like uh-uh, hell no!

Suge pulled his gold flask outta his pocket and spiked my tea for me nice and strong, and then I took it in the bathroom with me while I soaked in the warm bubbly water behind the locked door.

I laid back in the tub and closed my eyes, loving the way the hot liquor felt sliding down my throat and trying hard to let those rambling thoughts of Mama and all that other craziness that had gone down in New York drift right outta my mind.

After a few minutes Suge knocked on the door and said he needed to dip and go take care of some business, so I hollered good-bye and then kicked back again, sipping my yakked-up tea and soaking my aching ass. By the time the bubbles disappeared and the warm water started turning cold, both my body and my mind were feeling a little bit better and I was ready to concentrate on the gank at hand.

I got out the tub and dried off, and then rubbed some baby

oil gently into my skin. I had picked out a booty-hugging, ankle-length cotton dress that I was planning to wear downstairs to dinner, but as soon as I put that baby on I knew it wasn't gonna do. The banging little number was slinky and sleeveless, and Gutta had kicked up mad bruises everywhere he could get a hold of me. My chest, my shoulders, my arms . . . damn near my whole body was bruised up from one end to the other and I was gonna hafta cover up real good.

What I really felt like putting on was a pair of old sweats and a raggedy T-shirt, but rich folks like the Dominions didn't roll like that at the dinner table, not even on their worse damn days. So I put my hair up in a ponytail and pulled on some tight jeans and a long-sleeved clingy shirt, and then I swung by Bunni's room and we headed downstairs to eat.

Selah hadn't shown up yet, but the rest of the crew was already sitting around the dining room table. Dane, Jock, Fallon, Dy-Nasty, and Barron. Pilar's uppity ass had shown up too, and she had a tart look on her face like she had smashed her damn finger in a car door.

Dy-Nasty was sitting beside me with her elbows propped on the table and talking real loud on her cell phone. She was wearing my ear out and steady running off at the mouth as she bragged to some hood chick on the other end about all the fly shopping she was finna do and how much she was gonna pay for so-and-so luxury items from so-and-so expensive-ass stores.

Bunni was sitting on my other side, and I wanted to crack up when she leaned over and whispered in my ear, "That hood bitch is so damn *ghetto*!"

I nodded and then went straight back to iggin' Dy-Nasty's ass because listening to her talk I could tell she didn't know shit about no real shopping for no quality items. Matter fact, her guttersnipe ass wouldn't know classy if somebody slapped it on her breakfast plate and poured syrup all over it, because almost every designer she was naming was second rate and their gear coulda been had for basement-bargain prices at some slum little outlet mall.

I squirmed my aching ass around in my chair and tried to get comfortable as the kitchen staff carried in steaming platters of fried chicken, mashed potatoes, and corn on the cob. We went ahead and fixed our plates even though Selah hadn't shown up yet, but the only ones who seemed happy as fuck to be at that table was Bunni and Dy-Nasty, and both of them was about to work my last nerve.

Bunni was chewing with her mouth open and busy gnawing a chicken bone down to the marrow, and Dy-Nasty, with her wide-hipped self, was spreading about two inches of butter around on a thick hunk of white bread.

I barely had an appetite, myself. All I could think about was the fact that my backbone was on fire and my heart was still missing Mama.

I was glad when Selah finally decided to show up. Her eyes were damn near dancing in her face as she walked over to the table and stood beside her chair and said, "Good evening, everyone. Sorry I'm late, but I have some good news and I wanted to share it with everybody at the same time."

She was grinning all hard like she knew the best damn secret in the world and could barely hold herself together, so it was only natural that I started grinning too.

"Your father's doctors called today," Selah said with big-time excitement in her voice. "They summoned me to Houston right away, and Dy-Nasty and I flew down there almost immediately."

She glanced around the table, beaming like crazy at each and every one of us and then she finally spit it out.

"There's really no way to ease into something like this, so I'll just go ahead and tell you. Viceroy is awake! One of his experimental treatments worked and your father is *out of his coma*!"

Fallon busted out crying and Pilar looked pissed like a muthafucka.

"Hold up, Mama Selah!" Dy-Nasty wailed. "I'm the one who flew way down there witchu and you didn't even tell me Daddy was woke!"

"I'm sorry, Dy-Nasty." Selah smiled at her. "I wanted to keep it a surprise until we were all together and I could tell everyone at the same time."

I forgot all about the pain that was radiating through my body. I was so damned stunned by the news that all I could do was sit there frozen in my seat, speechless like fuck, but then Dy-Nasty started actin' up, and you can best believe when she jumped off into her grifter act I started cuttin' the hell up too!

"*Dadddeeee*!" she wailed, smushing her face down in her cold mashed potatoes as she keeled forward like her ass had been sniper-shot. "Ohmygawd!" she sniveled, and slobbered all in her plate. "Praise his name!" She slapped both her hands down hard on the table. "Praise!" *Slap!* "His!" *Slap!* "Ho!" *Slap!* "Lee!" *Slap!* "NAME!"

I tooted up my lips and shot her a killer look. No this trick *wasn't* tryna go to church on me! No this heathen *wasn't*! Well we could go to church, baby! We could damn sure go to church!

Bunni shot me a *go get 'em* look, but it wasn't even necessary 'cause I wasn't *about* to let that trick show me up with her back-alley praise words, so I went for broke and busted out with a few of minez too!

"I *knew* it!" I shrieked. I leaped to my feet like somebody had shoved a golden pole up my ass, knocking my chair clean over as I pogo-jumped up and down on two stiff legs.

"I *knew* my daddy was gonna wake up one day! Hallelujah!" I held my hands high in the air and shook 'em like I had two tambourines attached to my wrists.

"*Hosanna*!" I shrieked, and Bunni looked over at me like I had a snake comin' outta my mouth.

"Lawdhamercy! I prayed on my *knees* for this, Mama Selah! I swear to *God*, I got down on my knees and *prayed* for my father's healing and his salvation, Lawd, thank you, *Jezeesus*!"

I started trembling and gasping like I was catching the Holy Ghost, and I was performing so good that even Dy-Nasty had to pop her head up and kill all that weeping so she could see what the hell was going on.

But then Barron stood up and cleared his throat real loud. He walked over to me and put his hands on both of my shoulders, then he gave me a hard lil push like, *Sinner, sit your black ass* down!

"A'ight now," Barron said, walking back to his place at the table. "We understand everybody is extra happy"—he shot a smirk at me and Dy-Nasty—"because me and Mama are happy too. Daddy has a long road of recovery ahead of him and it's probably gonna be a tough one. The first thing we gotta do is make some real quick phone calls and let his aunts and cousins know he's awake and that he's gonna be okay. After that, we'll all fly down to Houston tomorrow so everybody can welcome him back to the world and show him some Dominion love."

"I've got the business jet lined up for seven a.m. sharp," Selah said, stepping back into the convo. "And Viceroy is expecting us. He's anxious to see everybody but as you all know, your father has been through a lot. The time he spent in a coma took almost as much out of him as his injuries did, and he's also undergone some pretty invasive therapies to help his brain heal and rejuvenate too. In light of all that, the doctors want us to be extra-careful that we don't upset him and that we keep his stress level to a minimum."

She took a real deep breath and then she stared dead at me and Dy-Nasty. I was still standing there sniffling snot and holding my imaginary tambourines up in the air, and that weeping-ass snake oil swindler Dy-Nasty had done cried herself outta her chair and was clinging to the table with one hand while she had one knee planted on the floor.

"That means," Selah continued with a disgusted look in her eyes, "that Mink and Dy-Nasty, you two will have to stay back here at the house tomorrow. I'm sorry, but I just don't think Viceroy is ready to handle all this"—she frowned and waved her hand in the air—"*drama* y'all got going on."

If we thought what Selah had just spit was bad, the shit really hit the fan big-time when she excused herself to take a call from Viceroy's doctors and hurried outta the room.

Barron looked over his shoulder until he was sure his mama was gone, and then he turned around and dropped a shit bomb down on the whole fuckin' table.

"A'ight, now. I hate to be the one to piss in your hair weave," he said, grinning real hard as he busted Dy-Nasty out, "but now that Pops is awake and back with us, that little bullshit vote the board passed to give all y'all three hundred grand a year is a *wrap*. Sisters and brothers, the door to the trust fund has been officially *closed*, and I'll be filing a motion to have the board's vote annulled the first thing tomorrow morning."

Pilar sat there grinning like a muthafucka but you woulda thought somebody had melted all the glue outta Dy-Nasty's ratchet-ass horse tail.

"Uh-uh," she protested, coming up off her knee and climbing back up in her chair. "Wait a minute! Wait a *goddamn* minute! What the hell did you say just now?" she blasted on Barron. "Come again?" Her cat-eyes flashed in her face and she looked ready to jump all over him and take his ass to the mat.

"Whatchu mean the trust fund is a *wrap*?" She wagged her head back and forth. "Naw, naw, naw to da *naw*! That trust fund ain't no wrap, *Bearrun*! Ain't nobody tryna hear that shit! You *owe* me, baby! I worked for minez, remember? I don't care if ya daddy done woke up or not. That first DNA test said *I'm* Sable, and I want everythang all the rest of y'all been getting except I want my dough all lumped up in a big fat ball right *now*!"

"Well the first DNA test said Mink was Sable *too*!" Bunni jumped in from the other side of me. "And Mink took her damn test first! So why should you get to keep the whole three hundred smack-smacks all to yourself?"

"Neither one of y'all is getting *shit*!" Barron hollered. "And if either one of y'all gave a damn about my pops and half a damn about my moms, then both of y'all would get'ta steppin' out the door like you had some goddamn sense!"

Barron looked spitting mad. He was grilling me and Dy-Nasty like he just *wanted* us to run off at the mouth. Like he was just itchin' for one of us to go on a slick lil lip trip.

But I wasn't about to bite at that bait. I just sat there and stared back at his stupid ass and didn't say shit. And really, there was nothing I needed to say any damn way. Because something told me that after hearing what she had just heard, money-grubbin' Dy-Nasty was about to do enough screaming, biting, and backstabbing for the both of us!

CHAPTER 13

After dinner me and Bunni went upstairs so we could get our heads right with dick-slangin' Dane up in his private little fuck-palace over the Dominion's eight-car garage. A hot Reem Raw track was flowing from his deluxe speaker system and glowing sticks of incense were burning in about five ashtrays.

Dane was one of them real tasty-lookin' niggas. Pure-dee eye candy. He rocked some real tight twisties in his thick, curly hair, and his chocolate skin looked so damn smooth and sweet it shoulda had a golden candy wrapper around it.

We were walking into his loft when Bunni tried to pinch me as she licked her lips and checked out his package. I was still hyped over all the shit we had heard at dinner so I elbowed her and rolled my eyes, but I could feel where she was coming from 'cause Dane was holdin'. His chest and shoulder muscles was all over the damn place, and his tight stomach had at least ten cans on it. He had on a baggy pair of white basketball shorts, and two phat diamond earrings glinted from his lobes.

He fired up some sticky green and him and Bunni got down on a little bit of hash. Both of them were tossing back double shots of yakkety-yak, but my stomach wasn't in the mood for no more firewater so I just got lifted on a whole bunch of weed and sipped on a Corona instead.

I could tell Dane was feeling real up now that me and Bunni had come back to Texas. The three of us stretched out on some big fluffy pillows on the floor in his loft and proceeded to get straight tipsy.

"A'ight now." Bunni puffed her weed and got right down to bizz. "I heard all that bullshit Barron was talkin', but what's the real dealio with our duckets now that Pappa-Doo done woke up?"

Dane shook his head and pulled real hard on his spliff.

"Bump told it right. Pops is up. Talking and everything." He gave a short laugh. "Talking *shit,* I should say. It's crazy. That cat is the biggest workaholic control freak I ever seen in my life. The minute those doctors let him outta there he's gonna head over to Dominion Oil and get back in the driver's seat and put the pedal to the metal. And once that shit happens all of our asses can kiss that three-hundred-grand payday good-bye for good."

"And why is that?"

"Because the fund can only be activated if Pops dies or gets declared incapacitated to serve in his position at Dominion Oil, remember? That's why it's so fucked up that the board's vote didn't go through. Bump said he got the call just when he was about to get that shit signed and notarized. Pops already said that once he gets back to work he's gonna kill that money provision and kill it quick."

"Damn!" Bunni got all hyped. "Daddy-Deep-Pockets shoulda stayed his ass asleep for a lil while longer! He's fuckin' up some major plans around here!"

"You got that right," I said, and elbowed Bunni. " 'Cause without that trust fund dough, me and you is ass-out with no place else to go. Especially once them DNA results come back." I frowned at Dane. "While you bullshittin', we *all* about to be ass-out."

Dane nodded and took a deep drag off the blunt. "You ain't lying. I was counting on that cash too. Them fools up at my school is still trippin', man."

"Why?" Bunni gave him the stank look. "You still tryna get up in them dorm rooms with all them freak-a-deek college bitches?"

"Nah." He shook his head. "I ain't even thinking about them chicks. It's that disciplinary board I'm worrying about. I gotta shake those sexual assault charges before they'll let me back in school, man."

He took another toke. "But this chick I know in the admin office put a bug in my ear. She said the deans are about to send my shit up to the prosecutor's office so they can hit me with a charge. And if that happens, then I might as well just bend over and kiss my balls good-bye 'cause my ass is gonna be out the door."

"But I thought you was tryna get a lawyer?" I asked, and then filled my mouth up with a gulp of ice-cold Corona. I knew Dane had been up in them dorms splashing around in college coochie on the regular, but he was the exact type of dude that chicks loved to throw pussy at. He wasn't no damn predator!

"Them lawyer niggas don't work for free, yo."

I swallowed and belched and shook my head as my throat burned from the cold acid. "But you ain't even push up on nobody! You gotta fight that shit, son!"

"I was *planning* on fighting it—when I got my hands on that three hundred large, remember?"

Dane took one more pull off his tree and then tapped the roach out in the ashtray. "Now that Pops is back in action there ain't no way I'm gonna get next to that kinda money without somebody finding out."

I nodded. Dane's ass had been sweatin' that trust fund cheese damn near harder than me. And then I got a bright idea.

"Yo, your brother's a damn lawyer, ain't he?" I giggled. "Hire his crooked ass to go to bat for you."

Dane looked at me like I had a big hairy nut sack dangling from my chin.

"I already told you, girl. B is my boy, but something ain't right with that dude, yo. And that's word. Ain't no way in hell I'ma put my dick up on the chopping block if Bump is walking around with a butcher knife in his hands. Besides, he would never get his hands dirty with this type of nasty shit. I know my brother. He wouldn't touch it with a ten-foot pole."

"That's because he's a fuckin' hater," I muttered, sipping my beer as I thought about how Barron had been dissin' me from my very first day at the mansion. "And I wouldn't trust his ass neither if I was you. He didn't know shit about me when I got here. He didn't hafta go at my throat like that and try to turn everybody in the whole damn family against me."

For some reason Dane thought that mess was real damn funny.

"Oh hell yeah he did, Mink!" He bust out laughing. "Bump did exactly what the fuck he was supposed to do when you showed up, baby! He went at your throat because you went after the *family jewels*! Pops left Barron standing guard in front of the vault! What the hell did you think he was gonna do when you showed up telling everybody you was Sable? Open up the safe and dish you off a couple of gold bars?"

Dane laughed again, then reached over and yanked on my big toe. "Rich people don't stay rich by just handing their money over to strangers, Mink. They fight like dogs in the street to keep every dime they've got. That's just the way it goes."

Dane drained his shot glass, and then he sparked up another fat blunt. He scrunched his face up as the smoke swirled around his eyes. Taking a real deep drag, he sucked on that shit like he had a vacuum cleaner stuck down in his throat, and then he let the smoke out real slow and sighed.

I felt sorry for my play brother. He looked shook in the face, like no matter how much shit he smoked up and drank up he couldn't get high enough to wipe all his problems outta his head.

"Man, y'all," he said, putting his blunt down and shaking his head, "if them fuckin' deans kick me outta school and Pop finds out about it . . . shit is gonna get real raggedy around here."

"Hmph," Bunni said. She had been steady getting lifted while she listened to me and Dane go back and forth at the mouth, and when I glanced over at her I saw something shifty glinting in her beady little eyes.

"See there," she sneered, "Pappa-Doo done woke up and threw salt in everybody's game! If you ask me, Ol' Mister Oil-Jackin' Dominion might need to lay back down and take his ass another nap!"

CHAPTER 14

The next day while Selah took the rest of the family down to Houston to visit Viceroy, Barron drove over to the Ducane manor and got ready to face the music. He had come up with a half-assed plan to cut Pilar off at the knees, but he knew it wasn't gonna be easy because his cousin wasn't the type of gold digger to throw her shovel down without a fight.

Barron knew better than to lay the bad news on her while they were somewhere in public where she could show out, but he didn't want her wilding out and getting stupid on him up in the Dominion mansion where Selah might find out either.

His game plan was to drop the heat bomb on her when they were someplace where she could scream and holler and get as nasty as she wanted to get, and then after she called him a long string of dirty muthafuckas and cursed him out real good, he could dip out and bounce.

So, Barron swung by the Ducane manor the next morning when he was sure his uncle Digger had already left for work. He surprised the hell out of Pilar when he rang the doorbell and stood there waiting with one hand hidden behind his back.

"Barron!" she said, frowning a little bit as she opened the

door still wearing her nightgown. Every strand of her hair was wrapped around her head going in the same direction, and she looked even sexier and younger without all her usual makeup.

"Oh my God!" She grinned and tried to hide behind the door. "What are you doing here so early in the morning, baby?" She peeked past him and glanced toward his car parked in the driveway. "Are you by yourself? Is everything okay?"

"Yeah," Barron said quietly. "Sorry I just dropped by like this, but everything is cool. I just needed to talk to you for a few minutes, that's all."

Pilar touched her hair and then stepped back to let him in as she looked him up and down with excitement in her eyes. "Well why didn't you call me first? I would've gotten myself together and put on something sexy real quick."

Barron shrugged with his hand still hidden behind his back. "I was on my way to a meeting," he lied, "but I wanted to swing by because I've got something to give you."

Pilar tried to peep around his body to see what he was hiding, and he frowned when she shrieked in pure delight and pranced through the kitchen grinning like crazy.

Barron felt like he had a brick in his gut as he followed her sexy, swaying frame into the stylish living room.

Pilar perched on the edge of a plush sofa and arranged the hem of her short champagne-colored satin gown around her toned thighs. Smoothing her hair nervously, she swung her bare feet around on the sofa and then giggled with excitement as she looked up at him and waited like a kid on Christmas morning.

Barron walked over and stood in front of her. Digging deep for some swag, he pulled himself up firm and tall.

"Oh shit!" Pilar giggled again, hunching her shoulders and grinning just like a little kid. "It's about to happen!" she shrieked. "It's really about to happen!"

Barron coughed and cleared his throat, and Pilar reached out and slapped him on his muscular thigh.

"Boy! You should have called me so I could have put on some clothes first! I can't believe you got me sitting here half-dressed for something like this!" She swallowed hard and locked her eyes on his. "Okay, what do you have for me, B? Huh? What's that you're hiding behind your back?"

"Um, P, you know how much I care about you," Barron started. He made his voice go real deep as he stared down into her gray eyes. Slowly, he brought his hand from behind his back and held out a small paisley-printed envelope. It contained a copy of the private entrance key she had given him so he could creep in on her whenever he got ready.

"But me and you are gonna have to chill for a minute, Pilar. Daddy's up and he's about to get back on top of things, and I need a little space so I can get my head together."

"W-w-what?" she said, eyeing the envelope as the smile fell off her pretty face. "What are you talking about, B?" She shook her head. "You're bullshitting, right? This must be a joke. You're bullshitting."

Barron didn't crack a smile and his gaze remained strong and steady as he slowly shook his head. "Nah. I'm not bullshitting, Pilar. I'm dead serious, baby. But this ain't on you, okay? It's on *me*. There's a lot going on with the family right now, and my pops ain't in no condition to handle the kind of shit we've been doing."

Pilar frowned. "The kind of shit we've been doing? You mean our *relationship*? Are you talking about me and you being together and having sex?"

Barron nodded.

Pilar leaped to her feet like somebody shot a cannon up her ass. "Well then you better tell your goddamn daddy that me and you been *doing* all the nasty, dirty shit your black ass wanted to do!"

Barron nodded again but he never broke his gaze. He gave her one of them dude looks that said, *This is the part where you're supposed to call me a selfish muthafucka. Go right ahead. I deserve that shit.*

"So what?" Pilar got up in his face like she was daring him to confirm his words. "You're tossing me to the trash, is that it? Oh, I get it." She smirked, looking him up and down like he wasn't about shit. "Your fully grown black ass is scared your *daddy* might find out you been having fun eating my pussy and yank you off his money tit, huh?"

Barron frowned. Just a little.

"I'm not *scared* of nothing, Pilar. I just think we're going in the wrong direction, that's all. C'mon, now. I was in a real bad spot when Pops got hurt and you knew that. And then I went through all that drama with Carla, and then I jumped right into this lil thing with you. I never had a chance," Barron told her truthfully, "to really think shit through and get my head straight, ya know?"

He sighed and looked down at her with affection in his eyes. "You're a beautiful sistah, Pilar, and I love you." He let his voice drop low. "But you deserve way more than this, and I just don't think I'm the right man for you."

Barron couldn't understand all the filthy shit that came flying outta Pilar's mouth because it was a mixture of jumbled-up gutter shrieks and low-down curses, almost like she was speaking in tongues. A couple of phrases came through pretty clear though like, *You bitch-ass pussy, you!* and *You stubby-dicked bastard!* and *You non-fucking weak-ass bitch!*

Barron nodded, cool with it. This was the part where he was supposed to say he was sorry and break for the door, and he had just turned away to make his move when Pilar landed on his back. Clinging to him like a pissed off little monkey, she screamed and sank her teeth down deep into the soft part of his neck and took a chunk outta his ass.

"What the fuck?" Barron yelped like a bitch. He whirled around and shook her off, then clutched both hands to his bleeding neck.

Pilar slid off his back and hit the floor hard. She jumped up quick as shit, then she snatched a figurine from the end table and hurled that baby at him like it was a fastball flying across home plate.

"Pilar!" he hollered and ducked as the figurine flew harmlessly over his head. "What the fuck is wrong with you?!"

"No, what the fuck is wrong with *you*!" she screeched. "You trying to *play* some fuckin' body?" She snatched up another figurine and hurled that shit.

Instinct made Barron duck and turn away, but the marble figurine caught him and busted him right upside his head, and a trickle of blood slid down his temple and darkened the collar of his cream-colored Stuart Hughes dress shirt.

"Yeah, you dirty *bastard*!" Pilar twisted up her face and hollered when she saw his blood. She was breathing hard and her plump breasts were jiggling under her gown. "That's what you get, *muthafucka*! You lucky I didn't knock your lying-ass teeth down your fuckin' throat!"

Barron touched two fingers to the side of his face and stared at all the blood on his hands, and then he ducked again as Pilar cursed and let a glass ashtray fly at his head.

"Stop fuckin' trippin'!" he hollered over his shoulder as he ran toward the door. "This shit is over, dammit, so just stop trippin'!"

"Trippin'?" Pilar raged in the doorway with her erect nipples poking through her see-through gown as Barron hauled ass back to his car. "You ain't seen *trippin'*, you weak-ass, no balls, son of a *bitch*, you! You fucked over the wrong chick, Barron Dominion! Believe me, muthafucka! You ain't seen *nothing* yet!"

CHAPTER 15

Pilar was not the one to fuck with, and she damn sure wasn't going down without a fight. The sun was barely up and it was early as hell, but she was already feening like a bird who was on a secret mission to trap a worm.

Her glossed-up lips were pinched tight as she drove through the large gates that guarded the entrance to the Dominion Estate. The grounds were quiet and she knew the family was still knocked out and slobbering in their high-class luxury beds.

The Dominion posse was planning to jet down to Houston to visit Viceroy later in the morning, and Pilar was hoping to sneak into Barron's room before he woke up so she could work a little corrective mojo on his ass.

She had packed a sex kit the night before that was designed to spice things up and blow his mind. She had brought along a nice bottle of wine, a couple of real kinky toys, a dominatrix whip, some spiked handcuffs, and lots of edible strawberry foam. She had even loaded some videos of their raunchiest sex play onto her iPad so they could watch themselves getting it on.

Pilar glanced in the rearview mirror and nodded at her perfect reflection in satisfaction. That fool wouldn't be able to resist her. She was on her game and clocking in at a dime from head to toe. She looked sweet and suckably sexy, and she was butt-naked under her hot-pink Chanel skirt and sleeveless silk top. The only part of her ensemble that was missing was the massive diamond engagement ring that she should have been flossing on her finger by now.

Glancing down at her naked ring finger, Pilar pinched her lips even tighter as she got ready to sneak between the sheets of the man she planned to marry.

As she nosed her sleek whip up to the front door of the mansion, Durant stepped out from under the awning and walked around to the driver's side and opened her door. Dude looked sleepy and surprised to see her so early in the morning, but Pilar just flashed him a smile, then slid out from behind the steering wheel and shimmied across the pavement looking and smelling like the most succulent piece of eye-candy that had ever stepped foot on Dominion soil.

She kept her fake smile plastered to her face as she carried her bag of toys inside the quiet mansion and headed toward the stairs, but deep inside she was smirking like a mutha. Barron must have been out of his damn mind when he rolled up at her crib trying to dump her! As bad as she had pussy-whipped his ass in and out of the sheets? There was no way in hell that fool had gotten enough of the sweet gushy she was packing, and Pilar was stepping up in the joint today to hit him with a little reminder of what he was gonna be missing!

She was still mad at herself behind that crazy little scream-scene she had caused at her house. It had been ugly as hell and dumb as hell too. But Barron had shocked the shit out of her when he blasted her with that breakup line. He had caught her straight off-guard. Her heart had been pounding with delicious excitement as she anticipated the brilliant diamond he was about to whip out on her. She had been *so* ready for him to get down on his knees and finally ask her to be his damn wife, but instead of making a romantic proposal that fool had used some tired-ass fraternity line to quit her and give her back her house key!

And that's where Pilar had fucked up. The last thing she should have done was gone ballistic on a keeper like Bump. She had played herself out of position and lost her damn head, but she was back on her game now and she knew what she had to do.

She had to get up in that mansion and wipe some coochie juice on Barron that was so damn hot and sweet it totally blew his mind. She had to put her thump-nasty thang down on her cousin and show him that couldn't no other woman on the face of the earth make his dick jerk and his toes curl the way she did.

Pilar had to get up in Barron's suite and go to *work.*

Barron had been up ever since the crack of dawn, and no matter how much he yanked on his meat and stroked his nuts, he couldn't cum and he couldn't go back to sleep either.

That fool Gutta had took his money and then jerked him around. Instead of floating with the fishes at the bottom of a river, Mink had come back to the mansion and her sweet hips, that fat ass, and those plump, juicy knockers she had on her still drove him wild. No matter how much Barron thought he despised her ass, the girl was stacked like a mutha and there was no denying the fact that he wanted to fuck the shit out of her.

It was a terrible thing the way that grimy chick stayed on his mind and kept his dick on brick. She mighta disgusted the ego in him, but she turned the dog in him right the fuck on.

And that's why he got up out of his bed and slipped his five-thousand-dollar Stefano Ricci pure silk and cashmere bathrobe over his red silk boxer shorts, and then headed back down to her room again.

Barron moved like a cat-burglar as he crept down the stairs and turned the corner on the second floor. The mansion was cemetery-quiet and a chill from the cooling system was in the air.

He tiptoed like an overgrown ballerina as he passed several guest rooms on his way to the suite Mink and Bunni shared. He stood outside of Mink's door and listened to the sound of silence booming all around him.

Convinced that she was still sleeping, Barron slowly twisted the doorknob and then pushed slightly. He opened the door in a two-inch crack and peered inside at the fine body that was sprawled on the bed and twisted up in the luxury sheets.

The sun was just beginning to peek through the blinds, and it took a minute for his eyes to adjust. But when they did, Barron felt like he had hit the damn jackpot.

Mink was stretched out face-down on the bed wearing a leopard-print sleeveless tank top and a pair of matching bikini panties. It looked like she had an ugly pair of white cotton drawers tied over her hair, and her comforter had been kicked down to the floor.

Barron damn near drooled as his eyes ran over her luscious hunk of ass. It exploded upward from her back like the hump of a question mark, and one side of her panties were hiked up and stuck in her crack.

Oh hell yeah, Barron breathed thickly as his lustful gaze roamed her toned legs and down to her slim ankles. His big black dick was so hard it had jumped straight through the pee hole of his boxers and stuck out in front of him like an iron rod.

It jerked when he gripped it in his palm, and he massaged Mink's ass with his eyeballs as he pictured himself licking the thick cheeks of her booty and inserting his tongue deep in her sweet hole.

Barron eye-fucked the hell out of her as he stroked his dick and clenched his ass cheeks tight. He pretended he was rubbing his swollen head in the valley between her big titties, then down over her slim back, and then of course he plunged his meat deeply inside the split between her thighs.

Deep in his heart Barron had been dying to fuck Mink for the longest, and even though he couldn't stand her ass, he went ahead and squeezed his wood as he licked her pussy out from the back until his mouth was actually watering from her juices.

It only took him two more strokes to shoot his nut off after swallowing her imaginary cream, and he couldn't stop himself from grunting out loud as he deposited a load of hot, sticky cum in his palm and then smeared it all over his throbbing dick before gently tucking it back inside his drawers.

Shame slammed into him the moment his wad had been shot. He was disgusted with himself for being so weak over a piece of stank pussy, and he felt damned lucky not to get caught as he quietly closed Mink's door and turned around and hauled ass silently toward the stairs.

Pilar was creeping her ass off.

She knew her aunt was an early riser, and the last thing she wanted was for Selah to bust her sneaking into Barron's suite to get some dick at the crack of dawn.

She was almost at the top of the second landing, and she was so busy concentrating on being quiet that she didn't even hear the muffled footsteps that came bounding toward her.

"Barron!" she yelped. He was jetting out of the wing of rooms with his bathrobe flapping open and nothing underneath it except a pair of red silk boxer drawers.

She was so shocked to see him that for a split second Pilar forgot that he had dumped her and she flashed him a smile. But then she caught the funny look in his eyes and she jumped on her game and went straight to work.

"Look, baby," she said, stepping right up on him and pressing her lips to his naked chest. "I know we're going through a little something right now, but I didn't mean all that stuff I said at my house and I don't think you meant what you said either."

"P-Pilar," Barron stuttered. His eyes looked wild as he tried to step away. "Hold up, now—"

"Now, I know I was wrong," Pilar said, getting up on him again, "and that's why I'm the one who's apologizing first, and just to show you that I'm serious and I've learned my lesson"—she slipped her bag of tricks off her shoulder and let it dangle from her arm—"I brought a little something for me and you to party with."

She snuggled up in his arms again and flicked her tongue over his bare nipple.

"P-Pilar, stop—"

"Oh, Bump," she moaned as she pressed her aching titties to his chest. "You make me feel so damn good, baby. Let's not argue anymore, okay? Why don't we just go upstairs to your room and start this thing all over? How about we just pretend that none of that craziness happened at my house and just have us a little fun this morning and start our day off right?"

"Pilar, I need you to—"

She chuckled and reached for his dick.

"Oh, I know what you need me to do," she said, smacking her lips as she slipped her hand down the front of his waistband and then squatted down and made a beeline for his limp piece of meat.

"You need me to—"

Pilar froze in mid-lick. She got cold as hell. Like a brick of ice had just smacked her in the back of her head.

"Ewww! W-w-what's this?" she stuttered, yanking her hand out of Barron's damp drawers and staring at her fingers like they had been dipped in doody. She grabbed her wrist and eyed the sticky, congealing mass of cum that coated her skin.

"B-B-Barron, what the fuck is this?"

She stared at the front of his gummy drawers and then

glanced down the hall toward the bank of double suites. Her brain calculated shit up like a computer, and Pilar let out a small, wounded cry, then reached into her bag of tricks and jumped up swinging.

"You bastard!" she screeched, smashing the bottle of wine across his head. "You been in there *fucking Mink*? You slimy, low-down, cheating-ass *bastard*!"

Barron didn't have enough time to throw his arm up or duck, but he did manage to turn away real quick. And that's when the edge of the bottle cracked into his thick skull right above his ear, and he yelped like a muthafucka as the thick glass shattered and bit into his scalp, and soaked him *and* his luxury bathrobe in hot blood and cold red wine.

CHAPTER 16

Thirty minutes later Pilar stomped out of Dy-Nasty's bedroom fired up and ready to shoot. If Barron had thought she had gone bonkers on his black ass before, she was really gonna slice him up now, and his dumb ass was the one who had given her the knife!

She had tried her best to smash his shitty brains in with that wine bottle, and not only was that fool gonna need stitches, he was gonna carry that scar she'd put on him all the way to his fucking grave!

But that wasn't all she had in store for his trifling ass, though! She was about to air him out! Barron was straight up busted because there was only one damn room he could have been creeping out of with all that cold cum gunked up in his drawers. *Mink's!*

Fumes had rolled off Pilar's scalp, and she was so mad that she had sweated her curls out. She grunted in satisfaction as she thought about how she had barged into Dy-Nasty's room and dragged her skank ass out the bed. In no time flat Pilar had pulled up a Web site on her iPad and showed Dy-Nasty a series of pictures that had bucked her sleepy little eyes wide the hell open! Pilar had made the girl an offer that she damn sure couldn't refuse, and now all she had to do was sit back and watch the show as she got her revenge without ever getting her dainty little manicured hands dirty.

Pilar's nostrils were flaring as she stomped down the steps and stormed out of the mansion. She gave a damn about waking anybody up and getting caught now! Fuck them Dominions! Fuck 'em all! Barron Dominion had crossed her up for the last goddamn time, and thanks to Dy-Nasty's dumb ass, payback was about to be a real motherfucker!

Dy-Nasty had no idea the walls had ears as she sprawled in a beach chair by the Dominion's hot tub and bitched into her cell phone.

"Mama! You ain't gonna believe this fuckin' shit! These fools over here tryna tell somebody the trust fund is a wrap! Uh-huh, I'm *dead* serious! *Bearrun* said it! For real, Ma. I swear to *God*, if that black bastard don't gimme my money I'ma set this whole fuckin' joint on fire!"

"Mink!" Bunni hissed as she leaned away from the open second-floor window and kicked the bed where her best friend lay on her stomach snoring her ass off. Bunni had been cracking sunflower seeds between her back teeth, eating the nut, and then spitting the chewed up shells outta Mink's bedroom window when she spotted Dy-Nasty sitting below and keyed in on her convo.

"Mink, get your ass up *right now*!" Bunni whispered. "That trifling bitch Dy-Nasty is outside on the phone talking shit to her mama!"

Sprawled out on the bed, Mink tooted her big ass up in the air and dug her head deeper underneath her pillow. "Lee' me 'lone, Bunni," she mumbled. "Dy-Nasty's mama is dead. Just like mine."

"No the hell she *ain't*!" Bunni whispered. She leaned toward the window with her ear cocked open wide as she listened to Dy-Nasty tell her mama all about the three-hundred-grand payday that had just been canceled.

"Nope!" Dy-Nasty complained into the phone. "I can't even get the lil hundred grand no more 'cause these fools done already gave it to that ugly bitch from Harlem, and her dumbass already tricked it up!"

"*Oooooh,*" Bunni sang quietly as she leaned back inside the room. "Mink that bitch just said you was ugly! Yep, she fuckin' called you *ugly*!"

"Ugly?" Mink flung the pillow to the floor and sat up in the bed in her skimpy leopard-print camisole and tiny little drawers.

"Who the fuck is that ugly bitch calling ugly?"

Two seconds later she was standing right beside Bunni and listening to Dy-Nasty talk a whole bunch of shit.

"Yeah, Mama, that might work too, but check this out! Barron's cousin Pilar came to my room real early this morning and showed me some pictures. They were pictures of Barron! On the Internet with lipstick on his lips and some nigga's dick in his mouth!"

Dy-Nasty twirled an ashy lock of beaver-weave around her finger and nodded.

"Yep, I'm dead fuckin' serious! You heard me right but I'll say it again. It was a picture of *Bearrun*! With lipstick on his lips and some nigga's dick in his mouth!"

Bunni's eyes bucked open wide and she reached out and pinched Mink so hard on her left ass-cheek that Mink had to bite her tongue to keep from hollering out loud.

"No, it ain't no cross-con, Mama. I seen the pictures with my own eyes! She showed them to me on her iPad. It was him! Barron Dominion!"

Mink jammed her heel down hard on Bunni's little hammertoe, and then she grinned her ass off as tears of pain flooded her girl's eyes and Bunni broke out in a sweat and started hopping around on one foot.

"Uh-uh," Dy-Nasty said below them. "I can't e-mail you the pictures 'cause they was on a Web site and I don't remember what it was off the top of my head. But Pilar said she's gonna give me the link, so as soon as I get to a computer I'll put the link up on my Facebook page so you can see 'em for yourself," she promised.

"*No*, Mama," Dy-Nasty said, sucking her teeth like she was exasperated. "My timeline is *private*. That's why I keep telling you to make you a Facebook account, damn! It's people way older than you that be on that shit runnin' they mouth all day long."

She listened for a few seconds.

"Uh-uh. No, you can't see my page from Shantel's account, neither. Me and her don't speak no more, remember? That hoe went and blocked me after I gave her ugly boo Tre'kwan that real bad dick infection, 'member? She started acting all shitty just because she caught it too! So no, you ain't gonna be able to see nothing I post if you on Shantel's page, but if you make your own page and friend me I'll confirm you, okay?"

Mink and Bunni were hanging halfway out the damn window now.

"Oh my goodness! For real, Mama? You think I should show them nasty pictures to his *daddy*? And send them to the Dominion board too? Ooooh! Mama you slick as hell! But you right though. You should see how that fake muthafucka be walkin' around here like he doo-doos out green money and it don't stink! Yeah, he so busy tryna fuck me outta my cash, let's see how that fool likes it when we fuck him right outta his!"

Wooo-hooo! Game *always* recognized game, and conmami Mink and pickpocket Bunni had to give Dy-Nasty her schemin'-ass props on this one!

"Okay, now," Dy-Nasty said. "I miss you too, Mama. I can't wait to get back home so we can have us a real big party! Bye!"

By now Mink had forgotten all about that pinch on her ass, and Bunni wasn't stuttin' her hammertoe! The only thing they was worried about was getting on Dy-Nasty's Facebook page so they could find that Web site link and peep them pictures of stiff-ass Barron Dominion wearing lipstick and kissing dick!

Dy-Nasty's critter-ass really did have a private Facebook page. Me and Bunni couldn't see shit she posted, especially no links to them nasty pictures of Barron, unless we were her Facebook friends. But Bunni wasn't about to let that stop her. So she opened up a dummy e-mail account and then logged on to Facebook and started a fake profile. I cracked the hell up when she called herself "Film Director Looking4 HotBigBootyTalent."

"*Sheeit,*" Bunni drawled as her fingers flew over the keys on the laptop. "Laugh if you wanna, baby! Just watch. Soon as that busted-lookin' trick peeps this page her thirsty ass is gonna be all over it. Trust!"

"You got that right!"

"Pull up your shirt!" Bunni ordered me as she went around behind me holding out her cell phone. "Unbutton your pants and slide 'em down ya hips and lemme see them million-dollar cheeks! Make sure your thong string is showing too. I wanna get some real good ass-shots so when niggas peep our page we can have 'em beating off in their fists and licking their computer screens."

I tooted up the bomb dook and laughed like hell as she snapped mad pictures of it from the waist down and from a bunch of different angles. Bunni posted a real hot shot of my booty as her profile pic, and then she uploaded the rest of the pictures into an album. After that she sent out a bunch of friend requests to random rap artists, urban authors, and big-titty models who were all tryna come up on their grind.

In no time flat her friend requests started getting confirmed left and right, and once she had enough friends to make her page look legit, she went back to Dy-Nasty's profile page and sent her a friend request too.

"That raggedy bitch better confirm me," Bunni said, and sure enough, just a few minutes later, Dy-Nasty did.

And now, all four of our eyes were crawling over Dy-Nasty's page like ants on syrup. That crab had a bunch of bomb ass-shots of her own, and we had to scroll through all that nasty booty she was holding before we found what we were looking for.

Bunni clicked on a link that had been shared with somebody named "Phat Pat" and it took us outta Facebook and to a Web page.

"Oh, shit," Bunni said quietly as the first shot of Barron came up on the screen. He was stretched out on a couch with his legs gapped open. He had on a short skirt and some stupid-looking calf-high black dress socks.

"Uh!" Bunni hollered like she'd been gut-hit. "That's a *bad-ass* fuckin' skirt that nigga got on! I wonder where he got that shit from?"

"Bunni, please!" I said, and turned the screen more toward me.

"Hold up. Is that his *dick* laying on the couch between his legs?" I peered at the picture tryna see if the thick shadow under Barron's skirt was actually his meat hanging out. "*Please* tell me that ain't his dick I'm seeing! 'Cause if it is, that nigga is a *piper*!"

"Um, yeah," Bunni confirmed. "That's a dick all right. I've seen one or two of them thangs before, and that looks like a nice big dick to me!"

We scrolled down the page and stared at every picture of Barron on the site, and by the time we was done looking I knew that nigga's foot-long hot dog was about to get *burnt*!

"Oh that bitch Dy-Nasty is fin'ta *fuck* your brother up," Bunni declared big-time.

"Um," I corrected her, "he's *her* brother. Not mine, remember?"

Bunni shrugged. "It don't really matter who damn brother he is. His shit is 'bout to get fucked up."

CHAPTER 17

"Oh God!" Selah moaned as Rodney Ruddman planted a trail of kisses down her tight stomach and rubbed his fingers through the mound of her neatly trimmed forest. "This shit feels so fucking good! I can't believe I'm doing this again. I can't believe it!"

Rodney's laughter echoed off the walls of his large penthouse suite, and he grinned as he spread Selah's creamy thighs even wider.

"But you *are* doing it, Mrs. Dominion," he reminded her heartlessly. "You're doing it and you're loving it too."

If Rodney was treating her harshly, then Selah knew she deserved it. They'd been playing the phone sex game, and she had gotten her satisfaction and then hung up before he could get his too, and now he was paying her back in cruel, delicious ways.

And it was damned delicious too! Selah sighed with pleasure as he spread her legs even wider. She had taken Jock and Fallon down to Houston to visit Viceroy early that morning, and she'd made it her business to get the hell out of there as quickly as she could. Viceroy had tried to pull that same old tired trick on her as they were walking out the door, but this time instead of going back to sit on his limp dick Selah had damn near knocked Jock down trying to get out of that hospital room.

"Let them kids go on ahead!" Viceroy had wailed as she broke her neck getting out the door. "Come back for a minute Selah and let me show you something real quick."

Sheeiit. Selah shuddered at the memory. She reached over and jacked Rodney's ramrod hunk of wood. Viceroy could just keep his little limp hot dog in his goddamn pajamas! Who the hell did he think wanted to sit on his rubbery little Louisiana hotlink?

She moaned louder as Rodney plunged his thick fingers in and out of her softness. Selah's juices sloshed in his hand as she panted and fucked up at him with her hips.

But it only took her a few minutes to get tired of all that. Hell, she had her own damn fingers. A man with a big stiff dick is what she wanted!

She grabbed Rodney's wrist and made him withdraw from her tunnel. And then she maneuvered her body until her face was in his crotch and his gigantic sausage stood up stiffly like it had a steel rod going through it.

"Yes, suck my dick, *Mrs. Dominion*," Rodney ordered her. He wound his fat fingers in her hair and guided her mouth to the top of his shaft. "Suck my big hard *dick*," he repeated as her lips swept down his pole and covered it in hot, soft wetness. "And act like it's your husband's."

Fallon was stretched out on her sofa getting her lips sucked just the way she liked. The strong pink tongue that slipped in and out of her mouth felt like moist satin, and the bright white teeth that were perfectly straight dazzled her mind.

She felt the hand that crept up her side to cup her firm breast but she didn't try to stop it. In fact, she wanted to be touched. She arched her back and poked her titties out and mentally begged for her nipples to be stroked.

The strong fingers squeezed her titty gently and thumbed her nipple, and then slid down across her belly and pressed against the tender spot of her triangle. Fallon sighed and let her legs fall open, and she was just thrusting her hips up to meet the sweet pressure that was bearing down on her clit when her phone rang.

"Don't answer it," her partner panted, but Fallon couldn't help it as she reached behind her and snatched the cell phone off the end table.

"H-hello?"

"Sup, baby girl."

It was her ex. Freddie. Fallon's body started cooling down as she closed her legs and struggled to sit up.

"Hey. What's up?"

"I ran into a little problem with Verizon," Freddie explained. "Them fools claim they can't find my payment so now they about to cut off my phone. I need you to hook me up with five hundred until I get paid, a'ight? Can you do that for ya daddy real quick?"

Damn! Fallon smirked. This was Freddie's third damn time calling for money this week!

Fallon glanced at the fine-ass dude sitting next to her. They'd been in the same class since the seventh grade and she liked him. He was naked from the waist up and his dick was seriously on brick.

She licked her lips, then reached over and covered his rock with her hand and gave it a nice, slow squeeze.

"Sorry, Fredericka," she said into the phone. "This isn't a good time for me. I have company so I'ma have to holla at you later."

Click.

"Okay, so here's what I want you to do," Pilar said, running down her final take-down plan and speaking slowly like

Dy-Nasty was brain afflicted. "Get in touch with Uncle Suge and put the hammer on him. Squeeze that nigga's balls! Bump is just a fuckin' tool, but Suge holds all the real cards. I want you to tell that fool you got something on his nephew that's gonna bring the whole damn family down! Tell him he better smack you in the pockets with a million dollars in cash if he wants you to keep your mouth closed, and if he gives you any bullshit then you show him the damn pictures and fuck him up!"

Pilar's face lit up with an evil, conniving grin.

"And after you make him crawl and you get that damn money in your hands, then you *still* fucking tell on Barron!"

Her eyes sparkled at the thought of using Dy-Nasty to do all her dirty work.

"Tell who?" Dy-Nasty asked.

"Tell *everybody*, stupid! I want you to print them damn pictures out and show them to Aunt Selah, and then you find a way to sneak them up to that hospital so Uncle Viceroy can get a peek at them too! By the time we get finished fucking Barron he's gonna hate the day he met us!"

"Hell yeah!" Dy-Nasty nodded with dollar signs lighting up her eyes, but then her hood instincts kicked in and she frowned and suspiciously grilled the pampered little rich bitch sitting across from her.

"Yo, why you all of a sudden tryna be so down with me, Pilar? Ain't you bonin' Barron? Whut? You tryna get you a lil cut of that Dominion cash too?"

"No." Pilar shook her head as a fire crept into her eyes. She thought about all that hot sticky cum that was in Barron's drawers when he left out of Mink's room. Yeah, cash was good, but butt-fucking revenge was always better.

"I'm not boning that asshole and I don't want a dime of that money either," she told Dy-Nasty. "I'll get my satisfaction when Barron is bent over and taking a fat dick up his ass!"

★ ★ ★

"I don't give a good goddamn," I snapped at Bunni as I waited in the downstairs parlor for Uncle Suge to come get me. "I'm *still* tellin'!"

"Mink you just too damned hardheaded! Why don't you just *listen* sometimes?"

Listen? I had heard every damn thing I needed to hear when we was up in that window listening to Dy-Nasty plot up on a scheme to blackmail Barron out of a million big ones!

I had igged all that yang Bunni was spittin' and politely called Suge and asked him to come pick me up. And as soon as he got here I was planning on dropping a big fat dime and telling him all about Dy-Nasty's grimy little caper.

But Bunni was acting like I had lost my damn mind.

"Look, you and Dy-Nasty was gonna get down together before, remember? Y'all was gonna split that three hundred grand trust fund money right down the middle and you was real cool with that shit! So what's different now? Why can't you just hit Dy-Nasty up on the sly tip right now and let her know you're up on her shit? You can tell her it's gonna cost her half of whatever she gets from Barron if she wants you to keep her lil gank under your hat! Why you just can't do that?"

" 'Cause I don't want shit that donkey-faced bitch got, that's why!"

"Mink!" Bunni went at me hard. "Is you fuggin' *crazy*? Is you on some new kinda dope? Do you know what we could do with half a million smack-smacks?"

"I don't care, Bunni. I'm tellin'."

Her nose flared and sweat beads popped up all over that shit.

"Girl you is *losing* it! *For real*. Why in the world would you do some stupid shit like that?"

"Because what she's tryna do ain't right, Bunni!"

"*So*? Look, I'ma need you to wake the hell up, okay? Yo ass is just getting too damn *soft*! You willing to miss out on half a mil in cash for that fool Barron? Girl, you know damn well that nigga don't even *like* you! If it was up to him your high-yellow ass woulda been drop-kicked straight into the toilet bowl the very first day we rolled up in this bitch! I don't know why you all of a sudden wanna help *him* out! He damn sure wouldn't do nothin' to help *you*!"

I igged Bunni and kept peeping out the door looking for Suge's truck, but on the real tip I knew every damn thing my partner-in-grime was spittin' was right on point. I couldn't hardly believe I was about to drop a dime when keeping quiet might make me a dollar, but I still wanted to do that shit.

'Cause Bunni was calling it correct. Barron hated me and I hated his black ass too! But I hated that greasy bitch Dy-Nasty *even more*! Yeah, I was a con-mami all down in my bones and grifting was my favorite pastime. Tricking niggas for their loot was a delicate game and I was a top-notch contender with a whole lotta wins under my belt.

But at least I had some respect for my profession! Some flow to my hustle! Dy-Nasty was just shitty for no good reason at all. She was lazy and trifling, and everything about her skunk-ass was way below the grime of the gutter and underneath the grunge of the hood!

Bunni grilled me and rolled her eyes hard enough to make one pop out and skedaddle across the floor.

"You can roll 'em till they fall out, Bunni. I'm still tellin'."

"Okay, but just what the hell is Uncle Suge 'posed to do about it anyway?" she demanded. "Tell that horse-headed wench to leave his Lil Bump alone?"

I just smirked at all that noise she was making 'cause I wasn't even tryna hear it. Bunni knew damn well what type of gully nigga Suge was. He had spent his life erasing criminal footprints for that street-thug turned billionaire brother of his. Shit, Suge Dominion wasn't nobody's joke. That dude was a closer. A quicker-cleaner-upper. There was no doubt in my monkey-ass mind that if anybody could shove a hot stick of dynamite up Dy-Nasty's ugly ass, it was Uncle Suge.

★ ★ ★

Uncle Suge had picked me up and I was busy spittin' something hot in his ear, but it damn sure wasn't about no Barron and Dy-Nasty!

"Ooooh, yeah, baby!" I moaned as I rode his beefy dick bronco-style. "Right there, Daddy!" My titties jiggled and I shuddered as Suge gripped my hips and pounded up into me. "Uh-*huh*! Put that thang right there!"

We had rode out to his crib and tossed back a few drinks. Suge had thrown two big cows on the pit and started cutting up all kinds of shit to make us a salad, but my pussy was even hotter than the grill and by now them damn steaks was probably burnt!

We was buck naked on his living room sofa going to town.

"I wanna take that thang from the back," I whispered, leaning forward as I stuck the tip of my tongue inside his ear. "I want you to fuck my lights out, baby!"

In a flash that big nigga had lifted me under my arms and flipped me around. I yelped as he mushed my head down in the couch pillows and yanked my ass up high in the air.

He slapped me on the ass like I was a horse he was sending to the stable, and then he fist-gripped his monster meat and guided it to the slit of my dripping pussy and hummed as the tip of his dick tickled me like a vibrator.

"How bad you want this shit?" he growled.

I glanced over my shoulder and damn near fainted at the sight of his muscle-bound chest, rocked-up arms, and forty-pack abs.

Instead of answering, I reached back and grabbed my own ass-cheeks. I spread them thick babies open slow and wide so he could see all the creamy juices that were leaking from my tight pink slit.

"Bad enough for my pussy to beg for it," I said, and then I giggled at the look on his face.

"Goddamn. This the prettiest damn pussy I ever seen,"

Suge declared, and then he dove up in my shit, forcing his thick tube of meat into my juicy opening and ramming that shit all up in my guts.

I grunted as his pole sank into me. And then I arched my back and twerked my ass and massaged the hell outta my hot swollen clit as Suge pounded me out like a pro.

By the time he licked the back of my neck and then busted his walnut deep up in my twat, I had already gotten me two big nuts and one little tiny one for the road.

We laid on the couch sweating and panting with the smell of burning steak coming in from the patio outside. I was still stretched out on my stomach and he was leaning most of his weight on his forearms and spooning me from the back.

"Now what was that you wanted to holler at me about?"

I pressed my face deeper into the pillows and frowned. I wanted to tell him about Dy-Nasty's shiesty little gank, but all I could hear was Bunni's warnings ringing out in my ears.

I don't know why you all of a sudden wanna help Barron *out! He damn sure wouldn't do nothin' to help* you*!*

Before I could say anything Suge's cell phone sounded off. I lifted my head and swiveled my neck around and eyed him as he leaned over and snatched his pants up off the floor. I felt some kinda way when he frowned at his cell phone, then swiped his thumb across the screen and backed up on his knees and turned away from me.

"Yo, what's up?" I heard him growl. "Oh yeah? A'ight, cool. I'm in the middle of something right now but I'll swing by in a few and we can holla."

"Who was that?" my nosy-ass demanded as he got up off the couch and I followed him up the steps to the shower. It was one of them bricked joints with stone everywhere and it was so deep it didn't even need no shower curtain.

"That was ya girl Dy-Nasty," he said over his shoulder as he turned on the hot water and it gushed out and sprayed from the soaker jets.

I felt my insides start to boil.

"Oh yeah, what that bitch want with you?" I blurted, scrunching up my face.

Suge shrugged. "She said she needs to get with me about something real crucial."

"Oh yeah?" I was really heated now. "So what, you gonna just jump up from bangin' me and run over there to see her?"

"Uh-huh," Suge said, and nodded. He reached out and cupped the back of my neck with his big-old paw and pulled my naked booty under the shower spray with him.

I pressed up against his hardness and let my tongue slither over his wet nipple.

"You really gonna leave me and go see her when you know I can't stand that bitch?"

He kissed me on my forehead and squeezed my titty real gently and chuckled. "Hell yeah. 'Cause when a cutthroat chick like Dy-Nasty wants to run off with her mouth, you gotta let her run it."

CHAPTER 18

Suge could feel Dy-Nasty grilling him on the sneak tip as he sped down the highway with her in the passenger seat of his monster truck. She was fine as hell but he wasn't impressed with her because he already knew the drill. Not only was he paid out the ass and powerful as fuck, he lived and breathed his hustle and it showed in his swag. Chicks were always tryna get at him, and this shiesty little street sweeper sitting beside him was no exception.

He was real comfortable handling the huge piece of truck he pushed, and he rode with his seat nice and low. Twirling a toothpick around in his mouth and driving with one hand on the wheel, Suge could tell Dy-Nasty was waiting for the right time to make her move, so he chilled and bided his time too.

She had hit him on his cell while he was laid up with Mink and asked him to give her a ride to a fish joint up in Dallas. Suge had picked her up from the mansion and now, igging the hungry, conniving looks she was throwing him from the corner of her eye, Suge nodded his head to the beat that blared from his deluxe package stereo system as he punched his gas pedal hard to the floor.

Dy-Nasty was still grilling him but Suge was cool with it.

A gutter chick like her was gonna throw down some game wherever she saw an opening, and all he had to do was sit back and relax and let her walk right into his trap.

And sure enough, by the time they pulled up outside the combination fish joint and BBQ pit that was in a little strip mall, Dy-Nasty was more than ready to spill every last one of her baked little beans.

"Okay, looka here, Uncle Suge," she blurted outta the slick side of her mouth as they climbed outta his truck and walked toward the restaurant. "I got somethin' I wanna get witchu about, and the only reason I called you to put you on is 'cause I can tell that you the one who's really runnin' this family bizz, 'cause you the only one who got some sense about yourself."

Suge tongued his toothpick as he side-eyed her. A slight grin was on his lips, but if her vision wasn't so faded by dollar signs Dy-Nasty woulda been able to peep the deadly frost that was lurking in his eyes.

"See now," she kept running off at the mouth as they walked inside, "I ain't even gonna fuck with none of the rest of them Dominions 'cause like I said, I already know who's really runnin' shit around here. All of them be steady kissing Barron's ass like he's some kinda fuckin' boss, but that's some bullshit 'cause Barron can't even get his own dick outta a pickle jar!"

Suge paid for her order at the counter and then they slid into a booth at the back of the restaurant to wait for the food. Dy-Nasty could barely wait for her ass to touch the seat so she could get back to running her game, and Suge laughed inside as the dumb little guttersnipe went into seduce-a-trick mode. He was amused as fuck as she slid her pink tongue wetly over her lips and then stared deep into his eyes and sat up straight, arching her back like a kitten. Pouting her lips, she pushed her round titties forward and stared at him through her false eyelashes as her body started giving off that old time-tested "come fuck the shit outta me" scent.

Suge wanted to laugh for real now. His dick didn't even

think about waking up as Dy-Nasty tried to throw her free-hot-pussy game down on him. His one-eyed monster kept right on snoring like a muthafucka 'cause this run-through trick right here wasn't the type of broad he woulda fucked with his toe, let alone with his precious dick.

"Check it out, Uncle Suge," she said, leaning across the table toward him. "I got me some dirt on Barron that's gonna fuck him up for life!"

"On Bump?"

Dy-Nasty nodded. "Uh-huh. On that stuck-up muthafucka who be tryna act like he so much smarter than everybody else!"

Suge's expression never changed.

"Oh yeah?" he said quietly, flipping his toothpick over with his tongue.

Dy-Nasty leaned in even closer and Suge peeped her entire hustle in the glint of her devilish eyes.

"Yep. Be'lee that. I found some pictures of him online. Wearing a skirt and sucking a *dick*!"

Suge never moved a muscle. His eyes looked like two ice cubes as he chewed his toothpick and grilled her. "Is that right?"

She nodded again. "Damn right. Check this out." She whipped out her cell phone and punched in a Web site, then passed it to him. She was grinning her ass off as Suge scrolled through a series of pictures of Barron in a bunch of different poses, each one more fucked up than the last one.

"*Okay*?" Dy-Nasty squealed. "See what I'm sayin'? And just like Barron was gonna use all that dirt he dug up on me and Mink to knock us off the block and keep us outta that trust fund, now my ass got something that I can use to knock him off his block too! And if that muthafucka wants me to keep my mouth closed about what he been out there doin' in the dark, then somebody is gonna hafta *pay* me!"

"Pay you?" Suge sat up straight and pretended like he was surprised. "How much are you trying to get paid, sugar?"

"I'm tryna get the same damn thang every damn body else got! I want Sable's whole inheritance plus a little bit extra! Matter fact, y'all can just go 'head and drop a quick *million* in my bank account! That's three years worth of trust fund money, plus the same hundred-grand inheritance dough y'all gave to Mink. And if anybody got a problem payin' to shut me up about these pictures then you can just *tell* me! I know y'all rich muthafuckas done heard of the World Wide Web, right? Well fuck with me and I'ma put Barron's down-low ass on the world-wide-*blast* and tell his daddy and 'nem ere'thang I know!"

Suge held up his hand like he was a peacemaker instead of a hit man.

"Now slow down, darling," he soothed her. "Ain't no need for all them threats, okay, sugar? Lemme see if I can work a lil something out for you. I can't promise you nothing or make you no guarantees, but trust me, I'ma do my best to make sure you get everything you need."

Suge dropped Dy-Nasty back off at the Dominion mansion and then zipped over to his man's office on the north side of Dallas. Two hours later he was back on the highway headed south and chewing a fresh toothpick as he hit a button on his center console and listened as the phone rang over the truck's speaker system.

"Lil Bump," he said when it was answered and he heard his nephew's voice on the other end. "We got us a little problem," he said quietly. "I need you to meet me at the Bat Cave, my nigga. And get there as soon as you can."

CHAPTER 19

The ten-acre ranch was located off a dirt road deep in the Texas brush, and if you didn't know it was there you never woulda found it. The structure was over ten thousand square feet of hard masculine wood and tinted glass, and Viceroy had built it twenty years ago as a secret refuge where him and his most trusted henchmen could retreat to when critical, and sometimes life-and-death, decisions needed to be made.

The ranch was fortified by some of the best security systems in the world, and an intricate set of codes had to be entered into a panel before a heavy, wrought-iron gate slid back on the fenced-in compound.

Admittance was by invitation only, and since the only two people who knew the codes to the security system were Viceroy and Suge, Barron knew his uncle had summoned him out there to discuss some real critical shit.

Suge was waiting for him near the gates of the compound, and when Barron pulled up in his brother Dane's Hummer, Suge punched in the code and then nodded and waved him through.

Barron parked on the paved lot right beside Suge's massive truck, and then he got out and followed his uncle inside. This was only the third time Barron had been invited out to the ranch, and he was still in awe of the place. It was a gangster's den. A place where dangerous men met to make crucial, cut-throat decisions. Barron stood in the middle of the large room and took it all in. The one-story ranch house was huge, and the fact that all ten thousand feet of it was spread out on one level made it seem even bigger.

There were several underground bunkers on the property, and Barron remembered Viceroy telling him that if the shit ever hit the fan and the country came under attack he needed to get with Suge and bring the entire family out here so they could hide out in the bunkers. According to his father, there was a ventilated air supply and enough guns, bullets, food, and water stored underground to last the entire Dominion clan at least three months.

"Goddamn, Bump!" Suge said as soon as he got a good look at his nephew. Barron had a nice round bald patch shaved in his head about the size of a quarter. "Who in the hell busted you upside your head?"

Barron shrugged as he thought about Pilar bitch-cracking him with that wine bottle. "It ain't nothing. I fell and nicked my head on some metal bleachers at the gym. I had to get ten stitches and a tetanus shot."

Suge smirked and raised his eyebrow but he didn't press him.

"Well come on in and relax yourself, B," he told him as he walked over to a large, well-stocked bar up against the wall and poured them both a stiff drink.

Barron sat down in a plush leather armchair and tried to get comfortable as he wondered for the fiftieth time what the hell Suge had brought him out here for.

Suge looked deadlier than a muthafucka as he handed Barron a double shot of Rémy, and then he sat down across from him and tossed his whole shit back in one swallow.

"We got us a situation."

There was no beating around the bush. Suge opened up on him and started laying shit down, and in that instant Barron knew exactly why his father had hired his baby brother as the leader of the Dominion war council all them years ago. 'Cause if your nuts ever got trapped in a metal vice or you woke up one day with your dick stuck in a real tight keyhole, Suge was the kind of take-care-of-bizz nigga you could call to get it out.

Barron sat there with his stomach caving in, and even before the first words dropped out of his uncle's mouth he knew exactly what the man was gonna say.

"I got a call from Dy-Nasty today. There's some bad pictures of you out there on the Internet. They ain't suitable for viewing and we gotta get rid of 'em. But it's gonna cost us a million dollars."

Barron bucked. "A million fuckin' dollars? Are you serious?"

"That's the askin' price," Suge said calmly, and then he grilled Barron hard, checking him with the ice in his eyes. "But you already knew about them pictures, didn't you?"

Barron sighed, then nodded and fessed up.

"This cat named Dopeman got me. He put a roofie or something in my drink and it fucked me up, man. That's how they got them pictures, Suge."

Suge got swole. "Listen here, Bump. When a Dominion man runs up on trouble we don't hide from that shit, you hear me? We come out here, right here to this *very room,* and we figure out how to kill that shit."

Barron hung his head low. The humiliation of getting caught on camera looking like a drag queen was bad enough, but to have that criminal-minded Dy-Nasty find out about those pictures and try to blackmail him was way fuckin' worse.

"That grimy skank," he muttered under his breath. "We gotta get rid of that bitch!"

Barron wanted to bend over and kick himself square up the ass. He'd thought Mink was a nasty scuzzball, but Dy-

Nasty was a scuzzball soaked in toilet water! He never should have brought her to Texas with him in the first damn place. He should have left her right up in that cruddy strip joint where he had found her ass, but *noooo.* He was so busy trying to bust Mink out that he had traded ghetto for gutter and ended up getting shit on instead.

"Dy-Nasty didn't find those pictures by herself. Who told her? Who put her dumb ass up to this shit? I bet you any amount of money it was Mink!"

Suge shook his head and frowned. "I don't think so. There's too much bad blood between them two. If I had to bet I'd say Mink would hop on your team over Dy-Nasty's seven days a week."

Barron frowned. Mink was the *last* damn person he would've expected to look out for him. Matter fact, he wouldn't count on Mink to piss on him if his ass was on fire.

He shook his head. "We can't pay that bitch no million dollars, Uncle Suge," he blurted. "Hell nah, we can't do that."

Barron had access to a nice hunk of money, but a payment that size would trigger an automatic audit on Dominion Oil's accounts, and with his father out of his coma and almost back up on his feet, there's no way in hell he could hide some shit like that.

"Uh-uh, man," he repeated. "We can't do that."

"Hell naw," Suge said, and shook his head just once. "We ain't payin' her ass shit. Look, this thing is bad," Suge told him quietly, "but it ain't as bad as it can get. I know where those pictures are. I had my boy sniff 'em out and he's an expert in this kinda shit. He traced the IP address where the files are being hosted, and we about to fry that shit like a pan of bacon. In about thirty minutes my dude is gonna send a fuckin' virus into that mainframe that'll make them pictures disappear forever, B, but there's still something else we gonna hafta handle, you know. We gots to handle *Dy-Nasty*."

Suge's killer eyes bored deeply into his nephew's, and as he ran down his gully plan, Barron saw something in his uncle's gaze that confirmed what he had always known.

I love you, Lil Bump, but I will straight fuck you up.

No matter what kinda bullshit went down between them, his uncle Suge was one hundred percent down for the team. Suge loved him, and he would lay his ass all the way in the gutter for him, if that's what Barron needed him to do.

CHAPTER 20

Even with all the scandalous shit going on at the mansion I still couldn't stop myself from thinking about the drama that had popped off after Mama's funeral. My stomach was on strike so I didn't have no appetite at all, and I walked around the crib feeling real fucked up in my heart. It finally got so bad that I just couldn't take it no more, so one afternoon I left Bunni up in the loft getting smutted out by Dane, and I went to my room and did what I had to do.

I dialed my grandmother's number justa hoping she had paid her phone bill and her shit wasn't cut off like it usually was.

"Hello?"

"Hey Granny, it's Mink. How you doin'?"

"*Mink*?" she hollered. It was loud as hell up in that camp, and the sounds of a drunk party almost drowned her out.

"Baby, what in the hell happened to you? Why you run off like that and leave us standing there like that at your mama's funeral? You know we didn't have no ride home! And where you at anyway? Some bad folks been coming 'round here lookin' for you. You got any money on you? Can you run up the street and put some numbers in for your old granny, baby?"

"I can't!" I hollered into the phone. "I'm outta town right now, Granny, but I'ma be back soon. Is Aunt Bibby there?"

"Who?" she shouted.

"Aunt Bibby!"

"Oh. Yeah, she's here."

I rolled my eyes. *Then why the hell you ain't ask her to run up the block and put your damn numbers in?*

"Can I speak to her, please?"

"Yeah, but don't stay on my phone too long, ya hear? I got some business going on and I'm waitin' on a real important call."

I twisted my lips up at that bullshit. Business, hell. Granny was a LaRue. A *lying-ass* LaRue.

It took Aunt Bibby forever to come to the phone, and listening to all them loud niggas partying in that cramped little apartment was giving me a headache. I was just about to say fuck it and hang up when somebody picked up the phone and said, "Yeah?"

"Aunt Bibby? It's Mink."

"Yeah?"

I could tell by that one word that she was good and juiced up.

"Umm, hey Aunt Bibby, can I ask you a question?"

"Yeah?"

"Do you remember that lady who ran up on Mama's hearse talking shit after her funeral?"

"Yeah."

"Who was that?"

"What? I can't hear a damn thing you sayin'!" my aunt slurred. "Lemme take this shit out in the hall."

I listened as she walked through the noisy apartment, and then I heard the front door slam as she stepped outside and into the hallway where it was a lot more quiet.

"Awright now! Why the hell is you fuckin' wit' me, Mink?" she slurred.

"I just wanna know who that lady was. You know. The one who ran up on us outside after Mama's funeral. The one who called Mama a bitch and said she was glad Mama was finally dead."

Aunt Bibby started laughing like crazy.

"Naw, naw, naw! Oh, hell *naw*! I *know* you ain't askin' me shit! I'm a damn liar, remember?" She mimicked me: "*You's a goddamn liar, Aunt Bibby! You's a old bald-headed lying bitch!*"

I smirked as she laughed in my ear.

"What?" she snapped all shitty-like. "You done finally got you some balls from somewhere? Now all of a sudden you ready to hear what's really real? Well *fuck you*, Mink! Somebody go outta they way to tryta help your ass and all you do is shit on 'em! *Fuck you*!"

I sighed and forced myself to chill.

"I ain't call to argue with you, Aunt Bibby. I just wanna know the truth about my mama. That's all."

"I *told* you the goddamn truth," she exploded. "I told you, I told you, I *told* your stupid ass! Jude wasn't shit! She wasn't *shit*, you hear me? The way she did my goddamn brother? The way she fucked around and killed my Moe like that?"

"But who was that *lady*, Aunt Bibby? Why she run up there spittin' and carrying on and talking all that shit about Mama?"

"That lady was your *aunt*, Mink! Your *aunt*!"

I frowned.

"What? How the hell she gonna be my aunt? Mama was the only child, dummy! She didn't have no sisters."

"*Ha*!" Aunt Bibby shouted, and then that drunk heffa kicked me dead in my throat when she hollered, "*Jude Jackson* mighta been an only child! But your *real mama* sure as hell wasn't!"

★ ★ ★

My ass was draggin' way down on the ground.

I was floored. Just fuckin' devastated. Aunt Bibby had put something on me that blew my little gaming head straight up. I felt like a brand-new sherm. Open as shit. Like a tender little mark who had been getting ganked by the throat my whole fuckin' life.

My head was banging and my heart was in so much pain that all I could do was ball up in a knot on my bed as Bunni pressed a freakin' ice pack to the back of my neck.

"Girl what the hell happened?" Bunni demanded as she wiped another snot bubble from my nose and started patting my back like she was tryna burp me. She had just got back from breaking Dane's back and found me in my room crying.

"I called home," I mumbled miserably. "I talked to my aunt."

Bunni sucked her teeth. "Did Bibby say sumthin' slick to you? Did she say sumthin' slick? I swear to God, Mink! If that tubby-gut hoe said sumthin' slick outta her mouth to you I'ma bust her one when we get back to Harlem!"

"She said I was *adopted*," I muttered as my eyes leaked a whole damn river of tears.

"Get the fugg outta here!" Bunni hollered. "First she told you that you got a twin, and now she's tryna say you was adopted too? That bitch sure knows a lot for a dummy!"

I coughed real hard and Bunni went from burping me like I was a baby to pounding the shit outta my back. "Hold up." She stopped pounding for a quick second and frowned. "Was that jailbird drankin' when she told you that shit? I bet that trick was pissy *drunk*!"

I sniffled. "Yeah, she was lit. She told me Mama adopted me right here in Texas and then brought me up to New York to live. Aunt Bibby swore all out that the lady who ran up on us at Mama's funeral was my aunt. My *real* mama's sister."

"Your real mama? No shit?"

I nodded miserably. "And if my mama ain't my mama, then that means my daddy wasn't my daddy neither."

Bunni's hand froze on my back again. "What kind of trifling shit is that? So where the hell do this real mama be, and what happened to your twin?"

I shrugged. Everything I had thought about Dy-Nasty was turning out to be true, and everything I thought I knew about myself seemed like one big dirty rotten lie!

"Aunt Bibby said my real mama died, and she thinks the other baby got adopted right here in Texas too. But that baby stayed here."

"Ooooh." Bunni had always been quick on the cap and it only took her a second to come to the same conclusion that was vexin' me. "So if the other baby stayed down here in Texas with the Dominions, then that means *she's* the one who got taken to New York and snatched up outta her stroller and kidnapped, huh?"

I nodded.

"Well damn! If Jude raised you, then who the hell raised your sister?"

"It musta been that chick she be calling Pat," I said, sniveling my ass off as I finally admitted what was crystal-clear and obvious. "That slick lady from Philly who told Dy-Nasty who she really was so she could come down here and go after her money in the first place."

CHAPTER 21

"I heard Pops is going bat-shit crazy sitting up in that hospital room all day long," Dane told us as we passed some piff around Bunni's room. "His doctors got tired of all his bitching so they gave Mama permission to get him outta there for a little while."

"Oh yeah?" I said, busting him a look. I was about to twist my lil lips right up because I damn sure didn't want Viceroy coming back to the mansion and fuckin' up my flow no time soon!

"Ain't he still too sick to be tryna come home already?"

Dane shook his head. "Nah, his doctors ain't letting him come *home* yet, but they do want Pops to have a little fun. He's itchin' to show all his business partners and associates that he's back up on his toes, so Mama's gonna throw him a big welcome back party at the lakeside mansion we have in Austin."

Dane sure had his info right because Selah confirmed it at dinner later on that night.

"We're having a barbeque tomorrow," she said. "We're all going to fly down to the house at Horseshoe Bay in the morning, and then I'm sending the jet to Houston to pick up your father and his nursing staff," she told us.

"Make sure you bring your swimsuits because the water is still warm and the lake is a lot of fun this time of year."

"Now remember, Mink," Bunni warned me the next morning as we picked out some fly gear to take with us to Austin. "Don't you be waving no white flag and surrendering on me 'cause this game ain't over yet! Matter fact, its just about to get poppin', yo! *Fugg* Dy-Nasty! That low-budget stripper can be Sable all she wanna be! That don't mean we gonna clock out on the job and sleep on what we brought our asses down here to do!"

"But the DNA results—"

"Forget them damn DNA results! All you hafta do is convince Big Daddy Domino that *you's* the kinda daughter he wanna show off to all them rich white folks he be hanging around, and Dy-Nasty *ain't*! You just act like one a them real sweet cream puffs when we get out there, ya heard? Ere'thang you do betta convince that loaded mofo that he can get with this," she said, pointing at me, "or he can get with that!" She twisted her lips up and pointed toward Dy-Nasty's room.

I sighed. "I don't know, Bunni . . ."

"Dammit, Mink, buck the hell up! Now, Peaches done trained you up right and you know exactly what you gotta do. You gots to get down there in Austin and *work,* mamacita! Lie your ass off, Mink! Be the type of Goody Two-shoes Oreo that rich old-head gangsta wants you to be! Do what you gotta do so we can get paid up in this bitch, ya hear me? 'Cause trust and believe, if you don't, then as soon as them DNA results come back these fools is gonna kick us straight up outta here! And when they put you out I'ma need you to remember something, Mink, a'ight?"

"What's that?"

"Your homeless ass ain't got no place else to go!"

* * *

I knew one damn thing for sure. Whether we was rich or we was poor, black folks knew how to throw a beast-ass barbecue!

The mansion at Horseshoe Bay in Austin was smaller than the one in Dallas was, but that bad-boy was still all the way live. There was food out the ass and bubbly champagne, cold brewskis, and top-shelf liquor was flowing like tap water!

Selah had flown a bunch of her staff down real early in the morning to set stuff up, and by the time the rest of us flew in right before lunch the waiters and waitresses had a huge spread laid out. The party was a mixed bag. Vans of Viceroy's gutterlicious family from Houston sat out on the grass getting zooted and mingling with a whole crew of clear people from Dominion Oil who were waiting around to welcome their head honcho back from the dead.

There were sawed-off barrel grills out the ass, and smokers full of chicken, pork, turkey, and brisket that was just'a falling off the bone. They had even set up a seafood-only grill where salmon topped with goo-gobs of butter and garlic was cooking on wooden planks, and shish kebab sticks were packed full of veggies and gigantic Texas-sized prawns.

I was the shit in my shimmering off-white Dior summer skirt that fit just right over my hips before tapering down and flaring out again above my knees. It was comfortable and sexy, and the stylish fabric moved with me as I swayed through the crowd. I had on a pair of silver Christian Louboutin's that had a funky wedge heel, and a plain white tank top that showed off my toned shoulders and arms and had my juicy titties looking nice and phat.

Bunni had picked out all my accessories, and she had done a damn good job too. I dripped a dainty pair of diamond earrings that we had charged on the Dominion's credit account at the rich people's mall, and a matching necklace that had a soft triangle of chipped diamonds that rested with the tip pointing right down into my cleavage.

Since I was gonna be meeting Viceroy I had left all my colorful Glama-Glos right in my suitcase. Today I was rocking my own hair, and I had washed it and let it air dry a little bit, and then twisted the ends with my fingers until they coiled around in shiny little curls.

About an hour after we got there a big commotion popped off in the front of the house, and when me and Bunni slid that way to see what was happening, we peeped a sleek black stretch limo in the driveway with a bunch of people standing around whistling and clapping.

"Uh-oh," Bunni said as the driver held the back door open and a foot slid out with a real expensive-looking men's shoe on it. "It's Big Daddy Domino, baybeee! Put ya game face on, Mink Mami! Get ready to hook this Texas fish and gut his ass out!"

Butterflies started beating all down in my stomach as I thought about how Viceroy's swollen-up eyeball had stared at me when he was in the hospital and supposed to be in a coma. Fuck what the doctors said, as soon as I walked in that room I just knew his ass was fake-sleep and was grilling me on the sly!

"Yo, I don't think Viceroy likes me, Bunni," I mumbled under my breath.

"Bullshit!" she snapped. "That fool don't even *know* you! Remember," she sang out, "ages eight to eighty, baybeee! Blind, cripple, and crazeee! Besides, look at all that!" She slapped me hard on my ass. "What straight dude you ever met who wasn't feelin' what you packin', boo?"

Selah had hired a couple of male nurses to take care of Viceroy for the day, and me and Bunni hung in the background and watched them get him outta the limo and into a wheelchair, and then push him down the stone path that led to the huge backyard on the lake.

"Pappa Doo is a G," Bunni said like she was real impressed.

Viceroy was sportin' some real casual attire, but his gear might as well have had big fat price tags hangin' off of it because from his imported alligator shoes to the bone-crushin' ring on his pinkie finger, to his fifteen-hundred-dollar Louis Vuitton Evasions, it was obvious that he was swimming in cash.

"He's skinny as a mug, though," I said as we followed the crowd that was following him. "Looks kinda light in the ass."

"Sho do," Bunni agreed as we rounded the corner to the backyard. "Dude needs to get up on a couple of them BBQ ribs and suck down a few cold ones. Fatten his narrow ass right on up!"

My eyeballs was on high-scrutiny mode as they crawled over every inch of that backyard. There was a white cloth awning set up for Viceroy to sit under that blocked out the sun, and underneath it were about five big folding chairs with fluffy pillows on the seats. His nursing attendants tried to help him get up outta his wheelchair but he waved them off, and with Selah holding him by the arm, everybody clapped and cheered as he walked real shaky-like over to the big chair in the middle of the row and lowered his bony self down into it.

Barron sat down on one side of his father and Selah perched her ass in a chair on his other side. For the party to be kickin' so live Mama Selah sure looked jacked in the mug. She sat next to her man tryna slime like it was a joyful reunion, but on the real, her lips were balled up and twisted like shit.

Barron was looking like somebody had snipped off one of his balls too. He was sitting right beside his daddy, but he was leaning far away from Viceroy's ass. Every now and then he would sit up straight and listen when Viceroy spit something out the corner of his mouth, but other than that Barron's mug looked hit too.

I glanced down at myself nervously. It was a damn good thing that Bunni had told me to go for the innocent-wouldn't-bust-a-grape look, because stupid-ass Dy-Nasty already had the slutty I-fuck-for-peanuts look on lock!

"Scab!" Bunni turned down her lips as Dy-Nasty swung her hips like baseball bats as she sashayed through the crowd of rich clear folks, talking all loud and grinning up in their faces. She had on a pair of purple dukey shorts like the kind those female volleyball players wear all the time. But Dy-Nasty's scandalous ass wasn't shaped like no athlete! Her thick yellow jelly was pouring outta them shorts like lemon custard pudding, and the lil top she had on wasn't even as big as a bra.

"That bitch ain't nowhere near as smoove wit' it as you are, Mink," my girl Bunni complimented me. "Naw, Dy-Dooky over there is just a straight-up loose-booty *scab*!"

I turned my lip up and watched as she walked right over to where Viceroy and Selah were sitting. Bunni had that shit right. The party hadn't been going but a hot-ass minute and Mizz Thang was already super tipsy and lookin' stank and raunchy in her coochie-cutter shorts.

I couldn't believe it when she bent her wide ass over right in front of Viceroy and dug around for a cold bottle of beer from the bottom of an icy cooler. She pried the cap off that baby with her back teeth, then gripped the neck and turned that shit up to her lips like a natural man.

Dy-Nasty's throat was so damn long, and she guzzled that brew so damn hard, that it started leaking all outta the corners of her mouth. And then, right there in front of Viceroy and all his rich white cronies, her dumb tail belched real loud and then laughed like crazy as she wiped at her wet chin with the back of her hand.

"Look," Bunni said, and elbowed the shit outta me real quick. "Check out ya play papa! Daddy-O ain't feelin' Stanky's ass *at all*."

Bunni was batting a thousand. The sneer on Viceroy's face was enough to say it all. He leaned over and whispered something to Selah, and she nodded a few times and then reached over and patted his hand.

"Ha!" Bunni said as she snatched me by my arm and we

walked past a smoking grill. She snatched a burnt hot dog off a platter that had been smothered in ketchup, relish, and onions, and gobbled up half of that shit in just one bite.

"Leggo Mink," she said, sashaying out into the crowded yard. "Get ready to put a big W in our column baby 'cause this here gank is 'bout to be a wrap. You ain't got a damn thing to worry about," she assured me over her shoulder as she switched her high booty toward the outdoor happenings. " 'Cause that lil amateur guttersnipe walking around in them stank purple panties ain't got shit on you!"

"What the hell you mean the Web site ain't there no more?" Dy-Nasty snapped with her hand on her hip. Her and Pilar were crammed together in the downstairs powder room while the rest of the party got their drink on and partied outside.

"I meant exactly what I said," Pilar muttered. "That shit isn't there anymore." She held her iPad up in the air and shook it like it was an Etch A Sketch.

"Well where the hell could it be?"

Pilar ignored the girl breathing down her neck as she refreshed the browser on her iPad and then typed in the Web address again.

And again, a PAGE NOT FOUND message came up on her screen and made her scratch her damn head.

Dy-Nasty whipped out her cell phone and started punching buttons.

"I know that million damn dollars better be in my goddamn bank account," she huffed. "Suge said he was gonna transfer it by 12 o'clock noon and that shit damn sure better be there!"

Pilar didn't say a word as she turned off the cellular data on her iPad and then turned it back on. She typed in the Web address one last time and came up with a fail again.

"Something ain't right," she muttered.

"It damn sure ain't!" Dy-Nasty hollered as she stared down at her cell phone. "I'ma fuck Suge up! There ain't but twelve damn dollars in my bank account!"

Pilar whirled around and blasted on the girl.

"You just couldn't keep your damn mouth closed, could you? Who else did your stupid-ass tell about this shit?"

"Whut?" Dy-Nasty rose straight up outta the gutters of Philadelphia. "Yo who da fuck is you callin' *stupid*? I didn't tell nobody but Suge! It ain't my goddamn fault that they done shut the Web site down! Who the hell else did *you* tell?"

"Why in the world would *I* tell somebody?" Pilar screamed on her. "I'm the one who tried to hook you up in the first place!"

"Stop trippin'! We can still gank they asses just as long as we can show them a copy of them pictures. You printed them shits out, didn't you?"

Pilar took a real deep breath. "No. I didn't print the damn things out. Did you?"

Dy-Nasty clutched her chest. "How the hell was I supposed to print 'em out? Do you see me walking around here with a printer and a goddamn computer?"

Pilar folded her arms over her breasts and peered at Dy-Nasty suspiciously. "Are you sure you didn't tell anyone about this other than Uncle Suge?"

"Hell yeah, I'm sure," Dy-Nasty lied as she thought about the convo she'd had with her mother. Technically she had told *two* people, but Pat didn't really count. "I did just like you told me to do! I got with Suge and squeezed his nuts. And that's the *only* person I told!"

Pilar looked Dy-Nasty up and down and then slapped her own forehead and snorted in pure disgust.

"I don't know what the *hell* made me trust you to do even the simplest thing right. What in the world was I thinking?"

"I don't know why I trusted your fake ass neither!" Dy-Nasty shot back. "You ain't do nothin' but waste my time!"

"Well somebody else must have found out about it," Pilar said, unlocking the bathroom door and reaching for the knob. "Because the pictures are gone. But that's cool, I'll just have to find another way to stick it to Barron because I'm out of it now. I have a feeling this shit is about to get way too messy for me."

"Oh, so now you just gonna be out and forget all about me? Well what about my damn money?"

Pilar looked down her nose at the grimy hood chick with the tatted up tits and the terrible weave and said, "I don't know, what about it?"

Dy-Nasty's eyes got real small.

"You stuck up bitch, you! I oughta wipe this whole damn bathroom up with you! I oughta stomp a mud-hole in your boojie ass and give you a head swirly right here in this god-damn toilet bowl!"

"Oh yeah?" Pilar said, turning around to face the tough Philly street chick head-up. "Go 'head and try it, bitch. You put one goddamn finger on me and what you *oughta* do is get ready to take your raggedy ass to *jail*!"

CHAPTER 22

Viceroy looked pretty damn decent for an oil blast victim, and the fact that he had come up out of his coma was cool and all, but Digger Ducane didn't drive all the way to Austin because he gave a hot goddamn about his brother-in-law. Hell no. He had come down to Austin to try to save his own ass.

He had called his sister Selah to see if she was still mad about him crossing enemy lines to work for Rodney Ruddman, and as soon as she answered the phone he could tell right off the bat that, yep, she was still pissed.

"Hey sis." He'd started out trying to smooth talk her like everything was everything and they were still all the way cool. "I heard Viceroy is out of his coma! God is good all the time, ain't he?"

"What do you want, Duncan?"

Oh, hell yeah. She was pissed all right. Selah hadn't called him Duncan since he was twelve damn years old!

"Pilar told me about the barbeque," he'd said, throwing his daughter's name in the mix because he knew his sister was a sucker for her niece. "I was just wondering if I could bum a ride down to Austin with the rest of the family."

Digger made sure he put a lotta weight behind that last

word. *Family*. Him and Selah were family and she needed to remember that shit. They had the exact same blood running through their veins, and no matter what went down between them, blood was always gonna be thicker than mud.

"Sorry," Selah had said coldly. "The business jet is full. If you want to come to Austin you're going to have to drive down."

That was some bullshit and Digger knew it, but he had waited for Pilar to get ready, then stuffed his fat gut behind the wheel of his Caddy and driven the two hours south anyway.

Viceroy was a big willie in the great state of Texas, and a lakeside 'que thrown in his honor had pulled a helluva turnout. Sitting under an umbrella table and sipping from an icy glass of vodka and orange juice, Digger looked around at the huge crowd of drinking and picnicking folks and felt a little lonely.

He had put in close to thirty years with Dominion Oil, and almost everybody out there had either ran the streets with him in the past or had been his close business associate or friend.

But all that shit had changed in a hurry when he defected from Dominion Oil and jumped in bed with their main competitor, Ruddman Energy. Yeah, Digger knew it took some real big Brooklyn balls for him to show his face in this crowd today, but he wasn't no grimier than those Dominions were. Besides, according to Pilar, Viceroy had woken up with a couple of screws loose. Hell, his marbles were bouncing around in his damn head so bad that they hadn't even told him about Digger leaving the company yet.

Digger sighed and swigged a mouthful of liquor. Viceroy used to be his main man and he felt real low for betraying him, but who the hell knew he was gonna wake up?

Digger watched as his old friend sat next to Selah and talked shit and cut up with all his old business partners. He missed being a part of that set. Yeah, the pay was definitely steady over at Ruddman Energy, but when it came to doing business Rodney Ruddman was one greasy-ass fuck! On the real, Digger doubted if he would even have a damn job when he got back to Dallas.

He thought about the call he'd gotten on Friday afternoon. It was from a secretary in human resources instructing him to be in Rodney's office with his logbooks and his company keys the first thing Monday morning at seven sharp.

Digger knew damn well that old fool wasn't calling him on the carpet because he wanted to go hit a few holes of golf. Nah, that little ruthless bastard was about to fire him, and Digger knew it. He had a feeling Ruddman wanted to stick it to him personally instead of letting human resources shut him down because that little bastard wanted to humiliate him first.

Digger knew he had it coming, but still, his pockets couldn't stand it. The thought of being broke and out of a job made him drain his shot glass and signal to a passing waiter to bring him a refill. He glanced toward the lake and spotted his daughter stretched out on a floater and his stomach clenched. The only way for him to dodge the unemployment bullet was to convince his sister to forget what he had done and let him come back and pick up his old contracting spot at Dominion Oil.

The problem was, Selah had already told him it would be a cold day in hell before she fucked with him again, and since the weather was a sticky eighty-something degrees and rising in the heart of central Texas, Digger knew his sister probably wouldn't be fucking with him today.

I had been watching Viceroy on the sly ever since he had rolled up at the party, and I still got the same creepy-ass feeling about him that I had gotten when he was laid up in his hospital bed.

Dude was a gamer, I could tell.

He had the look of a natural grifter about him. Like he had hustled up on some serious squares in his day. A working person could usually peep another working person right off the bat, and that's the shit that had me worried when Selah motioned me over and said she wanted to introduce me and Dy-Nasty to Viceroy.

"C'mon over here, Mink." Selah smiled and reached out to me as Dy-Nasty hung off her other arm like a stank lil rag. "It's time for the two of you to get to know Viceroy. I've told him a little bit about you ladies, and he's been looking forward to meeting you."

Bullshit, I thought as I busted the chilly look in his predatory eyes when he peeped the three of us coming his way. I couldn't speak for Dy-Nasty, but this cat was definitely not feeling *me*, and his animal instincts showed on his dark, handsome face.

"Viceroy," Selah called to him. Barron jumped up outta his chair and offered it to his mother but she waved him right off. "Listen, dear. I need to go inside and freshen up for a while, but before I leave I'd like you to meet Dy-Nasty and Mink."

What the fuck? I felt myself getting swole inside as Selah walked away and left us standing in front of her man like two greedy idiots. Why in the hell did she say Dy-Nasty's name before she said mine, when I was the one who got to the mansion first?

I stood there and tried to look all innocent as Viceroy's eyes rode rough over us like a scratchy black blanket. That ol' right eye of his wasn't swelled up like a hard-boiled egg no more but it was still scary as hell.

"Dy-Nasty and Mink," he growled with his top lip turned up like he smelled something stank. I just knew he was looking at us all funky 'cause of them nasty lil purple coochie-cutters Dy-Nasty had on, but then I realized he wasn't even paying her no attention and all that funktified eye-grillin' was aimed dead at *me*!

"Nice to meet you," I said, pulling my little hoity-toity

white girl voice outta my trick bag as I got ready to perform my ass off. "I'm so happy you're out of your coma. God bless, Mr. Viceroy! God bless you!"

"Really, Mink?" Dy-Nasty turned around and busted on me like, *Bitch, come up offa that bullshit!* "Really?"

She rolled her ugly eyes at me and then she reached out to pound Viceroy out like she was a dude giving up the dap.

"Hey, how you feeling, Pops?"

"Pretty good for an old fella," Viceroy said, and I almost shit when he dropped his frown a lil bit. "I'm hanging. I'm hanging."

Dy-Nasty bent over in her ass-almighty shorts and dug her hand way down in the bottom of the huge cooler that sat by his chair. She came up holding two ice-cold beers. She paused to lick the icy liquid off the bottom of both cans before holding one out to our play-daddy, and then she popped the tab on the other one and tipped that baby up and let it flow.

"Damn, Dy-Nasty!" Barron spit, eyeballing her stank cut-off shorts that were unbuttoned all the way down to the crotch and showing off her hot-pink bikini thong underneath. "You must have come down here with the cleaning crew because don't no lady suck on a can like that."

"Who said I was a lady?" Dy-Nasty belched and shot back at him. She glanced down at her plump cleavage and let her fingers skim over her thick thighs. "I'm a woman, though."

Viceroy laughed and passed the beer back to her, and I could tell that scandalous troll was appealing to the hood nigga in him. "Well have at it then, lil mama! You can kill this one too if you can handle it."

Dy-Nasty snatched the beer outta his hand and grinned as she plopped down in the chair on the other side of him. She leaned all up in his face and said, "Oh, I can handle it, Pops. I can damn sure handle it!"

She popped the tab on the second beer and grinned. "Now that you back it looks like we gonna have some fun around here! You just don't *know,* Papa Viceroy! I been on my *knees* praying for you to wake up, man." She leaned forward and busted a quick peek at Barron and grinned. "Day and night! I'm serious. I was on my knees!"

Viceroy looked interested as he kinda shifted his weight a lil bit so he was leaning in her direction. "Oh yeah, is that right?"

"Umm-hmm," she said, nodding. "See, what had happened was, I had found a little surprise present I wanted to give you, ya dig? Some real nice pictures that I just *knew* you would wanna see."

She took her eyes off Viceroy and smirked at Barron again.

"But some kinda way them damn pictures just went *poof!* and disappeared. I can't find them bad boys nowhere no more!" She grinned slickly. "But don't worry, Pops. I'ma keep on lookin' because I got a feeling them pictures woulda *blown your mind.*"

I busted a look at Barron. He had stretched his long legs out and was leaning back in his chair looking as chill as could be. Like a cat who had licked him some real sweet cream. I shook my head. Rich muthafuckas got on my nerves. If there was one damn thing money could buy that you damn sure couldn't get when your ass was broke, it was peace of mind.

Dy-Nasty cupped her hand around her mouth and started whispering something secret all down in Viceroy's ear, and I was about to say something slick so I could break that shit up, but then I thought twice about it.

Let that skag tell Viceroy any damn thing she wanted to tell him. Barron was getting exactly what the hell he deserved, and good for his ass too! He shoulda never brought that horse-tail heffa down to Texas tryna get at me in the first place, and whatever she put on his ass was exactly what he had coming!

The barbeque was bangin' and the music was loud and the liquor was flowing like a river. Barron had just watched Mink slink toward the side of the pool house with Suge hot on her ass, and that clown Dy-Nasty had killed her beer and her shiesty conversation with his pops and was now running up the back steps and about to disappear through the mansion's doors.

Barron smirked at the back view of her scandalous hips. He had almost laughed his ass off when that Philly stripper called herself busting him out in front of his pops. He had sat there in total confidence, silently daring that bitch to go ahead and get slick with it.

And he could afford to be confident too because he didn't have a damn thing to worry about. The dude his uncle had hired to erase those grimy pictures from the Internet was a top professional in his field. Not a single footprint of those pictures had been left anywhere on the Web. And as a precaution and a little punishment too, the server and the computer at the IP address where the pictures had been uploaded had been infected with a real nasty virus that it was *never* gonna recover from!

But still. Just the thought of what *could* have happened if Dy-Nasty had been able to show Viceroy those pictures sent a zing of fear shooting through Barron's nuts. He had wanted to reach across his father and choke the shit outta that two-dollar club slut and he couldn't wait until Suge worked his cold plan and that grimy bitch finally got what was coming to her!

Barron walked over to the edge of the dock and watched as a large group of people swam, splashed, and relaxed in the warm lake water. He spotted his cousin Pilar chilling on a yellow float about twenty feet away, and even though he still had stitches in his head, Barron couldn't stop his dick from stretching out and yawning as he eyed her firm, stunning body.

His eyes swept over the crowded lake and then zeroed right back in on Pilar. She was laid out on her back in a spicy-hot red bikini, and a pair of bright red sunglasses was covering her eyes. Her hair was pulled back from her pretty, caramel-colored face, and her lightly oiled body looked like it should have been the centerfold in *Beat Dick* magazine.

As much as this girl wanted to be his, and as hot as that sex thang between them was, Barron knew he had done the right thing by cutting her loose and giving all that shit up. With Viceroy out of his coma and getting back on top of the family's affairs, there was no way in fuck him and Pilar could've kept sneaking around bangin' each other like rabbits without getting busted. His father had been a real pussy hound back in the day, and there was no doubt in Barron's mind that it would've taken Viceroy about half a second to catch a whiff of Pilar's gushy on his dick.

And the last thing his father would have tolerated was Barron and Pilar causing a scandal that might put Dominion Oil in a negative light, and as much as he loved getting up in his cousin's guts and digging her out on a daily, Barron just couldn't afford to attract any more heat.

He must have been staring at her pretty damn hard because out of nowhere Pilar lifted her shades from her face and busted him watching her. Her eyes got real narrow and she shot him a look that was so damn evil that Barron almost stumbled backward.

He read her lips and caught the words, *Fuck you!* coming out of her mouth.

Oh hell yeah, Barron thought as she grilled him with the serial killer look on her face. His lil cuz was about to be a headache, Barron knew. Chicks like Pilar didn't get sat down every day of the week, and pissed off wasn't even the word for the look that Pilar had just shot him.

Hell nah. The look in her gray eyes didn't just tell him she was mad. That look told him she wanted her some *revenge*.

CHAPTER 23

Pilar laid back on her float and grilled Barron's fine ass as his eyes roamed all over her. At any other time she would have been dying to give him a nice hot go, but the sight of him creeping out of Mink's room with sticky cum in his drawers was burned into her memory, and so was the memory of those pictures that had up and disappeared.

Fuck you! she mouthed, and then hit him with an evil blast from her eyes that was so cold he took a few steps backward and then broke out and disappeared into the crowd.

Pilar fumed for a few minutes and then she paddled with her hands over to the shallow edge. Sliding her long legs around, she stood up on the sandy lake bottom and got out of the water.

Her eyes searched for Barron again but he had skyed up and disappeared.

Good, Pilar thought. That fucker must have thought she was one of those easily faded white girls he was used to banging! He didn't know who he was fucking with this time, she fumed as she pushed her way through the crowd and stormed inside the house. But he was about to find out!

Pilar's firm body glistened with droplets of lake water, and her bare feet slapped on the stone tiles as she stomped up the steps and left a trail of wet prints behind her as she headed toward her private guest suite.

She had just gotten to the top of the stairs and was turning the corner when she saw Dy-Nasty rushing down the hall toward her with one arm swinging wildly and the other hand gripping her crotch.

Pilar sneered and roasted that dizzy bitch in her hot glare as they stalked past each other like two snakes slithering in the grass.

"What's wrong?" she snapped, letting her gaze drop down between Dy-Nasty's thick thighs. "Crabs biting that ass?"

Dy-Nasty cracked up laughing as she cupped her pussy even tighter and waved her other hand in the air.

"You so fuckin' funny, Pilar!" she said, shaking her head just as hard as she was shaking her ass. "You's one funny fuckin' bitch. For real!"

Pilar rolled her eyes and stormed down the hall to her room. She walked in just as her fiancé Ray was pulling the sheets and blankets up on the bed, and he jumped in surprise when she yanked open the door.

"Pilar!" he blurted.

He was standing there in nothing but a pair of humungous checkered swim trunks and he looked like ten cans of chunky soup. Pilar busted the guilty look on his face and sneered at his lazy ass.

"Don't tell me your big ass was up in here sleeping," she hissed. "Why don't you go outside and get some fresh air, Ray? Splash around in the lake for a while and get some *exercise*," she said sarcastically. "Or better yet, try taking a walk! Do something besides laying up on your ass or watching television all day!"

To her surprise Ray swelled up on her. "You don't have to

talk to me like that, Pilar!" he said, glaring at her from his chubby face.

Pilar smirked as she eyed his man-titties and his jiggly stretch-marked stomach. His swim trunks were a size 3XL and they were still tight around his waist and bunched up between his stocky thighs.

"What are you gonna do about it, Ray?" she asked, taunting him as she stepped up in his face. "I can say whatever the hell I want to say."

Ray sighed. "I'm tired of you disrespecting me, Pilar," he said without backing down. "And I'm not taking this kinda shit from you no more!"

"Oh, is that right?" Pilar said, feeling herself as all the rage she was choking on because of Barron rose up in her and she got ready to throw it down on Ray.

"So what the hell are you gonna do about it, Ray? Leave? Are you fuckin' gonna *leave*? Well, get gone, then! I've been telling you to do that for the longest time. You finally ready to take the hint?"

"YEAH, BITCH!" Ray whirled around and blasted on her, barking in her grill so hard that he covered her entire face in a spray of spit. "Hell yeah! I'm leaving, you stuck-up *bitch*! I'm *leaving*! That's what you wanted and now that's what the fuck you got! I'm leaving! I'm fuckin' *leaving*!"

He whirled around and snatched his pants up from the floor, and Pilar stood there with her mouth open, straight stunned.

This fool had never opened up on her like that before. He had never so much as raised his fuckin' voice to her and she couldn't believe it. She just couldn't believe it!

"Ray!" she said, grabbing hold of his meaty arm as he stood on one leg and tried to stick his foot inside the leg of his pants. He stumbled forward and she grabbed his shoulder and twirled herself around him until they were face-to-face again.

"Uh-uh," Pilar said, peering at him with her gray eyes squinted up like a cat. "Hold the hell up. Come here, Ray!" Pilar yanked on his arm and got up on him so close that for a minute it looked like she was about to tongue him down. But then she stuck her nose right up under Ray's bottom lip and took two long sniffs. The first one was bad enough, but the second one damn near knocked her out.

"Oh, *shit*!" she screamed at the top of her lungs.

This fat muthafucka had *pussy* on his breath!

Pilar was going off like a whole pack of firecrackers as she wilded out and tossed her suite up.

"What the fuck is this?" she screamed as she snatched the sheets back and saw the outline of a drying puddle smack in the middle of her bed.

She stared at Ray and then caught a quick flashback of Dy-Nasty coming down the hall gripping her stank pussy like it was sore. And then an even uglier flashback hit her that fucked her up *even more.*

The fuck noises she had heard one night at the mansion when she was walking down the hall to Fallon's room came flooding back to her! At the time she had thought Bunni was in there trying to hit on Fallon's young ass, but now Pilar realized those noises had been coming from *Dy-Nasty's* room!

Grunting. Gasping and groaning. *Growling.*

"Yeah! Suck my clit! Eat this pussy, goddammit! Fuck me with that long-ass tongue and lick up all *my cum!"*

"You nasty *muthafucka*!" Pilar exploded as realization hit her and hit her hard. She lunged at Ray with her hands stretched out and started slicing into him like she had razor blades stuck to her fingers.

"You low-down fat bastard!" she screamed in disgust, clawing into his face and shredding his skin. "You ate her nasty pussy! You munched that dirty bitch *out*!"

Ray yelped and tried to cover his face. Pilar went for his neck and hands and got to shredding those shits too. He grabbed her wrists and yanked her arms up in the air. Pilar shrieked and head-butted him smack in the mouth like she had on a helmet. They both hollered when Ray's top teeth cut through his lip and her forehead too, and blood trickled down his chin and over the ridge of her nose.

"You dirty bastard!" Pilar wailed, gripping her bloody head as she brought her knee up hard into his fluffy crotch and then stomped her heel down on Ray's big toe.

"Owwww, *shit*!" Ray cried out and clutched his tiny nuts. Pilar reached up and clutched the back of his neck and tried to bite a hunk outta his nose. Ray hollered and let his dick go and grabbed his face. Pilar went to work on his ass. She kneed him in the gut and then pushed her face into his chest and sank her teeth deep into the softness of his right titty.

"Owwwww!" Ray bitch-screamed and shoved her hard with both hands.

Pilar went flying through the air and landed right in the wet cum spot in the middle of her bed.

She felt the slimy dampness under her hand and jumped up like she had an electric prod shoved up her ass.

She hit the floor running and grabbed a half-empty bottle of wine from the small bar near the sofa. She swung that bottle like a baseball bat and hollered in satisfaction when it cracked Ray right upside his skull.

"You fuckin' bastard!" she shrieked as the skin on his head split like a grape and bright blood trickled down his face and dripped off his chin.

Ray clutched his head and moaned and sank halfway down to his knees.

"I hope your fuckin' *tongue* falls off, you shit-eating bitch!" She stood over him and raged as she looked around for something else to bash his head in with. "I hope it falls off just like your little-ass dick fell off, you nasty *bastard*!"

"I'm sorry, Pilar," Ray muttered as he got up on his feet and staggered toward the door. He was crying too. Not only was his head busted, Pilar had scratched his mug down to the white meat, and his face burned like a muthafucka as tears seeped into the bloody welts that streaked every which'a way across his jiggly cheeks. "I'm sorry."

CHAPTER 24

Meet me in the pool house in five minutes.

Jock sat on a lawn chair looking bored as fuck as he came down off his high. The joint was packed out. The "Welcome Back from the Dead" party for his pops was getting bigger by the minute, and so was Jock's funky attitude. With Viceroy back on the scene a nigga couldn't even get lifted as much as he wanted to. He couldn't run up on none of these fine honeys walking around wagging their asses in itsy-bitsy bikini bottoms, and he damn sure couldn't kick back in the grass and puff no chronic or no yay.

Jock yanked the brim of his fitted down over his forehead and stared at the huge house next door where a big party was going on too. The Dominions were one of the few black families who owned waterfront property in Horseshoe Bay, and even though Jock had spent a lot of summers out here at the lake, he had never really fucked with the neighbors too much.

Except for the blond chick named Lisa who lived next door and who had been giving him the sweet eye for the past summer or two. Jock checked Lisa and her white friends out as they swam and paddled and Jet Skied in the Bay. Every now and then Lisa would peek over and wave at him all friendly, like white people do, and then go back to screaming and splashing in the water with her silly little girlfriends.

Blondie looked good as shit, Jock thought as he eyed her firm, creamy ass-cheeks. Her little blue bikini string was clenched between two sweet lumps of pale meat, and for a white girl she was nice and hunked up back there.

Jock slid down in his chair and opened his legs wider as his dick got hard. He tuned out the loud music and all the half-drunk conversations going on back and forth, till the only thing in his world was the sexy blond-haired white girl, her smooth white ass, and her nice jiggly tits.

Jock's bottom lip sagged as he fucked the girl with his eyes. He was sitting there fantasizing like a mutha about bending her over, twisting her up, and all the other freaky shit he wanted to do to her when outta nowhere she dove under the water and then burst up dripping wet and stared dead at him.

Jock jumped in his seat. He was busted. Her eyes were locked on his like she was reading his damn mind. And when she licked her lips and held her hand up in the air, waving him over, he straightened up in his chair a little bit and then aimed his thumb at his own chest like, *Baby is you talking to me?*

Lisa nodded her head, and then angled it twice toward her pool house, like she was tryna tell him to slide over and meet her at her crib. Jock angled his head that way once just to be sure, and when she nodded vigorously and started walking toward the sandy shore, he jumped up and beat feet through the crowd of partiers so he could get his black ass over there and get at her.

The last thing Jock was thinking about was putting on a helmet as he plunged into that tight piece of hot white trim. He was on a whole nother high as he cupped her juicy ass in his palms and stroked her so deep he battered her pubic bone.

The little snow bunny in his arms was burning on fire. She had dragged him inside the outdoor changing room and jumped his chocolate bones. Without hesitating, she had dropped down to her knees and yanked Jock's shorts down with her. He had almost screamed like a bitch as she went to work sucking his dick like it came in thirty-one delicious flavors.

For the last ten minutes Jock had been digging her out with his long hard shovel. Her pussy felt like a hot velvet suction cup as they squeezed each other's asses and fucked standing up.

But all of a sudden shit changed in a hurry.

"Shhh!" the white girl hissed through her teeth as she stopped humping and gripped his shoulders tight. She pressed her finger to her lips. "Somebody's coming!"

Jock froze in mid-stroke.

And then he heard what she had heard. Footsteps. Heavy footsteps. Coming toward the changing area.

He pushed against her hips and his cream-coated dick slid outta her in a big wet plop. He looked around, his eyes desperately scanning the fenced-in area for someplace he could hide.

But there was only one door. One way in and one way out.

Jock's eyes skimmed over the top of the wooden fence. Even if the stakes weren't shaved to a point, there was only about six inches of clearance room between the tips and the roof. Not enough space for even his long athletic body to get through. He looked down and saw it was the same thing with the gap under the bottom of the fence. Six to eight inches. He wouldn't even be able to get his big head through that!

The footsteps were closer. Right outside the swinging door. He could hear them talking.

"You're just going to have to buckle down and study harder this year, son."

"I know, Dad. I will. I promise."

Jock bent over and yanked up his swim trunks and stuffed his limp dick back inside. He stared at Lisa. She was scared shitless. Her green eyes looked panicked like fuck.

"It's my father!" she whispered. Her bare feet sank into the soft sand as she stood on one foot and scrambled to get her other leg back through her blue bikini bottoms. She covered her pink breasts with the cups of her bikini top and Jock's fingers fumbled as he tried to help her retie the strings on each end.

He had just gotten that bad boy tied when the door opened and Lisa's father and two of her brothers walked in.

"Lisa!" her tanned older brother shouted. And then his eyes met Jock's and they turned to stone. "You dirty son of a bitch!" he snarled, and barreled straight toward Jock with his thick wrestler's arms stretched open wide.

"What the hell is going on here?" Lisa's father shouted as he watched his ass-naked daughter hop on one foot with her bikini bottoms dangling from her left ankle.

By now both boys had jumped on Jock and knocked him flat on his narrow ass. The older one sat on his chest pounding him as the younger one tried to bury Jock's head in the sand with his bare feet.

"Did he rape you?" the girl's father roared as he stared at his daughter's naked coochie and thighs and the thin stream of cum that was running down her pale legs. "Did this nigger *rape* you?"

"Daddy, *no*!" the young girl wailed as she gave up trying to get into her bottoms and sank her naked ass down in the sand and covered her crotch with her hands. "Daddy, *please,*" she begged as tears of shame fell from her eyes. "Nothing happened! We didn't do anything! I swear to you, nothing happened!"

Rage washed over the older man as he eyed his little girl's skimpy blue bottoms hanging from her ankle. Her bikini top had been tied too tight, and it was hiked up so high that one of her juicy breasts was hanging out of the bottom.

He glanced over at his furious sons as they put a hurting on the black boy whose cum had been running down his baby girl's thigh. He was a grown man and he knew he should probably stop his boys before they killed the little nigger they were beating down in the sand. Yeah, that would have been the righteous adult thing to do, but he just didn't have it in him as he rushed over to the scuffle pile and jumped in swinging.

Hoards of partygoers smiled and waved as Selah walked over and sat down under the pavilion next to her man. She had gone inside the house to place a quick call to Rodney Ruddman. He had made Selah promise to call him during Viceroy's BBQ so they could play their sexy phone game, but when she got upstairs in her master suite and dialed his number, she had chickened out from shame and slammed the phone down before he could answer it.

Besides, here lately Rodney had been getting just a little bit too possessive. He'd been making noises about how she should leave Viceroy and move into his penthouse apartment with him, as if that crazy shit would ever happen.

Selah was dick-whipped but she wasn't no fool. Getting her backside banged a few days a week was one thing, but shaking up the foundation of her family was definitely out of the question. As good as Ruddman made her feel in bed, Selah knew their little secret trysts would eventually have to come to an end. She figured if she could get with him two, maybe three more times it might satisfy her love jones enough that she could safely walk away.

She glanced at Viceroy and sighed when she saw the look on his face. Selah had understood all the medical stuff the doctors told her about Viceroy's brain injury and how it could affect things like his emotions, his memory, and his reasoning skills, but that didn't make his mood swings or his growing demands for sex any easier to put up with.

"I want some head when I get to Austin, baby," he'd told her over the phone first thing that morning. "I don't give a damn about no barbeque. I'm a man and I need my dick sucked, Selah. I need you to wet it up for me real good, you hear?"

Selah had almost gagged. Wasn't nothing sexy about a dead snake! There was no way in hell she was sucking that man's limp, rubbery dick! Not when she could slobber on Rodney Ruddman's nice stiff pole whenever she wanted to.

The thought of sucking Ruddman off made her heart rate speed up. That man was like a drug, and she felt like a junkie who was dying to get clean, but just didn't have the willpower to leave the good stuff alone.

Not that Rodney would have let her leave him anyway. As brilliant as he was, he had begun to mistake hot sex for true love, and in the heat of one of their spectacular fuck fests he had *made* her promise to leave Viceroy so they could be together all the time. And with that rock-hard dick pounding up inside of her so deliciously, Selah had thrown her head back, climaxed all over that wood between her legs, and agreed.

Of course she hadn't meant it. She had no intention of leaving her husband for Ruddman. Hell, she would have said any damn thing just to keep that good feeling going in the sheets, and a man as smart as Rodney should have known that.

She took a deep breath and plastered a fake smile on her face and hoped she looked like she was having a good time. As the wife of a billionaire Selah knew she had a role to play, and she was cool with that. But Viceroy had been fronting and playing himself a role all damn day too. Skinning and grinning and coming off real smooth and silky when he was around his business associates and employees, but snapping like a bastard on wheels as soon as he caught her or one of the kids alone by themselves.

Especially Barron. That boy was really catching hell from his daddy. Viceroy acted like none of the hard work Barron had done while he was laying up there in a coma was worth shit now that he was awake. Poor Bump. Selah had watched him try to stay as far away from his father as he could all day long, but with so many industry people running around expecting them to look like one big happy family, either him or Selah was stuck sitting up under Viceroy just to make the lie they had gone back to living look like the truth.

"Yo," Viceroy leaned over and muttered in her ear as they watched the teenagers dancing and kicking up sand to the loud music that was blasting around the water's edge. "What's up with that button on Fallon's shirt?"

Selah sighed as she watched her youngest daughter twerk her hips to the beat in her rainbow-swirled bikini. There was a small gay pride button pinned to Fallon's bikini top that had caught her father's eye.

"Well, what the hell is it? What does that shit say?"

Selah swallowed hard. "It looks like one of those tolerance buttons, Viceroy," she finally said. "It's no big deal. It just means people who are a little different can count on Fallon to accept them and support them just the way they are."

Viceroy snorted like, *Nigga, please!*

"But that's a rainbow on her, right? That's them gay people's mess ain't it?"

Selah shrugged and nodded.

"So you sitting here telling me that them lil fruity faggots with the colorful skirts can count on my daughter to support them, huh?"

Selah sucked her breath in sharply. "They're not called *faggots*, Viceroy! That's just wrong! And just so you know, Fallon is almost eighteen and she can make her own decisions about who she supports! The world isn't as simple as it was back when we were her age. Kids are exposed to more options now. They accept more and they know more."

Viceroy bucked. "*My* damn kids accept what the hell I tell 'em to accept!" He leaned toward Selah, and then with a deadly look on his face and his cold-blooded eyes plastered hard on Fallon, he leaned in even closer and hit his wife with his wrath full-blast.

"So tell me, Big Mama. What in the hell was you out there doing when our baby girl was pledging her support to some damn freaks of nature?" he snapped with his lips almost touching her ear. "Tell me what kind of *mama* allows her only daughter to walk around wearing a button like *that* and embarrassing the shit outta her entire family?"

"What in the hell are you talking about?" Selah blurted and pulled away from him. "I'm not *allowing* Fallon to do anything!"

"Well did you tell her to take that shit off? Did you knock her on her ass when she told you she was supporting them tulip freaks?" A sneer of fury slid across Viceroy's face as he shook his head and grilled Selah with a look of rage in his eyes.

"You know, my poor mama worked three jobs, Selah. *Three* fuckin' jobs! She scrubbed floors, she scrubbed shitters, and she washed other people's funky drawers! But never *once* did she fall down on the job that was the most important thing her goddamn life: raising me and Suge."

Viceroy shook his head. "Now, if Frances Mae Dominion can scrub her damn fingers to the bone and still manage to raise two hardheaded boys to grow up and be some damn body, then the *least* you shoulda been able to do was raise Jock and Fallon half-assed right!"

Selah wanted to punch him in the face for low-rating her mothering skills! She wanted to smack him right upside that banged-up head of his and then drown his half-crippled ass in the lake! But with so many important people around and this fool acting so damned unpredictable, the best she could do right now was to get the hell away from him.

"You know what?" She gave Viceroy a smack-down under

her breath while smiling politely at their guests the whole time. "I'm about to beg your goddamn pardon for a little while because I have something a whole lot better to do."

He reached out and snatched her by the wrist and she quickly jerked it back and popped him on the back of his hand.

"Let me tell you one fucking thing, Viceroy," Selah said, coming straight up out of her Brooklyn bag. "I did a damn good job of raising my kids! There's nothing wrong with Grayson or Fallon! Both of my kids are doing just great, thank you, and that's because of me, baby. Not you!"

Viceroy shrugged. "That's a matter of opinion, sweetheart." He angled his head toward their daughter. "Fallon is over there shaking her ass, and the last I seen of Jock he was walking around here so damn high he was sniffing cloud dust! I don't know *what* you was laying around the house doing while I was in the hospital Selah, but you been slackin' hard, baby. You ain't been raising these kids right. You damn sure ain't been doing *that*."

Selah turned halfway around in her chair and stared at him. Oh, it was about to be on now. Fuck appearances. Fuck all their company. This fool had jabbed her in her mother-button and that shit *hurt*.

"You know what, Viceroy?" she said quietly, rising to her feet in one graceful motion as she got ready to go back in the house and make that phone call again. "How about you kiss my black ass, huh? Believe me. You've been slacking for a long time in some areas too"—she stared down at his crotch and then back up in his eyes—" 'cause trust me baby, there's a whole lot of shit that you *still* can't do right!"

CHAPTER 25

"Fucking *bastard*!" Selah muttered under her breath as she maneuvered her way through the throng of guests and stormed toward the back entrance of the lakefront mansion.

Viceroy had more nerve than a little bit, talking that bull-shit to her! The twenty-year-old flame that had been burning low in Selah's belly sparked up into a raging fire. No matter how hard she had tried, deep down inside she had *never* for-given Viceroy for the shit he'd put her through that day! All he'd had to do was keep his ass at the hotel with his family where he belonged, and they would have taken the kids out like they had planned, and her babies wouldn't have been stuck up in that room going crazy!

And if the babies hadn't been locked up in that little ass room, then Selah wouldn't have had to ask the concierge to call her a taxi to take them across town to Viceroy's office!

And if she hadn't taken her children to Viceroy's office, she never would have caught him with his dick in her sister's mouth!

And if her tramp-ass baby sister hadn't been sucking the skin off of her husband's rock-hard bone, then Selah never would have run out of that building and dragged her babies around the streets of Manhattan with her heart all broken up in little tiny pieces.

And if she hadn't been walking the streets of Manhattan with her heart torn up, then she never would have needed her a drink in the first damn place!

And if she hadn't snuck and drank up almost a fifth of liquor, then she wouldn't have had a reason to run inside that damn Duane Reade's drugstore to buy her some mouthwash.

And if she hadn't needed that mouthwash, she would have never left her kids waiting outside with a baby in the stroller with only a seven-year-old out there to watch them!

And if she hadn't left her seven-year-old son outside alone watching the kids, then her baby girl Sable wouldn't have been snatched out of her stroller in broad daylight!

And if sweet little Sable hadn't been snatched from her stroller and kidnapped by a stranger, then the scandalous fiend who had just busted out the back door and was coming down the steps sweating and holding her crotch wouldn't be in Texas trying to convince Selah that she was her child!

"Whassup, Mama Selah!" Dy-Nasty hollered as she bounded down the steps. "Whew! It's hot as hell out here! I'ma run and get me a cold brew. Want me to bring you one?"

Selah shook her head. "No thank you, dear," she said as she walked past Dy-Nasty and headed through the back door. "I'm fine, baby. But thanks."

Selah stormed inside the house and walked down the long corridor. She had just turned the corner and headed toward the staircase when she felt the floor shaking as Pilar's overweight fiancé, Ray, came barreling down the steps straight at her.

"Ray!" Selah yelped and pressed herself up against the wall so he wouldn't knock her down. "Goodness!" she shrieked as she saw the bloody ribbons of shredded skin hanging from his face. "What the hell happened to you?"

"It was Pilar," he blurted out. Tears were in his eyes and Selah saw a patchwork of blood-streaked scratches on his neck and arms too. "Your niece jumped on me and hit me in the head with a wine bottle!"

"Pilar?" Selah said in disbelief. "Why in the world would she do something like that?" He started down the steps again but Selah grabbed his arm.

"Uh-uh," she said, nudging him gently in front of her. "You just take yourself right back up those stairs!"

She shook her head and frowned.

"You walk yourself out there in front of Viceroy and his friends all scratched up like that and he'll have a damn fit. Uh-uh. Come on upstairs with me, baby. Let's put some peroxide and Neosporin on those scratches and get you bandaged up."

"She just went crazy," Ray muttered as Selah dotted his face gently with cotton balls soaked in peroxide. "She attacked me. Just jumped all over me! First she said I was messing around on her, and then she went bonkers and started scratching up my face!"

Selah frowned. "You? Cheating? That's ridiculous! There must be some sort of misunderstanding because really, that just doesn't sound like the Pilar I know." She dabbed at Ray's shredded skin and squeezed the cotton balls so the peroxide would drip foam as it cleaned out a few of the deeper scratches.

"Well it was her," Ray muttered. "Pilar's been acting crazy for months now. Fighting with me over the littlest things, ignoring my calls and talking down to me like I'm not worth shit! I don't get it, Ms. Selah. I'm a good catch! A good man! But no matter how much I try to do for your niece, she's just never satisfied!"

Selah treated his wounds and listened quietly as Ray poured his heart out. She wasn't one to get in other people's business and after hearing Ray out, that's exactly what she told him.

"Look, I can't explain Pilar's behavior and I can't excuse it either. All I can tell you is . . ." A feeling of deep regret and longing washed over Selah and she felt her heart quiver. "Just don't waste your damn life, Ray," Selah said quietly. "You only live once, baby, and every single day is precious. If a relationship isn't right for you then you'd be a damn fool to spend twenty or thirty years trying to make it right. What did the old folks use to say? If it don't fit, don't force it?"

Selah picked up a Q-tip and smeared Neosporin all over his face. What she was about to say was for Ray, but it was also for herself too.

"You have to live your life, Ray. And Pilar has to live hers. The last thing you want to do is wake up thirty years from now and realize you've wasted your whole life on the wrong damn person."

If Selah thought her little dust-up with Viceroy had gone down unnoticed she had another think coming.

Digger Ducane had a wide-open view of his sister and her husband as they sat under the white canopy and talked outta the corners of their mouths. Digger knew his sister, and he could see right past her fake smile and spot the fury flashing in her hazel eyes.

The music was too loud and Digger was sitting too far away to hear what Selah and Viceroy were saying, but judging from the set of Viceroy's jaw and the way he leaned in on Selah and gestured with his hands, their private little convo wasn't about nothing nice.

Digger knew he was on point when Selah jumped up from her chair and smirked down at her husband, and then rolled her eyes and walked off with her hips swaying as she left Viceroy sitting alone and headed toward the house. She never even looked back as she worked her way through the crowd and passed Dy-Nasty coming down the back steps, and then disappeared through the double doors.

Digger's first instinct was to run over there and knock the

shit outta Viceroy for upsetting his sister, but then he remembered that Selah wasn't even speaking to him and she had been giving him the shit treatment all day. Taking another sip of his drink, he settled down in his chair and kept one eye on Viceroy and the other eye on the back door where Selah had just disappeared.

Long minutes passed but Selah didn't come back out. Digger figured she'd gone inside to pull herself together or to use the bathroom or something, but after that little love tap she'd given Viceroy, something in his gut told him to go find his baby sister and make sure she was okay.

Taking the long way around so Viceroy wouldn't peep him, Digger skirted along the edges of the crowd and climbed up the back stairs. After shooting one last eye bullet at Viceroy, he pushed through the doors and walked down the hall, and then he headed up the stairs to go see about his sister.

Selah didn't have any excuse for what she was about to do and she wasn't trying to come up with one either. She had finished getting Ray patched up and then hurried down the hall to the master suite and locked the door behind her. She was pissed like hell, and what she was about to do was truly scandalous, but Viceroy didn't deserve her loyalty and she ignored the lively sounds of the guests outside as her fingers dialed the familiar number and she waited for it to ring.

It was his private line and it rang three long times before he picked it up. And when Selah heard his low, deep voice she almost slammed the phone down and hung up again.

But she didn't.

"Hello, it's Selah," she said simply.

"I know who you are, Mrs. Dominion," he said, and for a second she thought he sounded amused. "What can I do for you?"

"I, um, you asked me to call, so I'm calling."

"Okay."

There was a long pause on the line and Selah broke the silence first.

"Also, I was . . . I was wondering if we could, you know, meet someplace."

"Mmmm."

He was playing with her and she liked that shit.

"Come on," she said shyly, grinning like a kid from ear to ear. "I want to see you, Rodney. I do."

"Why? Would you like me to fuck you again?"

"Excuse me?" Selah giggled like a schoolgirl as a bolt of excitement zipped through her and she caught a cheap thrill.

"You heard me."

He was bold as hell.

"I said would you like me to *fuck* you again?"

Beads of sweat popped up on Selah's nose as she remembered how thoroughly his long black dick had plunged her out.

"Ummm . . ." She glanced out the window and saw her husband put his head back and laugh at something his business associate Hank said. "I was just wondering—"

"Come on now, Mrs. Dominion. We both know what time it is. Would you like me to fuck you? Or would you prefer me to lick your pussy first and make you cum?"

Selah blushed and pressed her hand to her groin.

"Yes, that."

"That what? Say it, Mrs. Dominion. Let me hear you say it."

"Yes. I want you to eat my pussy first. And then fuck me."

"Fine," Rodney Ruddman said in his deep, baritone voice. "Take off your panties and open your legs," he commanded her. "Then lay your head down on your husband's pillow and do exactly what I tell you to do."

Digger was just about to knock on the door to the master suite when he heard his sister's high-pitched voice coming from inside. Pausing with his fist in the air, he leaned in close until his ear was almost pressed to the door.

"Oh, yes, Rodney! Fuck me, darling!"

Digger frowned. *Rodney?*

"Split me with your rock-hard dick! Yes, that feels so damn good. Oh God, yes. I'm rubbing it for you. I'm creaming for you! No, no, no! Viceroy has never fucked me so good or made me feel this way!"

Digger pressed his ear right up against the door.

Rodney? As in Rodney Ruddman? And Selah? His sister and Viceroy's wife?

Get the fuck outta here!

CHAPTER 26

As usual, Bunni Baines was steady on her grind.

The BBQ was kickin' all the way live. I was chilling on the lawn sipping some Goose and juice with a few of the Houston cousins when my girl did the exact kinda shit that rich white folks expected hood rats like us to do.

Bunni had rounded up a group of about twenty corporate wifeys and lined them up side by side so she could teach them how to twerk it.

"Hey now!" she hollered as the stiff-jointed white women moved their bodies around in hard right angles. "I'ma need y'all heffas to put some hips in ya game, *okay*? You can throw a lil ass in it too, if you got any. Just be sure to make it whip like this . . ." She gapped her legs open and started rolling her stomach and snaking her high booty in S-waves like she had a roller coaster in her drawers.

"Ay!" she hollered and pointed. "You over there in the wrinkled-up shorts! What's wrong witcha hips, boo? That ain't it, Mami! That is *definitely* not *it*!"

Bunni marched down the line until she was standing in front of the stiffest chick in the bunch. She was a rung-out-looking white woman who looked about sixty, and even though she was real round in the middle, her eyes were bright and funny and her big Kool-Aid grin said she was down for what-eva!

"A'ight now, I want you to *feel* me, Mami," Bunni said as she turned around and tooted her round ass up and backed it into Grandma's flabby stomach. Bunni reached back and grabbed the old lady's hands and placed them firmly on her stacked hips.

"Now, wherever I move it," she ordered over her shoulder, "that's where I want you to move it too. You got that?"

The old lady nodded and giggled, and when Bunni dipped it down low and humped two times to the left, Grandma got down behind her and did the same damn thing.

"Yeah, *baybeee*!" Bunni hollered, egging her on. She leaned to the right and whipped her hips in two tight roundies, and Mami riding her ass swiveled her old hips around in a circle too.

Bunni grabbed the old woman's hands again and made sure she was gripping her hips real tight, and then she dropped it down even lower. Grandma said fuck it and dipped her damn chips too! She groaned like hell as her knees damn near gave out, but she got down on it!

And when Bunni got to twerking her fine, heart-shaped booty back up into a standing position, Mizz Thang behind her hung for the whole ride, and she twerked her square hips pretty damn good for an old chick too!

All the other ladies were clapping and cheering and lining up to take them a trip on the back of Bunni's ass next. My girl turned around and snatched up a little redheaded housewife. Bunni had just backed her ass up deep in the chick's stomach and gripped her pale hands to her hips when somebody stopped the music and a voice sliced through the air that was so damn sharp it made the whole damn crowd freeze in their shoes.

"Y'all heard me! I said cut that foolish-ass *fuckery* out!"

My eyes zipped all around tryna see who was barking. And then a bunch of mumbling went up in the crowd and bodies started parting like a muthafucka. I figured out real quick who had spit those words when I saw Viceroy's twisted-up face eyeballing us from his seat under the little white gazebo.

Bunni spotted him at the same time that I did, and my mouth went bone dry as Viceroy hit my girl with a hood-hardened killer look and growled out the corner of his mouth, "Who in the hell are *you*?"

He didn't know Harlem-born Bunita Baines wasn't one to be spit at, and I didn't know whether to laugh or pee when my rowdy put her hand on her little gapped-legged hip and barked right back on him, "Naw, who in da hail are *you*?"

Ah, shit! I almost choked on my Grey Goose!

Once again Bunni's little ghetto behind had taken shit too damn far!

The music had stopped and not a single tongue was flapping as Viceroy grilled my girl in his beastly gaze and based on her again.

"I *said,* who the *hell* are *you*?" he demanded.

"And *I* said"—Bunni posted up in a wide-legged stance and hit him dead in the mug with her stank camel toe—"who in da *hail* are *you*?"

All of a sudden it was so quiet out there you could hear the damn fish gargling in the lake.

Pack it up, Mink, I told myself as I watched the look on Viceroy's face go from one end of the pisstivity meter all the way to the other. *Pack ya shit up and move it along to the next gig, baby. 'Cause thanks to Bunni Baines our black asses are outta here!*

I just knew Viceroy was gonna pull out a gat and bust a cap straight up Bunni's ass, but then I got the shit shocked outta me right along with everybody else.

"They call me Viceroy," the old G said, bustin' out in a slick grin and then laughing his ass off. "I'm the HNIC in the place to be! Now who the hell might you be, lil mama?"

Work him! I thought as Bunni arched her back and threw both hands in the air, and then sashayed her big round booty over to Viceroy, grinning like a vixen as every male eye on the property either zoomed in on her chunky crotch or her high-humped question-mark ass!

"So *you's* Big Daddy D!" she giggled, sliding up to his chair like he was a tender little trick and she was going in for the kill. "I been dying to meet a big willie like you!"

Bunni was feeling herself! Mami was a professional!

If a man had at least half a nut in his sack she could *work* his ass!

"I'm Bunni Baines, so now ya know!" she laughed, dripping mad sex appeal all over his scrawny ass. " 'Scuse me," she said, waving Dane up outta his chair.

"Scoot over and lemme sit next to the Big Nacho, boo!" Bunni plopped her booty down beside Viceroy and reached over and put her hand all in his big plate of barbeque and got her a piece.

She was on her way back to her mouth with one of them bun-length franks when it slipped from her fingers and hit Viceroy's shoe before rolling into the grass at his feet.

"Oops!" Bunni laughed, snatching the meat off the ground real quick and kissing it up to God. "God made dirt . . ." She giggled, biting off half the damn frank and then shoving the other half under Viceroy's nose.

"And dirt don't hurt!" Viceroy said, opening his mouth and gobbling the other piece right outta Bunni's hand!

"So tell me sumthin'." Bunni chewed with her mouth all open as she reached in Viceroy's plate again and came out with a rib. "What's your thang, Big Daddy D? Do you like a lotta meat?" she asked as she sank her big white teeth into a juicy hunk of rib and let the sauce drip all from her lips. "Or are you into bones?"

★ ★ ★

Couldn't nothing in the world shut a rich people's party down the way a nigga with his dick caught in a white girl's cookie jar shut that sucker down!

I was standing across from Bunni watching her and Viceroy eat outta the same plate of barbeque when a big-ass commotion came from the side of the house.

"Pops!" somebody screamed. "*Pops*! Yo, get the fuck offa me, man! *Pops*!"

I peeped through the crowd and my eyes bucked out when I saw Jock being shoved forward.

"That's right!" a loud voice boomed from behind him. "Call your father—that is, if you even have one! Where is he? Huh? Where is he? And where the hell was he while you were trespassing on my property and *raping my little girl*?"

It felt like somebody had flipped the off switch up in that bitch and killed all our batteries.

Everybody froze like a muthafucka as some old-head white dude pushed his way through the pack of bodies, hemming Jock up and manhandling him like a lil bitch.

Baby brother looked *fucked*! His bottom lip was busted and his forehead looked like it had been kicked in. Blood was runnin' outta both of his nostrils, and the look in his eyes said he was scared enough to shit in his saggy pants.

"What the hell is going on?" Viceroy roared as dude stormed up on us with Jock on his tippy toes and his arm chicken-winged behind his back. "Get your fuckin' hands off my son—" Viceroy tried to come up outta his chair but Bunni snatched his frail ass back by his shirt and let Dane beat him to it.

"Yo!" Dane fist-thumped ol' dude in the chest and snatched Jock up outta his grasp at the same time. He flung Jock's skinny ass aside and then quick-gripped the white dude's throat as he power-drove him backward with a stiff arm and barked, "Ay, muthafucka! What the fuck is you doing, man?"

This shit was juicier than a T-bone steak, and my watery mouth was on the floor! You can best believe that me, Bunni, and every last one of Viceroy's friends and business partners were *all eyes and all ears*!

"Is this your son?" dude hollered. "I just caught him in my pool house molesting my daughter!"

Dane fist-gripped his throat again and dude grabbed at Dane's wrist with both hands and started digging his chin down toward his chest as he tried his best to get away.

"Let me go!" ol' boy bucked and croaked. "That bastard raped my little girl!"

Ahhhhhh shit!

A hush had fallen over the whole damn lake, and even the sun and the stars stood still up in that camp.

"Oh my." A real prim and proper little old white lady gasped and pressed her hands to her sunken, freckled chest. "That poor, poor girl!"

Murmurs went up in the crowd from the clear folks. They started looking around at our shaded asses like they had just woke up and realized they were in bed with a whole tribe of wild beasts.

"What the hell did you say?" Viceroy bellowed with rage flashing from his sunken eyes. "My goddamn son didn't rape anybody!"

"Hell no, I didn't rape nobody!" Jock hollered too. He had landed on Bunni's lap when Dane sling-shotted him and she had her arms crossed over his lil chest cradling him like he was her pet fool.

"Yo, your daughter *told* me to come over there!" Jock yelled, straining against Bunni. "She invited me because she wanted some of this! She's the one who was all over *me*!"

"You're a liar!" dude gasped as he turned red in the face

from that throat-clocking Dane was still putting on him. "I caught him! I caught him! He cornered her in my pool house and he *raped* her!"

Barron came busting up outta nowhere, and by now Viceroy had managed to pull himself up on his feet and was looking feeble as fuck. He tried to take a step forward and one of his male nurses rushed over and caught him under his arm.

"Let him go, Dane." Barron stepped in and pulled Dane off the white man who was straight up choking. "Turn him loose."

"Excuse me, sir." Barron tried to stuff the cat back in the bag as Dane un-assed ol' boy and Viceroy's business partners and their wives looked at Jock all crazy in the face. "I'm not sure what's going on here, but I'd be happy to sit down and discuss it with you."

Barron was tryna sound all educated and shit as he put his big black hand on dude's shoulder. "Would you care to come inside where we can talk about this in private?"

"Hell no!" Dude shrugged Barron off and got to storming back toward his house. He had taken about two steps when he turned around and jabbed his finger at Jock. "I *knew* something like this was gonna happen when *you people* moved into this place!"

"*You people*?"

Every Black person in the crowd hollered that shit at the same time, and that's when Viceroy came flying straight up outta his hood bag. Ol' rich-ass Daddy Dominion forgot all about his multi-million-dollar white homies as he staggered his bony ass toward dude and exploded, "Who in the *fuck* are you callin' *you people*, you redneck honky mutha*fucka* you!"

Everybody up in that bitch bucked. Including me!

"Heaven's mercy!" the white dude spit as he turned around to beat feet. "White children just aren't safe around here anymore!"

"Mutha*fucka*!" Viceroy raged toward him again.

"Yeah, that's right! Insult me! Call me all the names you

want, big guy! But just so you know, I called somebody too," he hollered over his shoulder as he hauled his narrow ass up off the Dominion property. "I called *the police*!"

Selah heard the commotion going on outside her window, and after peeping out and seeing her husband on his feet and her son hemmed up by a strange white man, she flung her cell phone to the floor and bust through the doors going a hundred miles an hour.

She had damn near flattened her brother Digger as he stood with his ear pressed to her bedroom door, but she barely noticed him as she ran down the steps with no shoes or drawers on to get to her child.

Digger had gotten the shit knocked out of him when Selah hit the door running, and he was just about to follow her when he spotted her panties and her cell phone laying on the floor near the bed.

"Hello?" he spoke into the phone as he picked it up. There was nothing but silence on the other end. But not the kind of silence you heard when a call had been discontinued. Nah, this was the silence of someone listening in, but just not responding.

"Hello?" Digger said again, and then a slick grin spread over his face.

I want you to eat me, Rodney. And then fuck me.

Digger couldn't believe his good luck. He'd caught his boss with his fat, greasy hand in the nookie jar! He didn't feel so bad after all, because not only had Ruddman stolen *him* from under Viceroy's nose, he'd stolen Viceroy's *wife* too!

"How's it going, Rodney?" Digger spoke smoothly into the phone as he thought about that Monday morning meeting in his boss's office that was never gonna happen now.

He chuckled when there was no response. "Sorry my sister threw the phone down in ya ear, my man! It seems there's some sort of emergency going on outside with her, um, husband. So I'm sure you understand why she didn't stick around to say good-bye."

Still no answer. Digger could tell Rodney was still there and listening, though. And he knew how to get that nigga to talking too!

"Speaking of good-byes, I got a call from your HR department the other day. They told me to report to your office Monday morning, and I hope you don't plan on telling me good-bye. Because if you do"—Digger lowered his voice and threatened—"I'll just have to tell Viceroy who's been creeping with his woman while he was laid up in that hospital bed. 'Yes, Rodney! Fuck me, baby! Fuck me *good*!' "

"Tell him!" Rodney Ruddman's voice came booming through the phone so hard and loud that Digger fumbled with it and damn near dropped that shit. "You go ahead and tell that muthafucka!" Ruddman hollered at the top of his lungs. "In fact, I'll tell him my goddamn self!"

Click!

CHAPTER 27

It was Monday morning and Selah slid her firm body into a peach-toned pantsuit as she tried real hard to push the ugliness from the barbeque at the lake house from her mind. Her womanly juices had been flowing like a river and she'd been finger-deep in an erotic phone fantasy with Rodney Rud-dman when she heard a commotion going on outside her bedroom window.

Kicking off her panties, Selah had slung the phone down and rushed downstairs to find Jock being questioned by the local police and Viceroy about to have a damn stroke.

Selah's face had been flushed red from the multiple or-gasms that Rodney's erotic instructions had stoked up in her, but when she saw her baby boy standing there looking terri-fied and being accused of rape, her entire body had flushed with hot guilt.

Viceroy was right. What kind of mother was she? While she was sneaking upstairs to get her phone swerve on, her son had been sneaking next door to get inside some teenaged girl's panties!

The police had taken a statement from the young girl next door, and since her and Jock were the same age and the girl admitted the sex was consensual and that *she* had initiated it, the police took Jock's statement but declined to take him in for questioning.

Selah knew the situation could have turned extra ugly, and she was grateful the white girl had told the truth, but to say her nerves had been shot out wouldn't have been saying a damn thing.

Peering in the full-length mirror, Selah smoothed the collar on her waist-length jacket and then turned around to check out her ass. It looked high and firm in her tight tailored pants. Satisfied, she turned around and eyed her hair and her lipstick, and then she grabbed her designer shoulder bag and walked out of her suite with sure, quick steps.

She had promised Viceroy she would fly down to Houston and have lunch with him at the hospital, but an early morning text message had killed those moves and changed her plans in a hurry.

Selah had been awakened by her cell phone vibrating on her end table, and when she raised her head off the pillow and clicked the backlight she couldn't believe what the hell she was squinting at.

It was a picture. Of a nice long chocolate *dick*. It had thick gobs of honey swirled all down the shaft, and it was sitting on a three-hundred-dollar fine-bone crystal platter.

The dick was pretty as hell and it was perfectly shaped. It was also ramrod stiff, and gripped in a thick fist.

Selah's heart had banged as her lower lips instantly became moist. She knew that dick. She knew it well. In fact, she would have known it anywhere because it was the dick that she feened for all day and the dick that haunted her in her dreams all night.

The caption beneath the picture had said, *Sexual chocolate. Served today at noon sharp*. Selah had licked her lips hungrily, and just like *that,* Viceroy was shit out of luck for that lunch date with his wife.

Too excited to sleep, Selah had texted her pilot and canceled her flight to Houston and then got up and packed a small overnight bag with a couple of her favorite toys: a pair of bondage handcuffs, a few colorful Hermes scarves, a black garter belt with a matching thong, a pair of sheer black stockings that came up to her thighs, and her favorite battery-operated toy.

Deep inside she had felt a brief pang of guilt for what she was planning to do, but it wasn't strong enough to slow her roll or to make her change her mind.

And now, as she waved off her personal assistant and headed out the door, Selah walked briskly toward her car so she could drive herself to her secret little lunch date.

She turned the dial to a talk radio station and listened to that bullshit all the way to Dallas, hoping the ridiculous conversation would take her mind off what she was about to do, but the shame of it all was a turn-on all by itself. Selah knew she was a beauty, and Rodney was damn sure a beast. There had to be some psychiatric explanation for this intense burst of lust she was feeling for him because it couldn't have been about his looks.

It's because Viceroy hates him and that makes him a no-no, she admitted to herself. By all rights, this man should have been way off-limits. Rodney was like a forbidden piece of fruit tantalizing her from a low-hanging branch. Not only was he rich and powerful, he was also her husband's worst damn enemy, and deep inside Selah knew that was the one true reason she couldn't get enough of him.

Selah's body was humming with excitement as she walked a half-mile from the parking garage to the Omni Hotel where Ruddman Energy was headquartered. Her shoulder bag was heavy with her sexual toys, and the stiletto shoes she had on weren't exactly meant for strolling, but Selah couldn't risk being seen parked anywhere near the hotel.

Rodney had given her a key to his private elevator, and

Selah hoped like hell nobody was watching her as she put on a large pair of sunglasses. She walked inside the hotel lobby with her head down and sped toward a bank of elevators on the left. Stepping into an empty elevator car that she knew would take her straight up to the top-floor penthouse, she stuck the key in the lock and turned it, then put her head down again and stared at the floor as the doors closed and she rode upstairs.

And at exactly twelve noon, when the elevator doors opened directly onto the building's executive-level penthouse apartment, Selah caught her breath and blinked rapidly at the delicious treat that was waiting for her.

"Mrs. Dominion . . ." Ruddman was stretched out butt-naked on a white satin sofa. His belly was a big round hill just'a sticking up in the air, and his dick was a foot-long hammer just'a banging in his hand. "Come on in, baby cakes. You're right on time. Lunch is served."

As usual, the sex had been outrageous but it was getting late in the day and Selah had to go home. Rodney had whispered sweet things in her ear and pounded her out real good, but his mood had changed when she told him she had to leave.

"Have you thought about the things we discussed, Mrs. Dominion?"

Selah shook her head. She was starting to hate it when he called her that.

"I haven't had much time to think about anything lately, but considering the circumstances I don't think the timing is right."

"First you said you couldn't walk away from your husband when he was down, Selah. And I accepted that. But Viceroy's good to go now. I heard he's back on his feet and ready to get to work. I think now is a perfect time for you to tell him about us."

Selah frowned and shook her head.

She thought not. True, she had agreed to a whole lot of

things while she was in the grips of passion with her over-weight lover, but didn't this fool know that shit was all pillow talk? She couldn't walk away from Viceroy and her family and move in with Rodney! Not now, and probably not ever!

"It's still too soon for me to make moves like that," she muttered as she slipped into her clothing. "Viceroy's not even out of the hospital yet. Besides, our children . . . they've been through a lot, Rodney. They don't need another disruption in their lives right now."

"So that means you continue to get everything you want, and I continue to get nothing. Am I right?"

Selah paused as she slipped her foot into her shoe.

She loved fucking Rodney but he wanted too damn much. Hell, all she'd ever wanted was sex, and now this fool wanted to own her!

"It's not like that," she lied as she threw her used sex toys back inside her bag. "I'm not trying to be selfish, Rodney. I just don't think the time is right to consider something so important, that's all. Can you feel where I'm coming from?"

Rodney's hungry gaze had looked sexy to her before, but now this fool looked like a man-eating wolf, and even though he nodded like he had caught her drift, Selah could tell he wasn't feeling her at all.

CHAPTER 28

Suge had finally caught up with that bitch nigga they called Dopeman, the dude who had fucked Barron up. He had stretched that old fool out on a cold piece of ice and he wouldn't be slipping nothing in nobody else's drink no goddamn more.

His boy had come through for him in a major way and gotten rid of those pictures of Barron on the Internet too, but their little problem still wasn't quite solved yet, and there was still something left undone.

So Suge called the family pilot and caught a ride in the *Dominion Diva* up north to Philly. He landed at a heliport, where three of his manz were waiting for him in a tricked out Lexus. They smoked a couple of trees and talked about the good old times, and then they swung over to the projects to pay a certain hustling chick a nice little visit.

I was planning on jetting upstairs to run some game on Mama Selah, but instead I ran into Fallon flouncing her lil grown ass up to her room.

"Hey, what's up?" I said as we switched our big booties up the spiral staircase side by side. Me and Fallon had gotten pretty cool with each other and I was actually feelin' her lil fast ass.

"Nothing much," she said, turning her sad puppy eyes on me and giving me the pouty-face look.

"Yo, what's wrong?" I asked, linking my arm through hers like we were pretzels. "What you lookin' all down about, baby sis?"

She twisted her lips. "I don't know. Probably because I just got off the phone with Freddie. I swear to God sometimes that girl be tripping."

I almost busted out laughing. Baby girl was having *man* trouble! I shook my head and grinned at her. "You know how dudes is, honey-boo-boo. You let 'em lick a lil titty and the next thing you know they tryna bang ya damn lights out! Niggas can *always* find some kinda way to trip out on us."

"Uh-huh," Fallon said, "but tripping ain't even the word for Freddie's shit! Come with me to my room for a minute," she said, pulling me down the hall toward her suite.

I hesitated for a quick second 'cause I wanted to get up in Mama Selah's bed before Dy-Nasty got her stank ass up under the covers, but Fallon jerked the shit outta me so I went ahead and followed her.

"I wanna show you these crazy text messages she's been sending me. I'm serious, Mink. Freddie's wildin' like she thinks I'm stupid or something."

Uh-huh, I thought a few minutes later as I lounged on Fallon's leather sofa and scrolled through the fifty million text messages from her slick-ass stud lover. Oh, Freddie damn sure thought baby sister was stupid. Stupid and *dumb* too!

"Damn!" I said giving Fallon the side eye. Ol' Freddie was on her pimp lean for real. "How long this damn dude been shaking you down?"

Fallon shrugged. "At first she just used to ask me for a couple of hundred every now and then. You know, to pay her light bill and stuff like that. But here lately she's been hitting me left and right, coming at me like crazy."

Like crazy wasn't the word, I thought as my eyes skimmed over Freddie's text messages. Didn't none of that shit surprise me. I was born and raised in the gaming life, so I'd seen this type of grind many, many times before. Freddie was a pussy playa. This broad wasn't nothin' but a grifting pimp-a-lina who had landed her a sweet little mark. She was gaming for dollars. Texting Fallon three and four times a day tryna get up on her pocket stash.

I scrolled through the text messages and smirked. A couple hundred my black ass! Freddie's hustling tail had been tryna stick Fallon up for a grand or two every couple of days! I was hoping like hell baby sis hadn't been stupid enough to fall for that shit.

"So how much dough you done dished off to her so far?" I asked with my lips all twisted.

Fallon took a long time to answer and she looked real stupid in the face as she shrugged. "Around ten grand," she finally admitted. "But not all at one time, Mink! She kinda eased it outta me a little bit at a time, and before I realized what was going on, almost all my spending stash was gone."

Stupid ass! I hissed inside. Not even in my *youngest, dumbest, darkest* days had I ever given a nigga a dime of my hard-earned loot! I didn't give a fuck how good a cat licked my coochie or how deep he planted his pipe, Mizz Mink was *always* on the receiving end of the yardage!

I realized Fallon was young and hard-headed, but I was about to bust on her anyway because not only was Freddie a moocher, she was the type of stud who liked threesomes. I used to run into them types all the time when I was on my stripping grind, so it wasn't no surprise to me. Ol' Freddie got her sticky off by watching Fallon strip for horny dudes, and then her and the dude would put Fallon's lil tender juicy ass in a fuckery sandwich and eat that sweet tail right on up!

"So," I asked her real slick-like, "Freaky Freddie still got you dancing for dudes or what? When's the last time she got you in a threesome so her and some nigga could freak you off, boo?"

I almost laughed as Fallon's face got all red and she started protesting.

"Uh-uh, Mink! Hell, nah. I don't even do that no more! All that club dancing is over for me. Besides, I ain't feeling Freddie like that. I hooked up with a guy I know from school and we've been kicking it really hard. I feel different now than I've ever felt before. Believe that."

I side-eyed Fallon to see if she was bullshittin' me, but all I saw was the truth shining in her eyes. Deep inside I thought Fallon was stupid as fuck, but I reminded myself that I had an advantage over her.

A chick like me had grown up scrambling on the streets of Harlem with junkies and hoes as my teachers and idols. Fallon, on the other hand, had been raised in the lap of luxury with a paid-out-the-ass daddy and servants who walked around waiting on her hand and foot.

Sheiiit, what lil mama needed to do was get her ass up outta this damn mansion and see how shit flowed in the real world! Fallon had been sheltered so tight by the Dominion dollars that she didn't even recognize a flimflammer like Freddie when she was tryna dig up in her pussy and her pockets at the same time!

"Umm, Fallon, boo, you seem like you already up on shit so I ain't tryna tell you what to do," I said as I got ready to tell her ass *exactly* what to do, "but you gonna hafta cut Freddie's ass loose, ya feel me?"

She nodded.

"And for starters, that tatted-up bitch gets no more free pussy, you hear me?" I demanded as I laid out the new rules of the game.

Fallon waved me off. "I already told you, Mink. I got a boyfriend now. I don't get down like that no more."

"Yeah, well," I said, igging that noise, "don't you give her thirsty ass not another dime, neither! Matter fact, the next time she so much as slides her crooked eyes over toward your pockets, you pick up the phone and call me. Hell, if that hustlin' heffa even *looks* like she wanna ask you to buy her a goddamn Happy Meal you hit my digits and put her ass on the phone, ya heard?"

Fallon nodded again.

"On the real," I said, sighing as I passed baby sister back her cell phone. "I told you this before. Freddie ain't no different than any other dude who's out there looking to stroll a chick. Let her buy some chips and rent herself a pole freak if that's what her bald-headed ass is into. Just don't let her freak *you.*"

Dy-Nasty sashayed her hips down the dark streets of Dallas cursing her ass off under her breath. She had bummed a ride into the city with Jock's young ass, and they had smoked up some good piff and killed a bottle of rum all the way there.

Ever since she tried to hustle Uncle Suge for a million dollars them fools up in the mansion had been acting real stank toward her and treating her some kinda way, but Dy-Nasty gave less than a fuck about all that attitude that was floating around.

Like Pat had reminded her, she didn't bring her ass all the way down to Texas tryna make no damn pizos. She was on the scene to gank these fools and to get up on some of that bank they was holdin', and just as long as she did what her mama told her to do she was gonna walk away from this scheme paid real lovely right outta her big yellow ass!

Dy-Nasty smirked. She was getting tired of them dumbfuck Dominions anyway, and she couldn't wait to get up outta that dead-ass mansion and find her some action to get into. She was a true-to-the-bone Philly hustler, and she'd been just a' lookin' for a party and just a' itchin' to shake her ass. So when Jock said he was going up to Dallas to find him some pussy and re-up on his stash, she had hopped up in his ride and told him to drop her off at the hottest club on the strip.

Jock had taken her to a joint called the Animal House, and Dy-Nasty had started working her mojo the moment she stepped through the door. Mad dudes tried to swarm her and push up on her fine body, but Dy-Nasty was a pole professional, and the only time a stray nigga got close enough to rub his dick on her was when he was coming outta his pockets with some greenery.

Shrugging off all the local ballas who was feenin' for some fresh meat, Dy-Nasty had picked herself out a mark who was sitting alone at the bar hunched over a drink. She had hooked him into buying her two double shots of Patrón before she zoomed in on another victim, and when mark number one started making noise like he was tryna get some kinda return on his drink investment, Dy-Nasty made like she was going to the bathroom and moved on to target mark number three.

She was violating like a muthafucka and she didn't give a damn neither. It was an unwritten rule that didn't no outside bitch go up in a strip joint hustling for drinks or nothing else. Chicks riding the poles would jump down off that stage and straight fuck a scab up, and that's exactly what happened when Dy-Nasty over-played her hand and over-stayed her welcome.

"I'm tryna *tell* your ass I don't fuckin' work here!" she had screamed on some drunk baller who kept slapping her on the ass and demanding she make it jiggle for him.

"Go slobber on one of them funky bitches over there!" Dy-Nasty pointed to some ratchet-ass chicks who were squatting over chairs and grinding on customers in the corner. "Fuck wit' one of them hoes!"

Suddenly Dy-Nasty's hood intuition came down on her. She felt a hot ball of hate coming her way, and she tried to duck through the crowd and keep it moving toward the door, but some jealous bitch had raised the alarm and all the other hoes had spotted her.

She had peeped an exit sign over a side door, and she was just about to bust up outta that bitch when she felt her weave jerked hard from behind.

"Skank!" One of the strippers yoked Dy-Nasty up and tried to quick-flip her down to the ground. "Who the fuck you think you is, coming up in here gamin'!"

There were three of them, and fighting to stay on her feet, Dy-Nasty cowered as they landed killer blows all over her head, back, and arms. The girl who yoked her was soft and juicy everywhere, and twisting into her body, Dy-Nasty sank her teeth deep into that bitch's pudgy upper arm like it was a warm buttered biscuit.

The stripper screamed and turned her loose, and Dy-Nasty ducked a punch from a girl with a red spiral wig and fought her way outside to the rain-soaked alley. She broke out running without looking back, knowing damn well them heffas wasn't gonna miss out on no dough just to chase her down the block.

Zooted up and breathing hard, Dy-Nasty stormed down the wet streets of Dallas cursing Jock out as she dialed his cell phone number and that shit just rang and rang off the hook. He was supposed to swing back by the club and pick her up, but she'd told him to come get her around two o'clock, and here it wasn't even one yet.

With her cell phone pressed to her ear, Dy-Nasty was swinging her big hips across a busy intersection when the screech of wet tires cut into the air and she looked back just in time to scooch forward so her ass didn't get clipped by a car bumper.

"Hey! Watch where the fuck you goin'!" she screamed as she whirled around and blasted the driver of a sweet silver BMW. "I had the goddamn light, you know!"

The windows were tinted and dotted with raindrops so she

couldn't see who was driving that baby, but she stood there posted up with her hands on her hips shooting eye-bullets in his direction.

She braced herself to curse him out from bumper to bumper when the driver's window slid down, but when she peeped the chubby old man sporting a thirty-thousand-dollar designer watch and grinning at her from behind the wheel, the first word that went through her mining-ass brain was *jackpot*!

And a jackpot was exactly what Dy-Nasty had hit as she rode down the wet streets kicked back and chillin' in the showroom-fresh luxury Beemer that belonged to some rich-ass oil tycoon who told her to call him R.R.

Dude had apologized fifty million times for almost ripping her ass on his bumper, and since it had started raining again he offered to give her a ride to wherever it was she was going.

Dy-Nasty was all for that shit as she pumped up the music in his whip and enjoyed the liquor buzz that was still rolling through her head.

"I'm going wherever you going," she had told him, cheesing all over herself. She recognized his whip as a fresh-outta-the-factory absolute top-of-the-line BMW, and everythang about that baby smelled brand-fuckin'-new!

And old dude was smelling pretty damn good too. Dy-Nasty's eagle-eyes had scanned over him like she was airport security, and in about five seconds flat she had peeped his platinum and diamond ring, his tailored sports coat, and the fact that his fat frog-lookin' ass had a quick eye for hot chicks with thick yellow thighs.

"I have a suite at the Omni Hotel," he'd told her. "It's only a few miles from here. We could go have a few drinks and relax for a while if you want to."

Dy-Nasty's eyes had lit up. Hell yeah she wanted to! And when ol' boy pulled up in front of some plush-ass five-star hotel and them valet boys broke their necks running outside to open their doors like he was the freakin' President of the whole United States, Dy-Nasty knew damn well she had hit the jackpot!

He took her over to a private elevator and used a key to close the doors. His spot was on the top floor, and when the elevator opened right inside of his penthouse apartment Dy-Nasty sucked her breath in deep 'cause that shit was bad as hell!

"Make yourself comfortable," R.R. told her as he took off his jacket and draped it over the back of a chair, and then walked behind a stone bar counter.

Every damn thing in the joint was marble and glass, and she could tell by the way it shined and smelled that somebody had been on their hands and knees scrubbing the hell outta every inch of it.

Dude brought Dy-Nasty her drink, and then he clicked a switch and some easy R&B filled the room. He sat down real close beside her and lifted the lid on a rectangular box that was on a low end table.

Now this is how you get a fuckin' party started! Dy-Nasty thought as he dug in the box and came out with a couple of joints and some nice-looking packs of fish scales too. They sat there getting buzzed and toasted up and talking all kinds of crazy shit, and she loved every minute of it.

Dy-Nasty was in the life, so she wasn't surprised not one bit when Mister put his pudgy hand on her knee and then slid it up her hot thigh. She stole a quick peek at his crotch and saw a fuckin' boulder stickin' up outta his lap, and dollar signs ching-chinged in her eyes!

"How about we," he said, angling his head toward the balcony on the other side of the room, "go outside and relax in the hot tub for a little bit?"

Dy-Nasty frowned. "I'm down but I ain't got no bathing suit."

"Neither do I," R.R. said, smiling as he stood up and unbuckled his belt. He unzipped his tailored trousers and let them shits fall down around his ankles. Then he pulled down his silk drawers and stepped outta all that shit and let his fat, foot-long dick wave in the air like a big black flag. "Neither do I."

CHAPTER 29

Selah was disturbed by the way things had gone down the last time she hooked up with Rodney Ruddman, but that didn't stop her from picking up the phone and dialing his number again.

It was late, and her hands trembled as she listened to his phone ring. She felt low as hell but her sex hormones were raging and she just couldn't help herself.

Rodney had seemed real disappointed the last time they were together, but Selah knew he got off on her just as much as she got off on him. She was counting on him freaking her with his Johnson bone at least one last time, but if she was waiting for him to pick up the phone and whisper something hot and nasty in her ear, she was about to wait a long time.

Rodney didn't pick up until the fifth ring and his voice was brutally cold right from the jump.

"Why are you calling me?"

Selah swallowed hard. Damn fool sounded like he was through with her. No *hello cat* or *hello dog.* No *Good evening, Mrs. Dominion.* Nothing.

"I said," he repeated, "why are you calling me?"

"H-h-hey Rodney," Selah finally stuttered over the sounds of the loud music playing in the background. She could tell by the hollow noise that he was driving in his car. "I . . . I just wanted to see what you were doing tonight. I figured maybe we could talk or . . . do something for a little while."

He hit her with a short, cruel laugh, and even over his loud music his scorn for her came through loud and clear.

"Oh, so now you want to talk?" He laughed again. "Talk about what? What you want me to do for you, or what I want you to do for me?"

"I . . . I don't know," Selah said, flustered like fuck. As cruel as he was, just hearing Rodney's voice had her woman juices flowing, and her heart started pounding with fear at the thought that he might hang up on her.

"Look, it's late, okay? I've got an early meeting in the morning. Why don't you try to get some rest? And if you can't sleep maybe you can hop in your jet and pay your husband a little late-night visit, huh? He's still in the hospital, isn't he? Maybe you can put on one of your sexy little outfits and pretend to be his night nurse."

"Fuck you, Rodney!" Selah's whole body flushed hot as she hissed into the phone. This fool was going way too far! He was trying to degrade her. To humiliate her for jonesing for him. And truth be told, it was working too. "Just fuck you!"

Rodney chuckled on the other end.

"Fuck me? No thank you, Mrs. Dominion. I don't think I'll be fucking you anymore, but maybe you should extend that offer to your husband—that is, if you can figure out how to get his *dick* up again."

"Motherfucker!" Selah shrieked from between her closed teeth. "Don't worry about my husband's dick! I want my ring back, Rodney, you hear me? I want my goddamn ring back!"

Even over the bass of the music she could hear the cruelty in his laugh.

"Sorry, Mrs. Dominion. I'm afraid I can't give it to you."

"What do you mean you can't give it to me? Why the hell not?"

"Because I don't have it anymore."

Selah broke. "Uh-uh. Uh-*uh*! Don't tell me you lost my goddamn ring!"

"No, no, no. I didn't lose it," Rodney said coldly. "I *gave* it away."

I had hung out in Fallon's suite for a good lil minute, and by the time I pranced over to Mama Selah's joint it was pretty damn late. I stood outside her door tryna decide if I should tap-tap-tap or straight out nigga-knock on that bad boy, but then I took a few steps backward and peered down and saw that her light was still shining out from the crack under the door.

"Mama Selah," I called out as I rapped my fist on her hardwood door. I didn't give it no po-po knock or nothin', just a couple of soft taps, but when she didn't answer I wondered if she mighta been taking a shower and couldn't hear me, so I pressed my ear to the door and listened.

And that's when I heard her.

Cryin'!

Mama Selah was crying! And they sounded like some big, fat gulping-ass tears.

I got confused for a second 'cause sistahs didn't usually cry like that! Hell, on the real, if I didn't know no better I woulda sworn it was a white chick up in there just'a boo-hooing like a muthafucka!

"Mama Selah!" I hollered, and this time I did nigga-knock on her damn door. "It's Mink! You okay in there, Mama Selah? Can I come in?"

"Just a moment," she called out but hell, by that time my hasty ass was already twisting the damn doorknob. And guess what?

It was locked!

"Mama Selah?" I hollered again. "You didn't lock yourself in there by mistake, did you?"

"Of course not, Mink." I heard the lock slide back and then she opened the door.

"Damn!" I blurted when I saw her red eyes and swollen nose. "You okay? Why you up in here crying with the door locked?"

She shook her head and sniffled as she rubbed her nose. "I wasn't crying, Mink. I have allergies. I locked the door because I was about to get undressed and I didn't want anyone to walk in on me."

"Uh-huh," I said, eyeballing her with the skeptic look. Yeah, okay. Mama Selah was gonna hafta come a whole lot betta than that. I was a Harlem chick, and as many scams as I had run I could damn sure spot some bullshit story when it was being laid on me.

"Well I just came to see what you were doing," I lied right back. "Actually," I slick-talked her as I brushed past her and walked deeper into her suite, "I was wondering if you would let me finish watching some of those shows you recorded."

She shook her head a little bit and I could tell she was about to say no, so I pounced on that ass.

"I mean, I guess I could watch them some other time, but for some reason I just don't feel like being by myself tonight."

She sighed real deep and I saw her whole body sag as she got all soft.

"Okay." She stepped back to let me in. "I could probably use a little company tonight too."

I felt like a gymnast as I vaulted my happy ass into her big-ass bed! While Selah went to take her shower I picked up the remote and scrolled through all the shows she had recorded until I found a couple I wanted to see.

I laid up in that bed feeling like a winner for beating Dy-Nasty's ugly ass to the punch, and when Selah got outta the shower and called downstairs to have a lil midnight snack delivered up for me and her, I started feeling like I could maybe get back good with her like I used to be.

We watched a quick rerun and then we cracked up laughing to a couple of comedy shows. And by the time I started getting sleepy I looked over and noticed that Selah was already knocked out.

Yeah, baby! I thought to myself as I clicked off the TV and grinned in victory. Dy-Nasty could forget about gettin' her tart ass up under these nice clean sheets tonight! I had claimed my spot on Mama Selah's throne, and for all I cared that hit-ass troll could take her ass back to Philly and sleep in somebody's doghouse!

I was snoring in my nice, comfortable spot in Selah's big old bed when the door banged open and all kindsa noise and funk came barging in the room.

"Mama Selah!" somebody hollered. "Where you at, Mama Selah?"

I lifted my head off the plush satin pillow and peeked through one crusty eye tryna see what the hell was going on.

Somebody was plowing through the room, bumping into all kindsa shit in the darkness and giggling under her breath.

"Dy-Nasty?" Selah sat straight up on the other side of the bed, and when I rotated my red eyeball in her direction I saw a look of confusion on her face.

"What the hell?" I muttered under my breath as I squinted at the clock. It was 4:48 and my head had just hit the pillow about an hour ago.

"Girl, what the hell is you doing!" I demanded as that drunk trick clicked on the lights and blinded me. I dove under the covers like I was a vampire frying under the sun.

"Dy-Nasty?" Selah said again.

"Yeah it's me!" that trick said all loud, and then she had the nerve to dive her ass straight into the bed right between me and Selah.

"Get the hell offa me!" I shrieked as she rolled her big booty over and laid on top of me butt-to-butt. I tried to buck her off but that heffa was solid meat, so I reached up and pulled a Bunni move and pinched the shit outta her!

"Owww!" she hollered like I had sliced into her with a damn razor blade. She scooted her ass off me and crawled over and laid her raggedy head in Selah's lap.

"Guess what? I just got back from Dallas!"

"Dallas?" Selah asked. "What were you doing in the city?"

Dy-Nasty giggled. "Hangin' out! Jock took me up there but I rode back in a fly BMW!"

That big fool dug her head even deeper into Selah's lap and grinned.

"Oooh, Mama Selah," she moaned like she was in heaven. "You ain't gone believe this, but I met me somebody."

"Prolly a damn pimp!" I muttered under my breath.

"What do you mean you met somebody?" Selah asked.

"Just what I said! I met this dude. Some old-head. He took me to this bammin' hotel and we had so much fun! He was so, so, so, so, so damn *rich*!"

I lifted my head off the pillow and started crackin' the hell up.

"You mean you picked up a 'customer' baby. A client. A trick. A john." I waved my hand and settled back into the softness of my pillow. "Stop frontin' and ga'head and call that little transaction exactly what it was. Bizzness!"

Dy-Nasty rose up on her knees and hit me with a nasty sneer.

"Do this look like something that got dished off by a trick?" She held out her hand and I saw a huge fake diamond ring flashing on her finger.

"Huh, baby, huh?" She grinned. "I bet nan'one of them

broke New York tricks you be rollin' with ever blessed you with nothing like this!"

I smirked as I eyeballed the glittering knuckle-duster she was sporting. It looked like a winner, but knowing Dy-Nasty she had probably dug that shit out of a Cracker Jack box. I was just about to get loose at the mouth and say something real slick but Selah shut me down when she stared at Dy-Nasty and blurted out, "That fool gave you my goddamn ring?"

She grabbed Dy-Nasty's wrist and stared down at her finger.

"*Your* ring?" Dy-Nasty snatched her hand away and hid it behind her back.

"Yes! *My* ring!" Selah snapped. "That's the very first ring Viceroy ever bought me and it's worth over a million dollars!"

She motioned impatiently with both hands like, *Un-ass my shit now! Give it up, give it up!*

"Uh-uh, hold up," Dy-Nasty said. She was still up on her knees with her hand behind her back, and now she poked out her lip and turned to the side, shrinking away from Selah.

"How you know my friend, Mama Selah? That dude I was with tonight. How did *he* get a hold of *your* ring?"

I couldn't stand Dy-Nasty but I was totally wit' her on that one, and all four of our big hazel eyeballs jumped halfway down Selah's throat because I was wondering the same damn thang!

Selah caught herself and tried to regroup. She swallowed hard and blinked a few times, and then she crossed her arms over her titties and shrugged.

"I don't know how he got it. M-m-maybe he found it. I lost it a long time ago, and he must have found it."

Dy-Nasty busted out with a slow, suspicious grin. Like she was reading poor Selah's ass like a book.

"Uh-uh." She shook her head and started crawling backward off the bed. "See, now. That there don't even sound right, Mama Selah. Hold up and lemme see somethin'."

I sat up as Dy-Nasty climbed off the bed and snatched her purse off the floor. She dug around inside it and came out holding a business card.

"Oooh," she squealed as she grinned at the card. "Ruddman Energy, CEO! Ol' boy is in the oil bizz too! Just like y'all!"

She cut her eyes suspiciously at Selah. "I wonder do your *huzzz*band know you lost your big ol' ring, and outta the blue this dude Ruddman found it for you? How about I show Daddy Viceroy my new rock and let's see what he gots to say about it?"

The look of horror that slid across Selah's face felt like a needle piercing through my heart.

"Uh-uh. C'mon now. Stop playing," I jumped in and shook my head. I came out from under the blankets and got up on my knees, grilling that skanky slut real hard.

"Give her back her ring, Dy-Nasty," I ordered her coldly and I wasn't fuckin' around with her neither. "Don't be coming in here in the middle of the night playin' no stupid games. Give her back her goddamn ring."

"I ain't giving her shit!"

That heffa started backing up toward the door.

"This is my damn ring!" she spit. Her hand was still behind her back as she wobbled drunkenly on her feet. "My *friend* gave it to me! Y'all ain't getting shit, 'cause I don't see no damn body's name on this bad boy, and it ain't on nobody's damn finger but minez!"

CHAPTER 30

Selah was burning up on fire as she barked into the phone.

"Do you know what you did, you sick son of a bitch?" she blasted on Rodney Ruddman. "That girl you picked up could be my *daughter*! My goddamn *daughter*!"

Ruddman was cool as a winter breeze.

"Your daughter? Well, how was I supposed to know that, Mrs. Dominion? I thought she was just a regular hooker. Besides, you've made your decision, so what does it matter anyway?"

"What does it matter?" Selah gasped. "What does it *matter*? For all I know you've fucked me *and* my daughter, and you're asking me what does it matter?"

Rodney damn near chuckled. "Well if that girl *is* your daughter she sure can teach you a thing or two about how to suck—"

"Shut up!" Selah shrieked. "You just shut your ugly frog-face the fuck *up*. Do you hear me?"

"That's enough, Mrs. Dominion," Rodney said calmly. "Name-calling is so unnecessary, don't you agree?"

"Kiss my black ass!" Selah exploded from the trenches of

her heart. "Your ugly ass can go eat a whole bag of wiggly dicks!"

Selah slammed the phone down and gasped for breath as she paced the floor of her bedroom. She was mad as hell! At Ruddman and at Dy-Nasty too! And she was definitely done with both of their asses. Completely done.

Rodney Ruddman could take his froggish ass straight to hell, and Dy-Nasty could get the fuck up out of her mansion! Oh hell, yeah. That girl had to get gone! She had to *go*. But not before Selah got her goddamn ring back!

While Selah was busy blasting on Rodney Ruddman, Dy-Nasty had made herself a little phone call too.

"You should see how they actin', Ma! That damn Suge lied on me and tried to beat me outta a million dollars, and now Selah is tryna take my damn ring!"

"Uh-uh!" Pat said. "They must think you stupid, baby girl! Now you *really* gotta gank 'em, Dy-Nasty! There's more than one way to skin a damn snake! You know how we do. It's time for you to trap they rich asses in a vicious cross-con!"

"I know, Mama, but I'm down here by myself! How am I gonna do all that?"

"Easy! You got that ring stashed someplace safe, right? So tell 'em you want *two* million this time! They didn't wanna pay up to keep you quiet about Barron? Well Selah is they prissy-ass *mama*! They damn sure gonna hafta pay you to keep quiet about her hoe-ass shit!"

"But we ain't got that much time," Dy-Nasty whined. "What am I supposed to do when them DNA results come back?"

"Well your ass ain't Sable so there ain't a damn thing you *can* do! You just betta get that money and get up outta there before the results come in, that's all!"

"But how am I gonna do that? Barron said they should be here any day now!"

Pat sighed. "Then you gotta make Mink drop her claim *before* the DNA results come back, stupid! Twist her arm up and make her tell them fools that *you're* the real Sable!"

"Mama! How in the hell am I gonna make her say that? Mink might be ugly, but that bitch is greedy too! She's tryna get paid!"

"Damn, Dy-Nasty! I *know* I taught you how to scheme harder than that! Just pretend you're only getting a million, then tell the damn girl you'll give her half a million if she drops her lil bullshit claim and lets *you* be Sable! That way, you get the cash and the inheritance money, and everything else the rest of them damn Dominions got too! Just try it. You heard what I said, right? Tell Mink you're gonna squeeze Selah for a million, and promise to give her half. Watch how fast her broke ass jumps all over you!"

Dy-Nasty pouted. "But I ain't tryna share none of my two million dollars with no damn Mink!"

"Girl please!" Pat growled into the phone. "Muthafuck Mink! We's scammin', remember? The only chick you gonna be sharing that money with is *me*!"

"That bitch ain't giving up that ring," I said, shaking my head.

"Well we just gone hafta *jack* her ass for it then!" Bunni declared.

"Mama Selah shoulda just beat her ass and took it from her that night. Now that trick is either gonna pawn it for some chicken change, or stash it somewhere outta sight."

"Where in the hell you think she's gonna hide it at?"

"I'on't know," I shrugged. "I just hope like hell she don't slide it next to that ugly piece of slum she be wearing on her hammertoe."

On the real, I had felt bad for Mama Selah when Dy-Nasty

ran up outta her suite with her precious jewels, but there was only so much that I could do. For one thing, *I* was a liar, okay? And a damn good one at that. And that's why I knew Selah was lying her ass off about some random oil billionaire just happening to find her damn ring and then sliding that shit to Dy-Nasty!

Naw, naw, hell to da naw! Rich Mama Dominion was gonna have to come a whole lot better than that if she wanted somebody to buy the load of shit she was selling 'cause it was sounding real wack from where I stood!

And for another thing, on the low I was still kinda pissed with Selah! She had kicked me straight to the curb as soon as Dy-Nasty came on the scene, and I had to practically beg her ass for every little bit of time and attention I got. Selah had made it real hard for me to throw my con game down on her, and even though I didn't like seeing Dy-Nasty twist my play-mama's thong up in a knot, part of me felt like Selah prolly deserved that shit for clickin' up with that rough-ridin' chick over me!

"We gonna have to catch Dy-Nasty out there at just the right time," I told Bunni. "If we roll on her in her room then we can beat the shit outta that slick-ass scripper and get that ring back before she goes blabbing off at the mouth about it."

"Yeah, let's do that." Bunni nodded and started taking off her earrings while I went in the bathroom to get the big jar of Vaseline. "Let's knock a hole in that bitch's back so deep we can stuff her whole damn head up her ass!"

We had stripped outta our finery and put our hair up and slapped Vaseline all over our faces and necks, but just as we were almost ready to creep down to Dy-Nasty's suite and put in some fist work, somebody banged on my door.

Me and Bunni stared at each other and frowned.

"Who is it?" I snapped like I was back in the projects somewhere.

"It's Dy-Nasty!"

I shot Bunni a look and she shot me one right back.

"Open the damn door and let the stank bitch in, Mink! Damn!"

Narrowing my eyes, I pranced my ass over to the door and flung it open wide.

Dy-Nasty stood there with her hands on her hips and poppin' hard on some pink Bazooka bubblegum. She had on a short skirt that didn't even fit her right, and she was about to poke me in the eyeball with them nipples of hers that stuck outta her tank top like two pointy darts.

"What?" I said, knowing I looked stupid as hell standing there with a bandana on my head and my face all greased up with Vaseline.

"Where you going wit' them fighting clothes on?" she said, giggling as she looked me up and down and peeped my sneakers and my battle gear. "Somewhere to get your ass kicked?"

I twisted my lips. "What the hell you come down here for?"

She chuckled as she banged her wide hips right past me and busted up in my room. "I came to *talk*, Mink. For real. I think it's time for you and me to have us a real long talk."

"What y'all got to talk about?" Bunni jumped in.

Dy-Nasty waved her off. "This here shit is between me and Mink. Your ass ain't even family so you ain't got nothing to do with it, okay?"

"Oh, Bunni's family," I said real quick. "She's family down to the bone, and blood is thicker than mud, baby! So whatever you brought your grimy ass down here to say you need to go ahead and spit it out while you still got all ya teeth!"

"Naw, I ain't sayin' *shit* in front of her ass, Mink! Bunni gots to *go*!"

I turned to my girl. "Gimme a quick minute, Bunni. I'll meet you downstairs in a few." As soon as Bunni switched her gangsta booty out the door I turned on Dy-Nasty and said,

"You got five minutes, trick. Four-fifty-nine now, and I'm counting!"

Dy-Nasty grinned. "All right. You ain't gotta get so shitty but since you put it like that then . . . handle this. You know that rich dude I met the other night, right? The one who slid me that bad-ass ring?"

"That's Mama Selah's ring!"

"Uh-huh," Dy-Nasty nodded and agreed, "it sure is, 'cause Mama Selah's been *fuckin'* him!" She smirked. "She been fuckin' that ugly beast for a real long time, and *that's* how he got her ring!"

"What the hell is you talkin' about?" I bucked hard on her even though what she was saying was some damn sure juicy-ass news! I couldn't even see Mama Selah getting her illegal swerve on, but hey, ya never knew what a horny bitch in heat might do!

"You heard me." Dy-Nasty shrugged. "That lil mush-faced nigga is her *boo.* And I can see why too. He's real fucked up in the grill but he got a monster dick and he can lick a mean cat."

I wanted to close my eyes and plug up my ears!

"You's a lying-ass dog, Dy-Nasty! And even if Mama Selah was fuckin' out on the sly that ain't none of your damn bizzness!"

"Oh"—she gave me a slick lil smile like my noise wasn't getting her pressed out in the least—"it ain't none of *my* bizzness. You sho' right about that. But I got a feeling Daddy Viceroy would love to hear all about it, and if Mama Selah wants her goddamn ring back, then *some* damn body better change my name to Sable quick fast, 'cause I'ma need me a cool mil if y'all expect me to sit on that."

"Y'all? How the hell you figure, *y'all*?"

Dy-Nasty put her hands on her hips and huffed. "It must be pretty fucked up to be ugly and slow at the same damn time, Mink! The reason I'm telling you is because I'm willing to split the loot with you, okay? Five hunnerd large each. Fifty-fifty. Right down the middle."

My lip mighta curled up in disgust but my eyes damn sure got big.

"Oh, you tryna gank Mama Selah big-time, huh? Even though she might just be your Mama?"

Dy-Nasty grinned. "Damn right! You might love her ass but I sure as hell don't!"

"Yeah, so what kinda stupid shit I gotta do to get that type of cash?"

"Nothing much," she said and shrugged all innocently. "You just gotta tell everybody that you really ain't Sable. And that *I am*."

I stared her down. "For half a mil? I'on't know about that, Dy-Nasty. Lemme think about it for a minute."

She nodded and switched her big booty outta my room.

"You think about it, Mink," she said slickly. "You go right ahead and do that."

Selah's forehead was full of worry lines as she thought about how she had practically begged Dy-Nasty to give her back her diamond ring. She had even offered to buy Dy-Nasty a ring for herself that was just as nice. But *noooo.* The young girl had refused to un-ass her property. In fact, she had threatened to tell Viceroy exactly who she'd gotten the ring from if Selah even thought about trying to take it away from her.

The threat on it's own was bad enough, but Selah knew she had stepped in some real stink dog shit when Dy-Nasty came to her room and told her she wanted to make a little deal.

"I know how bad you want your ring back, Mama Selah," the girl had said sweetly. "So here's what I think I can do for you. If you tell Mink to kill all that noise about being Sable and just get her ass on up outta here and go back to New York, then we won't even need them DNA test results and you can just tell everybody that I'm Sable and make me a permanent member of the family. Bet?"

Selah had frowned and shook her head.

"I can't do that," she tried to explain gently. "Mink has a right to her claim, and I can't make her drop it. Only the DNA results can prove which one of you is really Sable, dear, and they aren't back yet."

"Oh well!" Dy-Nasty went in hard as she put her hands on her hips and smirked. "I'ma hafta collect two million dollars if you want your little ring back, then!"

Selah had been stunned. "Two million dollars? Are you serious?"

"Damn straight," Dy-Nasty said, nodding. "Matter fact, I'ma need two million dollars *and* I'ma need you to tell everybody that I'm Sable. I don't give a damn what them DNA tests come back saying! If you want me to keep my mouth closed and give you back your damn ring, then that's what you gonna hafta do!"

Selah had stared deeply into the girl's cold, bottomless eyes.

"Could you really do something so foul to me, Dy-Nasty? Could you treat me this way even though you know there's a chance that I could be your mother?"

"Uh-huh!" Dy-Nasty bucked out her eyes and the truth was right there bold as day for Selah to see. "I sure the hell could!"

Selah had just stood there and stared at the girl. She had stared at Dy-Nasty Jenkins real long and real damn hard. And then she had walked that little bitch over to the door, pushed her trifling ass out, and picked up the phone to call the one person she knew could clean up a stankin' pile of shit like this with deadly discretion and lethal finesse.

She called Suge.

Bunni stared at me like I had a tampon up my nose.

"Five hundred grand? You went and told that bitch to kiss

your ass over five hundred grand? *Trick!* You musta bumped your head and scrambled your damn brains," she said, flouncing past me in a black g-string with her naked titties just a' jiggling. She bent over and mooned the shit outta me as she rubbed scented lotion all over her feet, calves, and legs.

"Girl you know damn well you ain't Sable! And soon as them damn DNA test come back ere'body else is gonna know it too! *Shoooot.*" Bunni stood back up and put her hand on her naked hip. "You better hop ya ass on that half a mil like a crab on a coochie hair, Mink. 'Cause once them test results come back you won't be getting *shit.*"

"Nah, Bunni." I shook my head as she grilled me with mad heat. "I don't believe Dy-Nasty and I don't *trust* her skank ass neither! That chick is foul, boo. I can't just let her do Mama Selah like that and get away with it!"

Bunni broke. "These *ain't your people*, Mink! You must be forgetting why we brought our black asses down here in the first damn place," she turned around and busted on me over her shoulder. "Remember, we came to rob these fools! Not to rescue they asses!"

"I'on't care." I folded my arms and doubled down. "It ain't just about what we came here to do no more, Bunni! I'm not about to just sit here and let Dy-Nasty fuck Mama Selah up like that!"

"*Mama* Selah?" Bunni screeched. "C'mon, now, homey! Be for real! Just the other day you was around here whining and bitching about how Selah be all the time treating Dy-Nasty better than she treats you! Make up ya damn mind, girl. You been slippin' for a minute now, ya know. Sliding right off ya game! I want my rowdy con-mami Mink LaRue back! Matter fact, you need to call that bitch Tasha Pierce and get her up in here real quick!"

Bunni stomped past lookin' at me like I was some kinda body snatcher who had come up outta a moon pod.

"I don't know who the hail you is, over here occupying

my best friend's brain, but your shit is way too watery to be the gaming-ass Mink LaRue I know!"

I just stood there fumin'. Bunni could talk that yang if she wanted to, but it still wasn't gonna stop me from doing what I had to do. She had one thing right, though. I wasn't Tasha Pierce no more, and I wasn't the same trifling Mink LaRue that had bust up in this joint on the Fourth of July! And I wasn't *about* to let Dy-Nasty shit all over Mama Selah neither, so for once in my life I was gonna have to buck up and tell the goddamn *truth*!

"You makin' a mistake," Bunni warned me as she rubbed her left titty and grilled me with the evil eye. "You's about to make a real big mistake, Mizz LaRue. I can feel it. Word."

I shrugged like whatever. Bunni had a radar built into her titty, and most of the time she was right on point with her shit.

But this time I seriously doubted it.

CHAPTER 31

Suge Dominion walked out of the Western Union office whistling a real sweet tune. In his hand he carried a copy of a sent money receipt that had been processed a few weeks earlier. It was in the amount of two thousand dollars and had been sent by Dy-Nasty Jenkins to a Patricia Jenkins in Philadelphia, Pennsylvania.

Getting his hands on that receipt had taken a little bit of work, but a nigga like Suge Dominion lived for that type of thrill every single day. Nothing made his nuts tingle more than going head up against some tough competition, and with the kind of money, power, and clout he carried, Suge bet on himself to come out on top every single time.

And today had been no exception. He was chuckling like a muthafucka as he climbed in his monster truck and tossed the piece of paper on his dashboard. The hefty white woman at the Western Union counter had damn near nutted in her middle-aged drawers when he threw his smooth Mandingo swag down on her and convinced her to search through her records for a particular transaction.

And when she found what he was looking for and Suge

slid her a crisp stack of hundred-dollar bills totaling five large, Big Mama had blushed like she was ready to climb up a pole and strip outta her granny drawers for him.

Suge thought about the phone call he'd gotten from his sister-in-law. He had never heard Selah sound so nervous and upset before, and there were a couple details in the story she had laid on him that he was gonna have to take with him all the way to his grave.

True, his first loyalty was always gonna be to his brother Viceroy, but Suge put in work for the entire Dominion family, and Dy-Nasty had definitely become a family problem.

"I shoulda took her ass out a long time ago," he had muttered under his breath when Selah told him how Dy-Nasty was trying to shake her down. He glanced down at the Western Union receipt in his hands. Some people were just too fuckin' greedy to be suckin' up air. And Dy-Nasty and her raggedy-ass mama were two of them.

We were sitting up in Barron's plush corner office surrounded by finery, and for once in my life I wasn't turned on by the fact that all eyes was on me.

I had called Suge and told him I needed to have a convo with him and Barron at the same time, and he had picked me up and we drove over to Dominion Oil headquarters and went straight upstairs to Barron's dope-ass office.

His spot was damn near unreal. Like something you would see on a television show. I had been wide open on Suge's bangin' executive suite, but he wasn't lying when he said his office didn't have nothing on Barron's!

I had expected to catch a shitty vibe from Barron right off the bat, but as my ass cheeks sank into his buttery-soft leather sofa, he sat behind his desk with an expression on his mug that even my cunning ass couldn't quite get a read on.

Uncle Suge had a curious glint in his eyes, like he was interested in finding out what all this back-alley bullshit was about, but Mister Bump looked like I had rolled up in his space to shake him down.

"Look, Barron, I asked Uncle Suge to hook up this lil emergency meeting because I got something that I really need to tell y'all."

With my eyes glued to the floor, I took a deep breath and did something that was straight up against my nature. I sacrificed myself for somebody else and let the *truth* hang out.

"I was lying when I told y'all I had to go back to New York because my boss got shot."

"Come again?" Barron said, and he said that shit real slick-like too. "You was what?"

"I was lying," I muttered, and then I took another deep breath.

"My boss didn't get shot. Matter fact, I don't even have no damn boss. I went back home because my mama was dying." I shrugged a little bit. "And then she died."

Barron smirked like he had seen this shit coming a mile away. "Yo, hold up. You told us your mother died a long time ago, remember?"

"I *said* I lied, damn!" I sucked my teeth. "She was alive that whole time, but now she's dead."

"So, wait," Barron said, shaking his head. "Who is this 'mama' you talking about, Mink? Is this Jude Jackson, the woman you told us kidnapped you?"

At first I nodded yes, but then I shook my head no real quick.

"Well see, yeah, Jude kinda kidnapped me, but she kinda adopted me too. She took me from my birth mother. Or my birth mother prolly gave me to her. But hell if I even know who that chick really is. Or was."

Barron leaned back in his chair and busted on me with a look that said, *Lies, lies, and more dirty rotten lies!*

Suge was giving me the funky face too so I knew I was gonna have to start all over and this time come correct.

"Look," I said, staring both of them dead in their eyes and hoping they could tell that for once I wasn't bullshittin'. "Here's the real scoop. Me and Dy-Nasty are twins. All right? We're *twins*."

Barron sat up with his eyes bucked. "So you lied about that shit too, huh? You told us you didn't even know that girl!"

"I *don't* know her ass!" I protested. "I mean, yeah, I think me and her are sisters and all that, but I don't *know* her. I never even laid eyes on that scraggly trick until you dragged her funky ass down here to mess my shit up!"

"Well if you don't know her then what makes you think y'all are sisters?"

"Okay, I ain't got the whole scoop, but from what I was told me and her was born right here in Texas, and then some kinda way my mama Jude adopted me and took me with her to New York." I shrugged at Barron. "And I guess y'all adopted Dy-Nasty and brought her out here to the mansion. She was the one you was babysitting outside that drugstore in New York that day. Not me."

Barron pounced all over me like the lawyer he was. "So you've just admitted that you're not Sable, and therefore you're not entitled to any financial assets from the Dominion family trust, correct?"

I shrugged.

"I ain't saying I don't want that money, but Dy-Nasty is Sable. I'm just me. Mink LaRue."

Suge looked relieved as fuck that me and him wasn't family, but Barron was still shaking his head and saying *hold the hell up*.

"So all this time you knew who Dy-Nasty was? You took a hundred grand from us and went through all that DNA testing when all that time you *knew* she was really Sable?"

I shook my head real fast. "Uh-uh! No I *didn't*! Nope! I already told you I didn't know shit about her, Barron! When I got that money I didn't even know her gutter ass was alive!"

"So where the hell is all this coming from, Mink?" Suge's deep voice was cool and calm but I could tell he was dead serious. "Why you coming clean with all of this shit now?"

I swallowed real hard. There was no way in fuck I could tell them the real reason I was fessin' up! Yeah, I was a shiesty money-grubber and I could run me one helluva con game, but I wasn't about to bust Mama Selah out and put her lil illegal swerve match with Rodney Ruddman on blast!

I thought about the way her face had looked when she saw Dy-Nasty wearing her old engagement ring. Mama Selah had been sweating in her bra over that shit! There was no way in fuck she coulda explained to her husband how his worst fuckin' enemy in the world had gotten hold of her ring!

"Um, to tell you the truth the only reason I'm telling y'all now is because Dy-Nasty is tryna talk me into getting down with her on a real grimy scheme about some nasty pictures she said she found on the Internet," I lied as I grilled Barron.

"For real, that broad is tryna twist y'all pockets up for a million hot ones. She's willing to tear me off half, if I get down with her, but if y'all mofos don't give up the loot she's gonna take her rabbit-ass straight to Houston and drop a big load of stank shit in Viceroy's ear."

Barron shot Uncle Suge a shook look and I smirked inside because now that nigga knew that *I* knew about his dick-sucking pictures too!

"And you can best believe," I said eyeballing Barron from his lips to his crotch, Dy-Nasty has some real sucky shit to drop in Viceroy's ear! On *everybody*!"

Barron looked cool as hell as he tried to front me off.

"Don't be so stupid, Mink. Dy-Nasty's just talking shit. She ain't for real. I don't think she's got a drop of dirt on anybody. Especially me."

"Oh, she's for real, baby. You better watch your back, dude. It's either lay that cheese on her or put it in writing that she's really Sable so she can get her a nice slice of the Dominion pie."

Barron grunted. "But just now you said Dy-Nasty is willing to give you half the money if you go along with her little scam, right?"

I nodded.

"So why don't you?"

"Why don't I what?"

"Why don't you just go along with her? Because if we declare her to be Sable, then you're ass out and you can't press a dime out of us. But if Dy-Nasty blackmails us for a million, then you just might walk away with half. What's up with that, Mink? Why in the hell are you *really* telling us all this?"

I thought about Mama Selah again. Bunni was right. Mama Selah had acted real shitty toward me over Dy-Nasty and her mess, and by all rights I coulda busted on her and hauled booty back to New York City with a nice lil gwap in my bank account and forgot all about her sometimey ass. But I wasn't no snitch. I had never dropped a dime on a pizo in my whole life, and I damn sure wasn't about to start droppin' none now.

"Your family's been through enough hell," I said, shrugging. "And I just don't wanna see nobody else get hurt."

Uncle Suge frowned. "So, what? You're just gonna slide the W over to Dy-Nasty's column and break out, huh? What? You and Bunni gonna head back to New York now?"

My heart fell and I dropped my gaze to the floor.

"Yeah," I said quietly. "I guess that's the plan."

"Cool!" Barron said, quick-fast and happy. He jumped up from his chair. "Run to the house and pack your shit up real quick and I'll buy both of y'all lying asses a one-way-ticket outta here."

CHAPTER 32

The doorbell rang just as Selah was approaching the spiral staircase in the Dominion mansion. Pausing with her foot on the top step, she glanced over her shoulder, and then turned around and headed toward the front of the house.

For the past few days her mind had been grinding on one single track. Viceroy's doctors were talking about releasing him from the hospital, and the last thing she wanted was for her husband to walk back into his house and get cold-cocked by all the drama that had been going down while he was gone.

Especially when it came down to her engagement ring. There was no doubt in Selah's Brooklyn mind that Dy-Nasty would stick that ring right up under Viceroy's nose if she didn't get the two million in cash that she was asking for. And there was also no doubt that Viceroy would recognize the ring that he had bought her as soon as he scrambled up his first real hunk of change and started rolling with the big boys. He had been damn proud of himself for bringing in the kind of cash it took to slide a piece of jewelry like that on Selah's finger, and he had been mad as hell when she lost it too.

Hell no, Selah thought as she hurried toward the front

door. There was no way in the world that she could let Viceroy find out where her ring had been for all these years. That fool would probably flip out and go on a killing spree and stab her all up in her throat!

Her assistant, Albert, was just closing the front door when Selah reached the parlor. He smiled as he turned toward her holding two large envelopes in his hand.

"That was the courier, Mrs. Dominion," he said, holding the envelopes out to her. "These came for you."

Selah accepted the packets from him and stared down at them. Her heart began to pound as she quickly scanned the addresses. Both envelopes were addressed to her, but one had come from Cross Type Laboratory, and the return address on the other said Central Dallas Testing Center.

Her hands shook as she thanked Albert and then quickly turned away. She felt flushed and her feet were unsteady in her five-thousand-dollar Loeffler Randall shoes as she hurried up the mansion steps and into the privacy of her master bedroom suite.

Closing the door firmly behind her and turning the lock, Selah forced herself to neatly peel the perforated edge of the courier envelope back and retrieve the set of documents inside. Her eyes skimmed over the page, landing first on Mink's name and then on the summary of results that had been compiled by the lab.

She stared at what was written there, and then the papers slipped from her fingers as Selah tore into the other envelope. Her breath got caught up in her throat as her eyes crawled over the DNA results that had been compiled from Dy-Nasty's blood samples.

"Oh fuckin' *shit*!" she whispered as she read all the way down to the summary on the bottom line. Her eyes skimmed up to Dy-Nasty's name again, and then they skimmed back down to the results.

Selah didn't want to believe it. She just couldn't fuckin' *believe* it!

The sheets of paper fluttered from her fingers and landed on the floor right beside Mink's test results, and Selah couldn't help it when her knees gave out on her and she sank down to the floor too.

"I don't know about this," Barron said as he paced the floor in Suge's expansive corner office. "Something about this shit don't smell right, man. Something just don't smell right."

Suge was sitting with his boots propped up on his huge desk as he toked on a three-hundred-dollar cigar. He stared at his nephew and then narrowed his eyes as the trail of smoke rose in the air.

"What's not to buy, Bump? Seems to me like the lil girl was just trying to come straight with us. She's got a thing for Selah and she don't wanna see her get hurt no more."

Barron shook his head like he still wasn't feeling it.

"A'ight, check this out," Suge told him. He swung his big feet down to the floor and sat up straight in his chair. "Remember that quick little trip I took up north a minute ago?"

Barron nodded.

"Well when I got there I hooked up with a few of my dudes from around the way. We put a sniffer out on some old fraud cases on Dy-Nasty and her *mother*. In *Philly*."

"Her *mother*?" Barron frowned.

Suge tipped his cigar and nodded. "Hell yeah. Dy-Nasty and her moms was in a city bus accident when Dy-Nasty was about two. Her moms hooked up with some slick-talking ambulance chasers and they pulled a fast one on the city. They sued them fuckers from one end of Philadelphia to the other, and once they got that first fat settlement check their asses got hooked and went on an accident spree after that."

"You went all the way to Philly just to find that out?"

"Hell naw," Suge said quietly and toked on his stogie as he thought about his little murderous trip to the projects where he'd had to knock a ghetto bird on her ass. "I already told you I went to Philly to dig through some trash."

He pictured the switchblade that crazy Pat Jenkins had pulled on him, and how her wild ass had tried to stab him and fight him like a man.

"The thing is, I ended up bagging that trash up and dumping it too." He flicked the ash off the burning tip of his cigar and into a thick marble ashtray and shrugged.

Barron shrugged too. "So?"

"So a while back I gave Dy-Nasty a ride to Western Union so she could wire somebody some money. I went back up there and got the name off the receipt, but something Mink said today kinda fucked with me."

"Just spit that shit out, man! What was it?"

"Mink said her mother's name was Jude Jackson, right? Well, the bag of trash I stuffed in a Philly Dumpster had a name on it too, and so did that receipt I got from Western Union. It was Pat Jenkins."

Barron leaned forward in his chair and peered at his uncle. "And Jenkins is Dy-Nasty's last name. Not Mink's."

"Damn right," Suge said. "And if Dy-Nasty was in Philly pulling ganks with that scheming bitch Pat when she was just two years old, then where the hell was Mink?"

A cold grin spread over Barron's dark, handsome face as he finally got it.

"Mink was right here in good old Texas. Hanging out with me and Dane. Running around chillin', and answering to the name of Sable."

Barron stood over Selah fanning her with a small stack of paper as she lay on her bead-embroidered chaise lounge with a look of distress pinching her face. He had come home from work to find his mother stretched out on the sofa with an empty flask of vodka wedged between her thighs, and judging by the fumes coming off of her she had spent the afternoon chugging down the whole damn thing.

"Calm down, Mama," he told her as he tried to cool her off. Tiny dots of sweat had formed on her nose and her upper lip. "Just take a few deep breaths and try to calm down."

"Calm down? Did you read that shit?" Selah demanded, pointing at the DNA results that Barron was fanning her with. She snatched them from his hand and shook them in his face.

"You told me those damn labs were clean! You said you checked them out yourself!"

"I *did*, Mama. I checked them. Both of them. You know I did. The results are right, and it's pretty easy to explain. Here," Barron said as he pulled out his phone and hit a number on speed dial. He waited until the line rang on the other end, and then he pushed the phone into his mother's hands. "Somebody wants to talk to you."

Selah sat up straight when she recognized the voice. It was Suge.

"Yes," she said as she listened to her brother-in-law's specific instructions. "Yes, of course. Uh-huh." Suddenly she frowned. "Wait, are you saying they're . . . are you sure about that?" She sighed real hard and then nodded. "Well, if that's the only way to get some peace then I guess . . ." Selah listened carefully and then nodded again. "Okay, I'm in. Yep, I understand. Absolutely. I'll do it. I'll get on it right away."

She clicked off the call and passed Barron his phone back. And then she reached for her own phone and called her personal stock broker and instructed him to place a large trade from her private bank account and deposit the proceeds into an account that had just been recently opened.

"Two million dollars, Mrs. Dominion?" her broker confirmed. "Did I hear you correctly? You want to liquidate two million dollars' worth of assets and deposit them into a third-party debit account?"

"Yes, George," Selah said calmly, as if she wasn't the least bit drunk. She got up and walked over to her desk and selected a bright red Magic Marker from a stack and held it in her hand. "You heard me right. That's exactly what I want you to do."

CHAPTER 33

It was the worst damn dinner of my life. Everything tasted like cardboard. Even the real expensive wine they had broke out for the grand celebration tasted like shit.

The whole damn family had shown up to hear the news, and all I could do was sit at that table stiffer than a damn statue as Dy-Nasty stole my props, my moolah, and my damn life!

Selah looked half-lit as she held some papers up in the air.

"The DNA results have finally come back and I'm happy to announce that we now know exactly who our daughter is!"

Selah separated the papers until she had one sheet in each hand. The paper in her right hand had a bunch of stuff typed out on it, and so did the other one, but the paper in her left hand also had the word NEGATIVE written on it in bright red ink with a big circle around it and I just knew that one was mine.

And I was right too.

"Dy-Nasty, darling,"—Selah smiled brightly—"these are you results," she said, holding up the clean piece of paper without all that ugly red scribbling.

Aunt Bibby was a big fuckin' liar! I screamed inside. I shoulda known not to believe nothin' her drunk ass said! Me and Dy-

Nasty wasn't sisters and we damn sure wasn't identical twins! 'Cause if we was then our DNA woulda came back an identical *match*!

"Come on, Dy-Nasty," Selah said grinning like she was all proud. "Stand up and take a bow, baby because you're the grand winner of this contest!"

You shoulda heard how loud them fuckers clapped for her! Even *Dane*! I mean, I expected Barron to be standing his stiff ass over there beamin' like a muthafucka, but I had always thought Dane was my nigga tho!

That Philly trick Dy-Nasty jumped up outta her chair squealing like she was on a game show, and on the real, I couldn't blame her neither. I mean, who wouldn't wanna be the long-lost daughter of a bunch of rich-ass oil tycoons? Everything she could ever want was now right at Dy-Nasty's fingertips, and the only thing I had to show for all my hard work and hustling was a plane ticket home in some scrunched-up seats way back in the cheap section near the toilets!

"See there?" Bunni leaned over and hissed in my ear as Dy-Nasty took a victory lap around the table and hugged and kissed her new family half to death. "I *told* your dumb ass not to turn that damn money down! You was so damn in love with ya fake 'Mama Selah' that they kicking our asses out on the streets dead *broke*!"

I opened my mouth to protest that shit and say something real mean and slick to Bunni, but then I closed it back again like my lips was glued shut. And they might as well have been glued shut too, because really, Dy-Nasty was a clear winner, and once you got a big L stamped in your column what else was there left to say?

Now that her ass was officially in and minez was officially out, Mizz Thang was prancing around the mansion like her feet didn't stink.

Barron had let it be known that since Dy-Nasty was wearing the crown that me and Bunni had to vacate the premises, and he wanted us outta the mansion quick-fast-pronto before Viceroy came home from the hospital.

"I can't stand that greasy bitch!" Bunni snapped as we watched Dy-Nasty order the servants to drag about a hundred designer bags and boxes up to her room from all the expensive stores she had hit in the rich people's mall.

That heffa had gotten real stupid about her shit too. Me and Bunni had grown up poor as dirt and hustling for every dime we could steal, but at least we knew how to act when we got a lil sumthin' in our pockets!

But not this here trick.

She had took her ass out there and tried to spend all the Dominion's cheese up at one damn time! She was flossin' all kinds of exotic labels and dripping icy jewels from her eyebrows and the top of her ears, and she even had a brand-new bangin' diamond ring squeezed around her big deformed-looking hammertoe!

"So when y'all ugly hoes gonna be getting' up outta *our* mansion?" Dy-Nasty asked as she flounced past me wearing a pair of skinny jeans with a slick grin on her face. This bitch was wicked grimy, and it took everything I had in me to keep from jumping on her ass and choking her with her brand-new extra-silky Rémy weave.

But Bunni was on her.

"We leaving when we get good and goddamn ready to leave," she said, blasting on Dy-Nasty like she wanted to slay her. "Yo ass might be a Domino now but you still ain't no shot caller up in this camp, baby! You betta recognize!"

Dy-Nasty just looked over her shoulder and grinned. It was almost like she couldn't even be bothered to argue with our broke, insignificant asses no more. We was just that low-rated!

"I oughta tell Mama Selah about that half a mil you was

gonna slide me to help you gank her for her ring," I muttered jealously.

That shit got her attention big-time, and Dy-Nasty turned all the way around to get me straight.

"Tell her," she said, grinning like a muthafucka as she reached down in the back of her stretch jeans and dug her tiny drawers out the crack of her thick ass. "Go right ahead and tell her, and then ask me if I give a fuck! My new mama done put *two* million big ones in my account already, baby, and just like this phat ass right here, there's plenty more where that came from!"

Barron had booked me and Bunni a one-way economy flight back to New York City, and booked Dy-Nasty a first-class round-trip ticket to Philadelphia. Since our flight was leaving just an hour before Dy-Nasty's, Barron had all three of us rolling out to the airport at the same time.

"Good-bye, my beautiful bed." Bunni's silly ass went around our suite kissing all the grand shit we would probably never see again in our lives. "Fare thee well, golden faucets. See ya later, marble tiles. Holla back, double-headed soaker shower!"

I was sad to be leaving the good life behind too, but I was gonna miss more than just the finery and the luxury. Plus, I was scareder than a muthafucka about going back home because I didn't know what kinda ass-kicking that fool Gutta was gonna have waiting for me when I got back to Harlem!

I had already said my good-byes to Jock and Fallon, but when I knocked on Selah's door before we left the crib she wouldn't even answer or let me in.

"That stuck-up bitch got herself a whole lotta goddamn nerve," Bunni said, sucking her teeth. "Doing you that way! That heffa oughta be kissin' your yellow ass from the left cheek to the right cheek for not tellin' on her! You better than me, Mink, 'cause if I was you I woulda snitched and told the whole damn world that Miss Goody-Goody's frontin' ass was fuckin' outta both drawers legs! *Everybody* woulda got the memo that the great Mrs. Domino's rich ass ain't nothin but a jump-off, out there getting' smutted on the side! Damn *skraight*! I woulda busted that trick straight the hell out!"

I felt where Bunni's pain was coming from, and it was a real hard lump to swallow especially since I had sacrificed my entire hustle just to make sure Selah's grimy game stayed hidden under the covers. But when it was all said and done, everything I had done was worth it, and I didn't regret a damn thing.

The mansion was buzzing with activity as the three young ladies from up north got ready to head to the airport. Selah's heart was full of a wide range of emotions, and after all the nerve-wrecking drama of the past few weeks, all she wanted was for her life to go back to normal again.

She had gotten in one last chat with Dy-Nasty before she left. Selah had caught the girl as she sashayed out the door and toward the Hummer where Barron was waiting.

"You *do* remember our little agreement, don't you?" Selah had asked as she clamped her hand down on the girl's arm. Things had changed drastically between them the moment Selah made that money transfer. Once she'd given in to Dy-Nasty's demands, the girl had gotten even rawer and more ghetto, if that was possible.

Dy-Nasty had glanced down at her arm and then jerked it out of Selah's grasp.

"Yeah, yeah, *yeah*!" she sang. "Don't worry, prissy mama. Your little secret ain't gonna get out. You lucky I'm such a stand-up chick from head to toe! I'ma send you a text message just as soon as we get out the gate. It's gonna tell you exactly where I left your precious little ring at, okay?"

Selah had swallowed hard. "I hope you're not playing

games with me. Because despite what you *think* you know about me, Dy-Nasty. I don't play."

The young girl had cut her eyes at Selah and flounced away giggling her ass off.

"Well *I* do! I play! But I ain't like you 'cause I play to *win*!"

"I'm sorry, Dy-Nasty," Selah said quietly with tears in her eyes.

"Next time don't be sorry," Dy-Nasty laughed over her shoulder. "Bitch just be *careful*!"

A few minutes later Selah's heart was pounding with anticipation as her cell phone vibrated in her hand. She glanced out the parlor window and watched the two vehicles drive through the gates and off the Dominion property. She frowned. Maybe Dy-Nasty was a woman of her word after all.

Clutching the phone, Selah glanced down at the screen and read the text message that the girl from Philadelphia had sent her. For a second she looked puzzled, but then excitement surged in her heart, and following the instructions in Dy-Nasty's text message, she took the steps two at a time as she rushed toward her bedroom suite.

Selah was breathing hard as she burst through her double doors, filled with joy at the thought of getting her hands on that precious million-dollar ring. But nothing in the world could have prepared her for what she saw as she approached her ultra-luxurious bed. There, sitting on top of her plush designer pillow with the mega-count Egyptian silk case, was a monstrous piece of ghetto slum that assaulted her eyes and rocked her world.

Right off the bat, Selah knew what it was. And she knew where it had come from too. The last time she'd seen this mold-green, tarnished piece of stainless steel with the chipped crumb of cubic zirconium in the center, it had been wrapped around Dy-Nasty's crusty big toe!

"I'm gonna fuck her *up*!" Selah screamed as she slapped that nasty shit off her pillow and sent it flying across the room. Rage seeped from her pores and spilled out into the big, empty house. She yanked at the zipper on her Fendi dress and practically tore it off as she ran over to her closet and started digging for something way deep in the back. "I swear to God, I'm gonna *fuck* that dirty bitch up!"

Me and Bunni were traveling pretty light compared to the first time we left up outta Dallas. Since I was no longer a Dominion there had been no marathon shopping sprees at the rich people's mall, no back-and-forth runs to the jewelry store, and no fifty-million pairs of new shoes to cram into our suitcases.

But Dy-Nasty had all that shit on lock for us though. It had took four big niggas to drag all her new shit down the stairs, and she was gonna rack up a helluva baggage fee before she got her ass on that plane.

Not that she was giving a fuck about loot these days.

"Look at this shit!" She had stuck a bank receipt halfway up my nose as she bragged on all the yardage that the Dominions had deposited into her new account. "Bitch I bet your mining ass ain't never seen this many zeros in your whole fuckin' life!"

I had rolled my eyes and waved her off, but on the real tip, she had that shit right. My eyes had damn near gotten googly from tryna count all those zeros!

Me and Bunni rode to the airport in Suge's truck and I grilled him outta the corner of my eye almost all the way there. I still dug the shit outta this dude, but I felt some kinda way now that all my lies had been exposed. I had been hoping Suge was feeling me enough to let me and Bunni crash at his crib for a minute until we could figure out our next move, but his ass didn't even bother to offer me nothing, and I couldn't fix my mouth to ask him for shit neither.

"Girl, you betta get over there and work his ass!" Bunni had barked on me when it really sunk in that we were getting sent back to New York dead broke. "All that damn sheet rippin' y'all been doing and now you scared to ask that nigga for a lil pocket change? *Sheiit.* You's a professional scripper, baby. That big nigga owes you some tips!"

It wasn't that I was scared to ask Suge for some ends. My damn *pride* wouldn't allow me to ask him 'cause I felt his ass shoulda *offered*! So, I rode to the airport sitting next to him broke as hell with my pride in my shoe and my lip poked out, and it hurt me to my heart when he looked real deep into my eyes with a blank expression on his face and then turned away and kept his eyes straight on forward all the way there.

That whole mad scene had my head spinning, and as I sat beside him sipping on some cold lemonade, I kept going back and forth between kickin' myself up the ass for fuckin' up my own damn hustle, and feeling like a winner for finally looking out for somebody other than myself.

We pulled up outside of the departure terminal at the airport. Barron had parked his SUV up ahead of us and him and Dane were busy stacking Dy-Nasty's fifty-million designer suitcases on the curb. I gave Suge one more long-ass look, hoping I would see something good in his eyes. He igged the shit outta me as he climbed outta the truck and went around back to get our bags, and that's when my lil heart got to beating so damn hard and fast I started sniffling and catchin' vapors.

"A'ight now!" Bunni warned me as she opened her door and got ready to climb out. "Yo ass betta not go falling apart on me, Mink! Let that muscled-up fool act as stank as he wanna act! Hmph! You better show his ass who the fine one is! Remember, you's a prime bitch, and ain't nothing changed around here but the weather, baybeee! Don't you *never* let a nigga see you sweat!"

I knew Bunni was right so I pulled myself together and put my game face on! *Sheiiit!* Fine-ass Mizz Mink LaRue didn't hafta slum around for no man! On the real, when one flaky nigga stepped off, the next one was damn sure gonna step right on up!

I opened my door and slithered outta that truck like the slick Harlem stunna that I was. I was just about to slide on my designer shades and switch my deliciously big booty across the sidewalk and inside the terminal when tires screeched on the pavement up ahead, and a midnight-black Mercedes damn near t-boned Barron as he climbed outta the Hummer.

"What in the *hail*?" Bunni hollered as a raging chick leaped outta the luxury whip and a good-old-fashioned street fight broke out! Even though mad fists were flying, long weave was being yanked, and some big-time noogies was getting punched up on foreheads, I still couldn't believe what the hell I was seeing!

It was *Dy-Nasty*! Getting her eye dotted by *Mama Selah*!

"Where's my goddamn ring, bitch?!"

All the Brooklyn had jumped outta Mama Selah's ass! Her face was shining with Vaseline, her hair was tied down with a blue bandana, and she had on sweats and a raggedy T-shirt. Miss cool and classy Michelle Obama was getting pure gutter with her shit as she yoked Dy-Nasty in the crook of her arm and pounded haymakers in her mug!

Dy-Nasty tried her best to get in some blows, but she'd gotten caught off guard and didn't have no wins. Her lil tiny pink skirt had flown up in the air and her entire ass was showing. "Yuck," Bunni said, and I didn't blame her. A light-blue thong was crammed up Dy-Nasty's yellow crack, and her monster cheeks were jiggling like lemon jelly as she took an airport beat-down.

"Bitch!" Mama Selah swung and caught her with one last punch before Barron and Suge broke them apart and wrestled Dy-Nasty outta her grip. "You've been fucking with the wrong one, dammit! The wrong one!"

Me and Bunni was speechless as we watched Barron muscle his sneaker-wearing Mama back inside her hundred-thousand-dollar Benz. Big Suge snatched me and Bunni up and manhandled us back down the street toward his truck so we could finish getting our stuff out.

I had just reached in the front seat to get my cup of lemonade when all of a sudden I realized there was *another* big commotion going down over by Barron's whip!

I whirled around and threw my hands in the air.

It was Dy-Nasty again! Poor mami was taking her *another* ass-whipping! But this time she was getting tossed the hell up by two white dudes who looked so regular and square they just had to be DTs!

My mouth fell wide open. "What in the—"

"Hold up, Lil Mama." Suge checked me with his big hand as I started to break out toward Barron's whip again. "Just chill out right here and relax ya'self, and for once I want you to keep your damn mouth shut and don't say shit, you hear me, Mink?"

Who in the hell was this nigga bossin'? My neck jerked all crazy and Bunni's did too, but neither one of us so much as parted our lips as we watched the knock that was going down right there in front of our eyes.

"Get the fuck offa meeeee!" Dy-Nasty kicked and screamed as the undercover jakes in dark business suits tossed her around and jerked both of her arms up behind her back. That scag looked a raggedy-ass riot with her weave flying, her ankles wobbling around in them eight-inch heels, and her ratchet cotton skirt flying all up the back of her stank ass!

"Get her!" I hollered, forgetting I was supposed to be keeping my mouth shut. "Tase that nasty trick! Yeah! *Tase* her fuckin' ass!"

"Now wait a damn minute!" Bunni blurted out. She stood posted up with her hands on her curvy hips and her fat camel toe winking its eye at the whole world. "Hold up!" she screamed. "Hold the hell *up*!"

She hit Uncle Suge with a beastly glare. "Why in the hail is they cuffin' that poor girl up like that? I can understand about Mama Selah and her ring, but since when did being stank and crusty become a federal offense?"

Suge crossed his arms and leaned back on his monster whip and grinned as the two white dudes balled Dy-Nasty up and threw her in the back of their unmarked car. "Oh they got a lil bit more on her than that," he laughed.

"Oh yeah, like what?" I wanted to know.

Suge shot me a fine-ass grin and then shrugged them big ol' country ham shoulders of his. "Like blackmail, extortion, bank fraud, identity theft, and whatever the fuck else Bump and them lawyer boys feel like hitting her with when they throw the book at her criminal ass."

CHAPTER 34

"If these mofos drag us into *one more* goddamn meeting . . . ," Bunni bitched as we got dressed to go downstairs. "I'on't know how these rich fools be getting that cheese 'cause all I ever see 'em do is talk each other to death!"

I shrugged and ignored Bunni as I peered in the mirror and combed through my fake eyelashes with a tiny little brush. Suge had brought us back to the mansion after the feds drove off with Dy-Nasty kicking and screaming in the backseat of an unmarked car, and I was so glad to be back in the lap of luxury instead of riding on a flight back to New York or locked up and sitting in somebody's pissy bullpen that I couldn't care less about going to another family meeting!

But I *was* curious about why Barron had called one, I admitted as I stepped into my thigh-high white knit Pucci dress and slipped on a pair of real sweet spiked heels. Barron's ass had barely glanced at me at the airport as he watched the cops haul Dy-Nasty off to the bing. He had made sure they lassoed her ass up nice and tight, and then he headed back to his ride and nodded at Uncle Suge like, *Leggo!*

I had been shocked outta my thong when Suge opened

the passenger door and told me and Bunni to get our asses back in his truck, and I had reached over and *pinched the shit* outta Bunni when she bucked and opened her big yakkety-yak and started whining about how the check-in lines was already out the door and he was gonna make us miss our flight.

Fuck that flight!

I had jumped back in that truck so damn fast I busted my kneecap on the edge of the door, and when we got back to the mansion and Suge took our bags out the back and told a couple of servants to carry them upstairs to our rooms, I jumped up on that big plush bed and did me a real stank stripper's version of the I'm-so-happy dance!

Bunni was still bitchin' as I adjusted my diamond clip-on earrings and patted the platinum-white Glama-Glo on my head that I had just brushed into brilliance. It was a real fly pageboy cut and it brought out the hazel in my eyes. I checked myself out in the mirror, admiring my stacked package from all angles until I was satisfied that my shit was set from head to toe.

I turned toward Bunni and examined her gear.

She had changed into a pair of hot-pink jeggings and a tight peach-colored tank that showed off her round titties and her toned, flat stomach. Her camel toe had a split going right up the middle, just the way she liked it, and her hips looked real cute and curvy in contrast to her tiny little waist.

"You ready?" I asked, giving her a quick nod of approval. Mami looked nice and stank with that big ol' hoe gap showing between her legs and she knew it too.

Bunni smirked. "I was born ready, baby." She popped her lips and smoothed her shimmery pink gloss around and grinned.

The minute we walked out the room I felt my nerves starting to get shot out. Alarm bells rang in my ears and the sour taste of dread jumped all in my mouth.

"Yo, why you think they brought us all the way back here,

Bunni? What you think they taking us to Dominion Oil headquarters to say to us?"

My girl shrugged and shook her Harlem ass as she turned around and headed for the door. "I don't know what in the hell them fools is gonna say, Mink. All I know is they better not'a brought us all the way back here just to kick our black asses right back out, ya heard?"

Suge's office was bad as hell, and Barron's office would sho'nuff snatch your breath away, but Viceroy's office screamed mucho-mucho-mega-moolah from the ceiling to the floor!

It looked just like one of them stupid, mind-boggling joints you saw in billionaire's pads on TV. It was spread out bigger than our whole damn apartment back in Harlem, and smoove and sleek as hell. There was expensive furniture and high-tech gadgets everywhere. There were so many books on his built-in-the-wall shelves that they just had to be for show because there was no way in hell one man coulda read them all.

Everybody was sitting around a conference table as me and Bunni made our grand entrance. I tried to stroll in all cool and carefree like my ass wasn't about to be homeless just a minute ago, but Bunni stepped up in there real lively-like, poppin' gum with her hips wiggling and titties jiggling every damn where.

I glanced around and checked shit out as I sat down. I had figured Pilar would have her greedy-ass front and center, but to my surprise there was nobody there but Barron, Suge, Dane, Fallon, Jock, and Mama Selah.

Barron stood up as soon as my ass hit the seat good, and when the first thing he did was clamp his hard glare down on me, I knew something truly fucked up was about to go down.

"Well! We're glad you could make it, Mink," he said.

I rolled my eyes at his stiff ass. This dude was a wanna-be

white boy for real! He ain't have an ounce of chicken grease in his whole damn soul! I grilled him hard, but there wasn't a damn thing to be read in his eyes, so I just smirked at him standing up there looking like an Oreo in his lil Brooks Brothers suit.

"Mama," he said, "can you pass me those DNA results please?"

Selah dug in her purse and came out with an envelope. She pulled out two sheets of paper, and when I saw the one with the big NEGATIVE circled in red marker I almost shit.

Barron took both pages from her. He looked around the table like he had some real big announcement to make.

"Okay, we read y'all Dy-Nasty's DNA results the other night, and despite what went down at the airport, we told the truth too. Her results really *were* a match for Sable. So today we're gonna read you Mink's results. And I'm sure everybody wants to know exactly what they say."

No this muthafucka didn't! I screamed inside. He did *not* bring me way back here just to put my shit on blast again!

But oh yes the hell he did. I realized this when Bunni snorted real loud and looked at me like our shit was cooked. My heart fell to my feet as I closed my eyes and started sliding down in my seat.

"I don't really see the point in all this," Fallon spoke up and said exactly what I had been thinking. "I mean, Dy-Nasty's results already came back a match so we all know who the real Sable is, don't we?"

Barron nodded. "Yeah," he said, with a smug lil grin on his mug. "You got that shit right. We *do* know. But I wanna read Mink's results out *loud*. In front of *everybody*."

Bunni wasn't having it.

"You mean to tell me you called another meeting just to tell us some bullshit we already know?" She cocked her eyes at Barron and fumed. "Man, gimme a break!" She threw her hands up in the air. "Y'all done already stabbed my girl in the heart, a'ight goddammit? And now you wanna twist the knife all up in her chest too?"

Barron shot Bunni a *bitch please* look, then he set the piece of paper that had the colored red marker on it face down on the table and held the other sheet up in the air and started reading real loud.

" 'In summary, the DNA sample submitted by Mink LaRue and tested by our lab has been compared to the DNA sample of Sable Dominion, and through extensive analysis has been determined to be a . . .' "

Barron paused in the middle of his sentence and grilled the shit outta me.

"We know the truth about who you are now, Mink," he said quietly.

"I *know* you know the truth, dufus," I snapped real stank. "I was the one who told you in the first damn place, *remember*?"

Barron shook his head. "Nah, we know the *whole* truth now. We know *everything*, and for one thing, it didn't go down exactly the way you said it did."

Okay, he had me. I sucked my teeth and threw my hands straight up in the air. He had my ass for real this time, because I had told so many lies that I didn't know which one he was talking about!

"You told us you had a twin, isn't that right, Mink?"

Bunni jabbed me in the ribs with her pointy elbow and whispered, "See! I *told* you not to tell them niggas nothin'!"

I glanced around the table real quick, then cocked my head to the side a lil bit and mumbled, "Yeah. I said I had a twin because that's what my aunt Bibby told me. But she was lying as usual, and anyway I didn't know nothing about it when I first came down here. I just found out."

Barron smirked, and then went after me like he was handling a murder case in the courtroom.

"Yeah, but you also told me that you and your twin were born somewhere right here in Texas. Ain't that right?"

Outta the corner of my eye I caught Dane's head jerking in surprise, and I nodded. "Yeah, uh-huh. I told you that."

"And you said that both you and your twin were adopted. Am I right?"

I cut my eyes at Barron's tight ass. It was so damn quiet in there you coulda heard an ant belch. Every damn eye at that table was on me, and for somebody who loved the spotlight my gorgeous ass was starting to sweat!

"Yeah!" I jumped *real* defensive. "I *kinda* told you that because that's what my aunt Bibby told *me*! She said we was adopted! So *what*?"

I was done with this fool, but Barron had his foot on my throat now and that sucker was pushing hard and going in for the kill!

"*And* you said your mother's name was Jude Jackson," he kept right on sweating me. "She adopted you here in Texas and then y'all moved somewhere in New York City, correct?"

"That's right," I snapped. "Harlem, baby. *Harlem*!"

Barron pulled back a little bit and nodded.

"Yeah, that's exactly what you said, Mink. But you were wrong because none of that is true."

I twisted my lips. "Come again?"

"You heard me. You were wrong. Jude Jackson didn't adopt you down here in Texas, and she didn't move to New York with you either."

"Huh?" I side-eyed Bunni and hunched my shoulders at that incredible nigga! "How you figure?"

"You *were* adopted right here in Texas, Mink. But not by Jude. And this is where you stayed. At least until our family decided to go on vacation in New York City."

"*Whaaa*?"

"Just tell her, Bump!" Uncle Suge cut in. "Stop with all the bullshit and just tell the girl. Damn!"

Barron glanced down at the paper and started reading again.

"'In summary, the DNA sample submitted by Mink LaRue and tested by Cross Type Laboratory has been compared to the DNA sample of Sable Dominion, and through extensive analysis has been determined to be a . . . *positive match*."

Barron grinned and let the paper fall from his fingers as me and Bunni both looked confused as fuck.

"Welcome home, Mink," Barron said with a small smile on his lips. "I never thought I'd be saying this, but you *are* my sister Sable."

"She *is*?" Bunni bucked.

"I *am*?" I screwed up my face and shot him the stupid look.

"Yeah," Barron said and glanced at Mama Selah. "You are."

"Whoa. Hold the hell up. I mean, yeah I would love to be Sable, but there's no way in hell me and Dy-Nasty could both have positive results unless y'all lied or unless me and her . . ." My eyes got big as shit.

"Unless you and Dy-Nasty are identical twins," Barron said. "And your DNA results prove you are. That's why her test was a positive match too."

"But then how do you know which one of us is . . ." My voice trailed off again and I stared hard at Barron.

And then I stared hard at Suge too. His eyes looked funny, but there was a small smile on his face. Like he was happy and sad at the same time.

"Hold up. I . . . I don't get it," I stuttered. I thought about that conversation where I fessed up to Barron and Suge and I wanted to holler, *Y'all niggas know goddamn well I ain't Sable!*

"I mean, I'm up on the DNA thang and all, but how you figure, Barron?"

"Yeah, how you figure, Bump?" Jock butt in, shaking his watermelon head. "You said Mink is really Sable like you know it for sure. If her and Dy-Nasty are twins and they got the same DNA, then you really can't prove which one of them is really real."

"Yeah we can," Suge said quietly. "Because Dy-Nasty was in a bus accident up in Philly when she was about two years old. Her and the lady who adopted her both got hurt and they sued the city for a gwap. I got the court records. The pictures, the doctor's reports, the whole nine. Dy-Nasty and her moms got a nice fat check and they started liking that shit. So they spent the next ten years pulling slip and fall schemes and accident scams and filing fake claims all over the city."

Jock shrugged. "That still don't tell us who is who, though. How you know Mink wasn't the one up there in Philly pulling off all those scams?"

Suge grinned. " 'Cause I got the adoption records too. And the woman listed on the adoption papers for Dy-Nasty Jenkins is the same woman who's listed in all the court cases against the city of Philadelphia. Her name is Pat Jenkins. She's Dy-Nasty's mother. I rolled up on her in Philly and convinced her to give up a little info on Dy-Nasty's birth mother. I found out her name was Valentina, and that she was your mother too, Mink."

Valentina? My heart banged. What the hail? That's the chick who was married to big Moe before he hooked up with Jude!

My mind was boggled. "Yo, did y'all tell *Dy-Nasty* about this shit?"

Suge grunted and frowned. "Hell no. If she'da found out we woulda never got that hellraiser outta here."

Dane scratched his head and held up his hand. "But hold up. If all this stuff is true, then where the hell was Mink while

Dy-Nasty was in Philly and all them accidents and court cases were going on?"

"Oh, I can tell you that," Mama Selah said, opening her mouth for the very first time since I walked in the room. "Mink was right here. At home with me and the rest of our family." She looked at me with tears in her eyes. "Except back then, baby girl, we called you Sable."

CHAPTER 35

Me and Bunni didn't waste no time moving outta the suite we shared. It was a real big house and there was plenty of room, so stank Mizz Camel-Toe got her own extra-large suite and you can best believe I got me my own suite too!

Finding out that my biggest lie had actually been my biggest truth had really fucked my head up. Every time Bunni walked past me she pinched the shit outta me and whispered, "Mink you is rich! You is really, really *rich*!"

Yeah, Bunni mighta accepted that shit one hundred percent, but I'd been playing the con game for so long that I couldn't hardly wrap my mind around it at all.

I mean, all this shit was just so twisted up and tangled!

It wasn't like I could just call Mama up and grill her. Daddy neither. And this Valentina chick? They was all telling me she was my birth mother but I wasn't buying that shit. I didn't even know what that woman looked like!

Nah, there were just too many dead people in the mix and too many secrets and lies that had been kept and told. So even though I ended up getting exactly what I came to Texas for, plus a whole lot more, it wasn't like I just jumped off the poor train and landed all happy on the rich wagon, you know.

Climbing in the bed one night swearing all out that you was one person and then waking up the next day and finding out that you was somebody totally different wasn't as easy as that shit sounded.

I'd heard all the yang Suge and Barron had spit about what they thought had happened to me and Dy-Nasty, how we had gotten split up as babies and then ended up coming back together just to fight over a hunk of cash, but on the real tip I *still* didn't know exactly who the hell I was!

But even though just the thought of it slammed me straight in the gut, I knew exactly who I *wasn't*.

"Big Moe . . ." I'd moaned when I called my aunt Bibby crying like a baby after Selah announced that I was definitely the little girl she had lost in New York City that long-ago day. "Big Moe ain't my daddy!"

"Oh yes the hell he is!" Aunt Bibby declared after I hipped her to the whole crazy story, minus the part about me getting my hands on some money. "Jude mighta been a lyin'-ass criminal but she wasn't no fool, Mink!"

"Huh?"

"Them people are right, Mink. Valentina *was* your mama. And Moe sure as hell was your daddy."

"But how could Jude have known that when she took me?"

"She *didn't*! But why the hell you think she snatched you in the first damn place, huh, stupid? When Jude walked past that damn drugstore and saw a baby girl sitting up in that stroller lookin' *just like* her man Moe, there was no way in hell she coulda passed you up! She *had* to snatch you, Mink! If Jude was gonna keep my brother tied to her titty then she needed her a baby who looked just like *you*. And why? Because you look just like *Big Moe*."

Aunt Bibby chuckled. "The fucked-up thing is, Jude never even realized that she was actually snatching Moe's real child. Her stupid ass never even knew!"

I was still kinda skeptical about all that, but the more Aunt Bibby talked the more I believed her. I mean, look at me! There was just no way I could be anybody else except a LaRue! And if I was a LaRue, then Dy-Nasty's cruddy ass was damn sure one too.

Which explained why we was *both* such good-ass liars!

I didn't climb in my big plush bed until real late that night, but when I did I slept solid like a rock. And as soon as I opened my eyes the next morning I looked around my new room and pinched the shit outta myself to make sure I wasn't having a crazy-ass dream.

It was almost time for breakfast so I took a quick shower and then walked around my spacious new suite bare-coochie naked. I kinda missed having Bunni right next door, but I was digging on my privacy too. Especially since Uncle Suge had slipped up in my suite to chill with me.

"I know you're family now baby girl, but I still don't wanna let you go," he had told me late last night as we laid twisted up in the sheets together. "What me and you got going on might not look right to the rest of the world, Mink, but it feels right in here." He tapped his big barrel chest. "It feels real right in here."

I had shocked the shit outta myself when I let loose and started crying in his arms. Just straight up bawling. Slingin' snot and ere'thang! Hell, I didn't wanna give up the good thang I had going with him neither! We wasn't *really* related! Wasn't none of Suge's blood runnin' through my veins! Big Suge treated me *right*. In and outta the sheets!

For the first time in my life I was chillin' with a grown-ass man who was diggin' on me for who I really *was*, and not because of the way I moved my body on a stripper pole or for the phat hunk of ass that puffed out my back pockets! I liked Suge! I liked the way his cowboy ass spoiled me and made me feel!

Tears had flowed between us and we held on to each other

all night long. But by the time the sun started coming up and Suge had to leave, we still didn't have no answers. All we knew was that we was really diggin' each other and neither one of us wanted to let that go. And what was wrong with that?

Suge was still on my mind as I massaged some warm vanilla-berry scented oil all over my naked body and put my hair up in a bun. And then, after grinning my ass off in the mirror, I slipped on some jeans and a T-shirt and walked barefoot down the stairs to eat breakfast with my new peeps.

Viceroy was out of the hospital. He had only been home for about a week but you could damn sure tell he was there. He had a team of therapists who came out to the mansion and worked with him every day, but he got around pretty good with his Mister Biggs cane and he kept shit lively with his loud mouth and cocky hood attitude.

"Daddy has really changed a lot since his accident," Fallon told me one day.

"Oh yeah? How so?" my nosy ass asked.

She shrugged. "For one thing he's a whole lot looser now. Easier to be around and not so damn intense all the time. For real, Mink. He used to be even worse than Barron. Tighter than an asshole. Everybody always had to say the right things and look the right way just so he could keep his public image up. Especially Mama. That shit was crazy."

I laughed. "Well he sure as hell ain't got no stick stuck up his ass now. That man's got some hood in him!"

"Yeah, I guess he woke up out of his coma and realized life is too short to be fronting all the time."

I thought about all the posin', frontin', and stuntin' I had done over the years tryna keep my image up and connive my way up on a dollar, and I didn't have no answer for that.

"Whateva," I told her. "I kinda like him. He's gutter as hell, but he ain't half as mean as I thought he was. Besides, who gives a good goddamn about what other people think any damn way! Life is to be lived, baby sister. At some point you just gotta let all the bullshit go and just live the life you got. Your daddy done finally figured that out."

"*Our* daddy," she reminded me.

I got quiet on that one. Viceroy was cool and all, but I was *Big Moe's* baby! But Big Moe was gone. Long gone. I still loved the hell outta him and I missed him too, but just like I had told Fallon, sometimes you just needed to let go and live the life you had. I think that's what Big Moe woulda wanted me to do.

"Yeah, okay," I finally said and grinned. "*Our* daddy."

CHAPTER 36

We were sitting around the dining room table after eating a big Sunday dinner. The servants had just cleared away all the dishes and quietly left. Dane got up and closed off the doors at both ends of the room. Viceroy sat at the head of the long table. He waited until Dane sat back down, and then he got to talking.

"All right, now. It's come to Jesus time for this family and I'm gonna get right down to business. I've only been back at my office for three days and lips are already flapping. I wanna know *everything* that went on while I was laid up in that hospital and I wanna hear that shit straight outta the horse's mouth!

"Y'all know how I roll. I built my empire up outta the *dirt*, and I'll be damned if I'm gonna let anybody fuck it up. Especially y'all."

Viceroy pinned ere'last one of us in his deadly black glare and fixed his eyeballs on us real tight.

"So, this is amnesty time, y'all hear me? I'm gonna give everybody *one chance*, and one chance only, to come clean and lay their dirt on the table because I don't want nothing sneaking up and knocking the shit outta me while I'm out there hustling my business in this cut-throat world!"

I snuck a glance around the table and I almost busted out laughing. Viceroy shoulda known better! The first law of the scheme game was Thou Shall Never Tell on Thou Goddamn Self, Even When Faced With Video Evidence! Just who in the hail did this fool think was about to raise their hand and fess up all their dirt?

Viceroy went on, "But no matter what you say in here today I swear I'm not gonna whip nobody's ass or break nobody's neck. You got my word on that. But remember," he said, narrowing his eyes, "this is gonna be your *only chance* to come correct. Y'all got that? If I find out later that you lied to me or left something out, your ass is gonna be grass and I can promise you that!

"So let's do this. Tell the truth and shame the devil! Y'all better not keep one more goddamn secret or tell not one more lie! Just lay it all out there! All of it! From right to left, fess up and put all your funky shit on the line and don't hold a damn thing back."

Since Jock was sitting to Viceroy's right, he got to go first.

He looked scared as shit as he opened his mouth and closed it real quick a few times, and I almost laughed when I realized that this was probably the first time I had seen his ass when he wasn't half-zooted.

"Um, I . . . I got caught in a little jam a while back," he finally managed to choke out. "In the pool house."

"Oh yeah?" Viceroy's eyebrow went up and he gave his son a cold look. "What the hell kind of jam, boy?"

"Nah, nah, it wasn't like the stuff that happened down at the lake house with that white girl, Pops!" Jock insisted, and I had to stop myself from hollerin', *Nah, fool! It was worse!*

"Come on, son. Don't make me ask you no whole lotta questions. Just spit it all out!"

Jock swallowed so damn hard I just knew his tongue had flipped over and slid down his throat!

"I took a honey in the pool house," he mumbled. "We was getting nice and then she, um, overdosed."

"What the hell?!" Selah damn near screamed, but Viceroy held up his hand and shut her down. "Uh-uh. It's amnesty time, remember?"

"But it wasn't even my fault!" Jock blurted out. "That stupid white girl took a bunch of pills! She just snatched them up off the table and started swallowing 'em. And then we, um, had sex, and then she . . . um . . . she died."

Viceroy hurr'up and broke his own damn rule!

"Goddammit!" He slammed his fist down on the table. "You brought a white girl on my property and she died in my muthafuckin' *pool house*?" He turned to Selah. "Where the hell were you when all this shit was going down, Selah?" He swung back around to Jock. "And what the hell did you do with the body?"

Jock stared down at the table like he didn't wanna tell on nobody, but Suge stepped up like the gorilla he was.

"What you think he did? He called me and I came over here and got her." He flipped his toothpick around in his mouth and stared at his brother and then shrugged like stashing a dead body was a small thing. "Hey. That's what I do."

Fallon was next on deck and her little ass was already squirming.

"I ran away while you was gone, Daddy," she confessed. She had this sugary-sweet, innocent look on her face like she was his little girl for real, but I knew mami had a swinger *and* a pole freak living inside of her!

But lil mama had her daddy wrapped around her finger and Viceroy looked like his heart was about to hit the floor.

"Baby girl!" His face crumpled and he sounded pressed the hell out. "What you mean you ran away? From *my* house?"

Fallon nodded. "I got mad because Barron kicked my girlfriend out. I got caught dancing for her—"

"*Pole* dancin'," Bunni had the nerve to butt in.

"Whatever!" Fallon said, waving her off. "I was *dancing* and Barron put Freddie out. So I snuck out the house and just left. I went to a shelter for gay and lesbian teens but Barron found me and made me come back."

"Fallon! Are you telling us that you're *gay*?" Selah blurted out, then clamped her hand over her mouth when she remembered the rules.

Fallon shook her head. "No, Mom. I really don't think I am. I think I hooked up with Freddie because I was lonely and bored and it seemed like the 'in' thing to do. She claimed she was in love with me, but Mink kept saying Freddie was just using me, and it turned out that she was right."

"So you're sure you're not gay then?" Viceroy side-eyed Fallon as he questioned her.

She nodded. "I'm pretty sure. I was needy and let myself get pulled into that lifestyle but my head isn't in that same place anymore."

"But you know your daddy would still love you, no matter what, right?" Viceroy asked quietly. "You know you would *always* be my baby girl, even if you were gay."

Fallon nodded. "I know, Daddy." She flashed him a small smile. "Thanks."

I could hardly wait when it was Dane's turn to fess up because I didn't think bruh-man had the nuts to go head-up with his daddy. But Dane shocked the shit outta me when he took a deep breath and jumped right on in the water and got soakin' fuckin' wet!

"Yo, Pops, I got kicked outta school, man. Some hater started a rumor about me pushing up on a drunk girl for some sex, and even though it never happened they brought me up on charges anyway. I had to go in front of a disciplinary board and without even hearing my side of it, they gave me the boot. But I swear, I never touched that girl. Yeah, I had a lotta honeys on a string, but I ain't never mishandled a woman. I was gonna fight the charge but I'm kinda short on cash right now and I didn't wanna ask Bump for nothing while you was down." He looked around the table and flashed a handsome grin. "So that's it, y'all. I might not have graduated, but I'm finally outta college."

It was Barron's turn next and I scooted my chair up closer to the table so I could catch every word that fell outta his hypocritical mouth!

"I got messed up at a frat party, Pop. Somebody slipped a hot one in my drink and I passed out. I don't even remember getting in my car, but I must have because I hit a kid. Ran right over him. I was so tossed up that I didn't even know nothing until the cops came and arrested me."

"Arrested you? Boy, I *know* ain't no son of mine got locked up!"

"I did, Pop. I got locked up, but only for a minute. I called my boy from law school and he hooked me up with your friend, Judge Halley. He tried to make it go away but the chief of police wasn't going for it and the kid's father ended up taking me for five hundred grand."

Selah sat up straight. "But you told me you only gave him two hundred and fifty thousand!"

Viceroy bucked. "Selah, you knew about this?"

Barron shrugged. "I did give the kid two hundred and fifty. At first. But then his father threatened to go running his mouth to the media unless I doubled it. So I did."

This was my first time hearing about Barron dishing off some blackmail money, but I wasn't surprised. He had tried his damnedest to stop me and Dy-Nasty from sharing a measly three hundred grand a year, but he had no problem sliding half a million outta the vault to keep his own ass outta a ditch! Fuckin' *hypocrite*!

Still, I prolly woulda let my new big brother slide on all that other stuff, but Bunni was tracking like a hound dog as she grilled Barron and said, "Yeah, whateva, two-fitty, five-hunnerd, that's all well and good, but what about them pictures boo?"

Barron was cool as sleet.

"What pictures?"

My girl got sassy. "Stop frontin'! You know what pictures I'm talking about!"

He shrugged. "Nah, I don't know, Bunni. But what's up? You got some pictures you wanna share with everybody?"

I smirked. Barron knew damn well that Web site had been shut down! Me and Bunni shoulda printed them bad boys out when we had the chance because no matter how many times we tried to get back to that site, we never saw those damn pictures again!

It was my turn to confess my crimes, and once again I was sitting in the hot seat with a spotlight on my forehead. I felt kinda shitty because even though almost everybody in the room had turned out to be a dirty rotten liar, I was ten times grimier than they were because all my lies had been designed to gank the very people that I belonged to.

"Umm," I said, and then cleared my throat and scooched my ass around nervously in my seat. I was too ashamed to look at Selah, so I stared at a little black spot on the table instead. "The only thing I did was I . . . um . . ."

All of a sudden a frog jumped up in my damn throat and I coughed as I tried to get my shit together real quick.

"I . . . um. Well, I lied," I finally admitted. "I tried to pull a big one on y'all. The only reason I came down here in the first place was to get my hands on Sable's inheritance money. I called the 800 number tryna get next to y'all, and then Bunni got with the dude at the DNA lab and um . . . we paid him five grand to give us a positive match on my blood test."

"Yo!" Barron jumped bad. "Y'all paid that fat bastard Kelvin Merchant? So did I! Man, I oughta kick his ass again! I tore him off *ten grand* to give me a *negative* match on you!"

"Uh-uh." Bunni glared at Barron and shook her head in disgust like we wasn't the ones who scammed Kelvin first. "That's just a shame, Barron," she muttered. "Just a goddamn shame."

I shrugged. "I'm sorry but I didn't know nothing about y'all when I first came down here. I guess I didn't care neither. Me and Bunni was just tired of being broke and we needed some money."

I finally got the nerve to look up at Selah, and even though I saw a whole lotta pain and disappointment in her eyes, I still peeped a little bit of love up in there too.

"Well goddamn!" Viceroy spit. He shook his head like we was a bunch of scandalous-ass crabs. "This shit is worse than I thought! I guess it's your turn," he said, turning to Suge. "What you got for me, bruh?"

My ass got tight as I hoped like hell Suge didn't tell everybody we'd been swerving. But Big Suge never even blinked as he flipped his toothpick around in his sexy mouth and shrugged.

"Nothing, bruh. I ain't got shit."

Viceroy nodded as he turned to Selah. "What about you, baby? You got anything you need to come clean on?"

Bunni reached under the table and pinched *the shit* outta me and for once I wasn't mad at her! I just knew all hell was gonna break loose when Mama Selah fessed up about her nasty lil fling with Rodney Ruddman, but instead of spilling them big ol' beans mami pursed her lips and shook her head all prissy and proper-like.

I thought about that bad-ass diamond engagement ring that Viceroy had bought Mama Selah, and about that rich-ass fool who had banged the shit outta Dy-Nasty and then tossed the ring off to her like it was a trinket of trash.

Sheiit, I knew damn well mama-duke wasn't gonna tell all that!

“I’m good, Viceroy,” Selah finally said eyeing him coolly as she gave him a small smile. “How about you, dear? Do you have anything you need to tell us?”

Viceroy shook his head real quick and grilled her right back. “Nah, baby,” he said, holding both his hands up in the air. “They washed me so good up in that hospital that I’m clean, sugar. I’m squeaky clean.”

Selah’s eyes glinted as she gave him another sweet little smile.

“Good. Because so am I.”

I glanced at Selah and she gave me a quick wink. I sat there and beamed. Like mother like daughter. I was proud of her ass! Shit, she was a damn good liar too!

CHAPTER 37

Being a Dominion was da bomb and being rich was even better! It seemed strange not to wake up every morning with a brand-new hustle or a scheme on my brain, but now that my pockets were permanently swole I didn't have to plot on a damn thing!

And after all that lying, stealing, wheeling, and double-dealing we did, none of us ended up getting the three hundred grand a year we were hoping for, but we did get Papa Viceroy back from the dead, and for a broke-ass chick from Harlem I didn't do too bad.

Every year for the whole eighteen years I'd been gone, Viceroy and Selah had stashed fifty large in a bank account that had been opened especially for me. And just two weeks after I was officially declared to be Sable Dominion and the word FOUND was stamped over my picture on all those posters and milk cartons, over nine hundred grand, plus interest, was transferred into my bank account without a single damn string attached!

As bad as I had been feenin' and fantasizing about being rich, now that I had a shitload of cash at my fingertips I couldn't think of a damn thing to with all that loot! Bunni got it in her mind that she wanted to open up her some kinda head shop and that we should fly out to LA and get us one of them reality shows, and she had producers out the ass blowing up our phones tryna make us a deal.

Viceroy had gone back to work at Dominion Oil full-time, and Selah was back volunteering at her lil charities and rich people's functions just like she was doing before I came barging into their lives and slinging shit all over the fan.

Believe it or not, things between me and Barron had changed too.

"Mama wants me to quit with all the guilt now that we got you back home in the fold," he told me one day.

"Hell yeah," I waved him off. "Give that shit up, dude! You ain't really lose me anyway."

"Oh, I lost you," he said, and I couldn't believe the way his eyes got all sad. "But I'm glad I found you too. I really dug being your big brother back in the day when we were little kids, Mink. And I'm gonna do my best to learn how to start digging you—and looking at you—as a sister again. Just a *sister.*"

Life with the Dominions was turning out to be all that, and I was starting to feel Dallas a lil bit more, but every now and then I missed the fast pace of New York City. I didn't miss it enough to take my ass back to Harlem and risk running into that fool Gutta, but it was good to have the *Dominion Diva* waiting right outside, because me, Dane, and Bunni zipped to Miami, Atlanta, and even Los Angeles to party on the regular.

The one thing that had been bugging the shit outta me and Bunni both though, was Peaches. He was living in our old apartment all by himself, and even though I broke him off some real nice ends and sent them to him through Western Union every two weeks, Harlem was a cut-throat town and that nigga Gutta had Peaches bobbin' and duckin' and lookin' over his shoulder left and right because of me.

Bunni got fed up with all that shit, and she just broke down one day and poured her heart out to Viceroy.

"Hey now, Daddy-O," she told him as he sat in the parlor after work sipping on a stiff one. "I needs me a little hook-up, okay? My brother Paul is up in New York and I miss him a whole lot. This is a real big house. You think he could stay with us for a lil while until I get on my feet and find me a place?"

"Your brother?" Viceroy looked kinda faded. "You want him to come stay here?"

Bunni nodded.

Viceroy picked up his drink and chugged it. "I don't know, Bunni. We just got rid of a lotta drama up in here you know."

"Uh-uh!" Bunni blurted. "My brother ain't about no drama! He's a man's man, Papa Doo! For real though! He's one of the chillest cats I know. C'mon, Pops. Just let him come stay for a little while?"

Viceroy had barely nodded his head good when Bunni plopped her ass down on his lap, grabbed his chin, and put two wet smack-smacks on his cheek.

"Thanks, Papa-Doo! I don't care what kinda yang your stank daughter Mink be talking about you! You is one cool-ass dude to me!" She hopped off his lap and jetted across the room.

"Just wait till you meet my brother!" she gushed, grinning like hell. "I swear to God you're gonna love him!'"

Bunni snatched the front door open and hollered, "Yo, Peaches! It's all good, baby! Papa Viceroy said you can stay! Come on in!"

I almost fell outta my chair when Peaches pranced through the door styling pussy-pink from the top of his Glama-Glo wig all the way down to his big twisted toenails! At six feet five and clocking two-fitty, he stood wobbling in a pair of bright pink drag-queen pumps and his pink satin Fendi dress looked like it had been sewn together from two extra-large tents!

"What the *hell*?" Viceroy caught a look at him and jumped up off the couch so fast he spilled his drink all over his hand. "This is your goddamn *brother*?"

"Errm-herrm," Peaches said, flinging his weave back as he pranced through the door dragging his suitcases and batting his fake eyelashes in a cloud of sweet perfume.

"Your *brother*?" Viceroy hollered again, and then squinched his eyes closed real tight and hollered, "Damn, damn, *damn*!"

AND THEN . . .

Viceroy Dominion sat at his desk shuffling through a huge stack of papers. A lot of shit had transpired while he was stretched out in a coma, but he wasn't the trusting type so no matter how long it took him he was gonna read through every single business document that his company had generated while he was gone.

He glanced around his large, luxurious office. He was a task-master who demanded maximum effort from his staff at all times, and he was surprised to see so many of them were actually happy to have him back.

He looked down at the mess on his desk. There were stacks of get-well cards that he hadn't gotten a chance to open yet, bouquets of flowers, and boxes of candy from his account holders and business associates. Even the inbox on his e-mail account was jam-packed with virtual good wishes from all over the country.

Viceroy clicked a button and scanned his personal incoming e-mail folder. There were tons of unread messages in his box, but the "from" address on one stood out boldly.

Moving his mouse, he clicked on the e-mail and opened it up. Viceroy frowned as he stared at a photo of a virtual box of limited edition Gurkha Black Dragon cigars that his arch-enemy and major business rival, Rodney Ruddman, had sent him.

"That cheap bastard," he muttered. A box of the real ones came soaked in cognac and cost over a hundred grand. The seven cigars shown were stacked like a pyramid, with three on each side, and one in the middle.

Suddenly Viceroy leaned toward the computer screen and peered closely at the cigar in the middle. He felt his heart thump. He knew he wasn't seeing what the fuck he thought he was seeing! He *couldn't* have been seeing what he thought he was seeing. He better fuckin' *not* be seeing what he thought he was seeing!

He clicked on the "view" tab at the top of his screen and then zoomed in on the picture and magnified it by fifty percent.

And there it was. Selah's very first engagement ring. The one he had bought her right after he stole his first million dollars. The ring that she claimed she had lost after that trip to New York City. Yep, there it was. Glittering like a muthafucka! Slid halfway down the base of the top cigar like it was still on her goddamn finger!

A look of rage crossed Viceroy's face when the cold reality that Rodney Ruddman had his wife's ring hit him and shook him all the way to his bones.

"No the fuck she didn't!" Viceroy hollered as his blood boiled over. He pushed away from his desk and jumped up so fast that his chair toppled over and fell to the floor behind him.

"I'ma kill that bitch!" he roared as he pictured that fat fuck Ruddman holding Selah's legs up in the air. Blinded, Viceroy swung his arm in a wide arc and smacked his computer screen right off the desk. The monitor crashed down to the floor and so did his telephone, all his framed photos, about twenty gold-plated pens, and over a thousand sheets of company paper.

Just watch, Selah had once said. *I'm gonna pay you back with your worst fucking enemy!*

"That dirty rotten *liar*! I'ma fuck her ass *up*!" Viceroy screeched, diving off the deep end of fury as he started tossing his whole damn office up. The sound of footsteps storming toward his office rose in the air as his panicked staff rushed in to see what the hell was going on.

"I swear to God I'm gonna *kill* that bitch!" Viceroy hollered. He stomped his foot and crunched the shit outta him and Selah's wedding photo as his administrative staff burst through the door and swarmed all around him.

"Y'all better hold me back!" he hollered. "I swear to God y'all better hold me back! 'Cause when I get next to that bitch I'm gonna kill her! I'm gonna fuckin' *kill* her!"

A READING GROUP GUIDE

DIRTY ROTTEN LIAR

Noire

About This Guide

The discussion questions that follow are included to enhance your group's reading of the book.

Discussion Questions

1. Con-mami Mink LaRue has been on one helluva misadventure. Why in the hell was her "mother" Jude Jackson so bent on Big Moe LaRue? How different do you think Mink's life would have been if her father had lived?

2. Jude Jackson was the mother of all liars. Was it understandable that she saw a baby who looked like the man she loved and then "snatched her up" so she could give Big Moe something no other woman could give him?

3. How did you feel when you found out that Mink was in that car when Jude drove it off the dock? What kind of woman makes desperate moves just to keep a playa in her pocket?

4. At the age of thirteen Mink was traumatized and nearly killed by the one person who was supposed to love and protect her above all others. Does that horrible experience explain her "gotta get minez" mentality?

5. Aunt Bibby might have been a trip and a half, but when it came down to Jude's foolishness, she knew what she was talking about. Was Mink's aunt just another hatin'-ass LaRue, or was she down for whatever when it came to Mink? Do you think Bibby did the right thing by telling Mink the truth about her birth mother and her twin? Is it possible to love a family member without really *liking* them all that much?

6. Barron lusted after two things: Mink and money. Was he crazy for dumping Carla and falling for Pilar? And even

though he and Pilar weren't blood related, did the fact that they were breaking down beds throw up flags for you?

7. Pilar was the type of spoiled, conniving diva who thought the world owed her everything. Tell the truth. Were you hollering, "Good for your ass!" when she landed in that wet puddle and found out about Dy-Nasty and Ray?

8. Bunni Baines is a true ride-or-die. She's Mink's ace in the hole and her straight-up rowdy. Now that Mink is rich and rolling in cheese, what do you think she should do for Bunni? Tear her off half of her inheritance? Set her up with her own crib and her own business? Bunni definitely earned her stripes. What should she get out of this crazy misadventure?

9. Selah was an elegant and classy socialite. How did you feel when you realized she had a little freak in her and was getting her illegal swerve on? Should she have accepted Rodney's offer and kicked Viceroy to the curb? Was her fling with Rodney just a physical thing? Do you want to see her and Viceroy get past their little bedroom issue and get to tearing up some sheets?

10. You could tell that Viceroy had bumped his head from the minute he woke up, and it seems like he got up just in time too. What kind of changes do you think he should make at Dominion Oil? He's been kind of moody lately and it seems like he's reverted back to his good old hood days. Since the Dominions are stupid rich and they'll never run out of money, is it time for Viceroy to step out of the way and let somebody else take over so he can chase his wife and count his cash?

11. Smoove Uncle Suge is a real bronco-buster. Mink is really feeling this dude and he's damn sure feeling her too. Now that Mink is family, is their little love thang out the window? When did it go from being just sex to "a whole lot more" between the two of them, and should a little DNA test stand in the way of true love?

12. Dy-Nasty got totally busted in all her little schemes, and when she was declared to be Sable, she gave everybody, especially Mink, her ass to kiss. True, she was a fraudster, a grifter, and a dirty rotten liar, but she wasn't no worse than Mink! What do you want to see happen to Dy-Nasty now that the feds have knocked her? Should somebody in the family feel sorry for her and help pull her ass out of a hole, or should she catch the maximum charge possible and get flushed straight down the pipes?

13. At the end of this misadventure, Mink finds herself paid out the ass and living the good life. No more stripping, no more capers, no more scandalous double-crossing schemes are required. How do you think living in luxury and having endless loot will affect her? Will con-mami Mink LaRue change her ways and elevate up out of the trenches, or will her mind-set—and her hustle—stay grimy forever?

What happens when beautiful, twenty-year-old petty thief and ex-stripper Mink LaRue finds out she's a dead ringer for the age-progressed photo of the missing oil heiress Sable Dominion?

Find out in

Natural Born Liar
by Noire

Turn the page for an excerpt from Natural Born Liar. . . .

CHAPTER 1

The Rip-Off

Pussy sold for pennies on the dollar on Friday nights in Harlem, and if you were looking for a couple of hot whirly-whirlies, then Club Wood was damn sure the place to be. Located on a busy corner off 125th Street, Wood stayed packed out with coochie-sniffin' niggas who were deep on the prowl, and some of the baddest bitches in the city of New York stripped, danced, and hosted private fuck-fests in the club's back rooms.

I had twirled around the strip poles earlier in the day, but I was taking the night off so I could collect some dough from a mark that me and my best friends, Peaches and Bunni, had recently ganked.

We'd schemed up a plan to lure a switch-hittin' old head into a motel room, then we snapped a bunch of shots of him sporting a sexy red bra and taking some real thick pipe up his ass.

Dude was a high-profile principal at a private boys' school and he didn't want no trouble. He didn't want no publicity neither, and in less than five minutes he had agreed to give up twenty g's to stop a picture of his hairy balls from being posted to his teenaged daughter's Facebook page.

The lick had gone down perfectly, and I was chillin' at the bar sipping slut juice and congratulating myself for a job well done when outta nowhere I caught a funny vibe.

Something wasn't right.

I got the feeling I was being watched. I had a bag full of blackmail dough slung over my shoulder, and something in my gut told me to get the fuck up outta Dodge.

I slid down from the barstool and broke for the door, but Hova's latest banga came on, and every pole freak in the house broke out in a mass stanky stroll. The strippers jumped down from the stage and hit the floor rolling hard, booties twerkin', hips grindin', stroking their pussies and sending a wave of horny niggas rushing down the aisles straight toward me.

WHO GON' STOP ME? WHO GON' STOP ME, HUH?

I crashed into about thirty sweaty niggas as I pushed through the crowd and tried to fight my way outside. I was shaking fools offa me left and right as their horny asses pulled me in all directions and tried to feel me up. A few of my regular customers offered to get me toasted, some wanted me to slide over in the corner so we could smoke some yay, and even more begged me to go in the back room and hit 'em with my patented-move, double-hump lap dance.

Somehow I made it past them, and I was *this close* to getting my ass outta there when a strong hand clamped down on my shoulder and a deep voice boomed, "Excuse me, ma'am."

I almost shit. I didn't know if I should turn around swinging or make another break for the door, but I knew I was busted. The twenty racks I had just hustled from that principal felt like a ton of bricks weighing down my bag. This was supposed to be an easy little gank, and I couldn't believe that greasy old dick-rider had called the cops on me!

Getting arrested was gonna be a real big problem for me. I was already on probation for writing bad checks, and a thousand lies flew through my head as I thought about the bus ride to Rikers I was about to take.

"I said, excuse me, ma'am," the voice boomed behind me again, "but is your name Nicki Minaj?"

I spun around so fast my pink-and-blond Chinese bangs swished across my forehead. I eyeballed the hand that was still gripping my shoulder. It sported a five-thousand-dollar platinum Versace ring on the pinkie finger, and I'd seen that fourteen-thousand-dollar Rolex Prince Cellini on sale at a jewelry store on Broadway.

"Oh! My bad." Dude busted a grin as he checked me out. I was styling pussy-pink from the top of my Glama-Glo wig all the way down to my toenails, and it was real obvious that he was feeling my flow. "You look *just like* Mizz Minaj from the back, but you're even finer than she is in the face."

I stunted on him. I was a con-mami, a pole dancer, and under the right circumstances I could be a big-ass thief. A chick like me had ninety-nine hustles but a rap star wasn't one of 'em.

I breathed a sigh of relief as I checked him out right back. Dude was handling his. He had pretty brown skin and real white teeth. His dome was freshly-lined and he stood at least six-five.

My eyes rolled over his gear as I added up his digits. Chocolate-brown Polo shirt, baggy jeans, Cool Grey Jordans. Uh-huh. He was thuggin' it and I was lovin' it. Papa was stackin' some real mean paper and he wasn't shy about flossin' it. I could almost see the fat money knots swelling up in his pockets and the hard piece of wood that was starting to rock up in his drawers too.

"I'm serious." He grinned again and hit me with his dimples. "I didn't mean no disrespect, shawty. You just look so damn fly, so damn . . . *New York*. For real. My bad."

His mistake was understandable because my shit was put

together super-tight. I was rocking Fendi from my diamond-trimmed pink shades down to my tight pink miniskirt. My jewelry was pink mother-of-pearls from Tiffany's, and my pink-polished toenails looked nice and suckable in my peep-toe heels.

"No problem." I grinned and played it sexy-classy. "Men take me for Nicki Minaj all the time."

"Hell, yeah, with that kinda body I bet the fuck they do," he growled. His voice was full of mad appreciation as he introduced himself. "My name is Dajuan," he said. "Dajuan Latrell Sullivan. What's yours?"

"They call me Tasha," I lied, sliding my shades off so he could peep my hazel eyes. "Tasha Pierce."

"Look, I don't mean to come at you, Tasha, but I'm just visiting here tonight. Me and my brother own a club in Philly and we're thinking about opening up a joint around here pretty soon too. You look like you know this city. Can I buy you a drink so we can kick it for a while?"

A businessman? A club owner? I was definitely down for that!

"Nah, I don't think so," I fronted. "I don't drink with strange dudes. For all I know you could be the Harlem River Strangler."

He laughed and pulled out a business card. "I'm a balla, not a killer," he said, passing it to me. "That's real talk. Look, I ain't tryna push up on you, I just want some good conversation, that's all. I ain't askin' you for no lap dance or nothing like that. I got a nice little spot over in the VIP joint, and we can have a few drinks together and then I'll have my driver drop you off anywhere you wanna go. You feelin' that?"

"Your driver?" I played him off, but I had never been the type to turn my back on a knockin' opportunity.

He looked through the glass doors and pointed toward the corner where a shiny black limo was parked right at the curb.

An old white man was sitting behind the wheel, and when Dajuan waved at him the old man smiled and waved back.

I glanced down at his business card. The lights in the club were pretty dim, but I could tell it was made of thick, cream-colored card stock with heavy gold trim. The initials D.L.S. were scripted and embossed in large red letters, and a bunch of other words were printed on it real small.

That right there did it. I felt a rush coming on. God, I loved this fuckin' hustle! Hoodwinking niggas felt as good as the first hit on a crack pipe, and I had to stop myself from squealing with excitement. This Philly fool was gwapped out. Swimming in cream! Did I wanna sit in his VIP booth and have a drink with him? Did a wino piss on the stairs?

I shook my head again. I was wide open but I still had a role to play.

"Nah, I can't. I got other plans for tonight."

I was praying he'd come at me one more time 'cause I just knew his deep-ass pockets were dying to get tricked out.

"So that's how y'all treat company around here? A Philly nigga can't get no Big Apple love?"

My bag was already full of dough, but a hustlin' chick like me was always good for one more con. I did the math in my head as I let Dajuan hold me by my waist and lead me back through the crowd. I was in debt with some real dangerous cats for some real crazy cash, and this was gonna be a great opportunity to get my weight up. Between his watch and his ring alone I could probably rack up at least ten grand at the pawnshop around the corner.

I switched my plump apple ass toward the VIP booth while Dajuan walked behind me watching it move. He seemed like an all right cat, but he was on the young side too. He was fine, but he didn't look like no genius. I was planning on getting his horny ass naked and doing a little dip and zip. Peaches and Bunni were expecting me to show up at the crib soon, and

I figured I could lure Dajuan into the hotel next door and get the whole bizz over and done with in less than an hour.

I slid into the VIP booth just a' crackin' up inside. Somebody's mama shoulda warned him about pickin' up strangers 'cause this was about to be a mismatch. But what the hell *ever*! Niggas these days were just beggin' to get got, and even with a pocketbook full of cash I could always find time to roll an unsuspecting mark with nothing but pussy on his brain!

Coming soon

Millionaire Wives Club
by Tu-Shonda L. Whitaker

Four deliciously dramatic divas bask in the attention of their own hit reality TV show, *The Millionaire Wives Club*. But the spotlight isn't always so flattering. . . .

Turn the page for an excerpt from *Millionaire Wives Club* . . .

The Club

Millions of dollars in premier fashions and champagne diamonds were on display at Manhattan's 40/40 Club as four ultrarich and ubersuccessful women—America's newest addition to reality TV—strolled the red carpet and smiled at the flashing lights of the paparazzi. The clicking of their designer stilettos was like exquisite steel-pan beats as they crossed the club's threshold, and the sultry sounds of Maxwell's live performance filled the air. Despite their individual insecurities and doubts, at this moment as they sauntered into the sunrise of superstardom, what mattered most was that they'd gotten their own piece of the latest in rich bitch candy.

"Ladies, ladies," a reporter from *E! News* said, motioning for the four of them to come together and meet him across the room. "Can you all tell us a little about yourselves?" He looked at the woman to his left. "May we start with you?"

"I'm Milan Starks, wife of the great Yusef 'Da Truef' Starks, number twenty-three on the New York Knicks." A lovely mix of her cinnamon brown Dominican father and golden-skinned African American mother, Milan had an effortless beauty that didn't require makeup or facials to be perfect. She had a Marilyn Monroe mole on the corner of her top lip, hazel eyes, and her Beyoncé-like hips were a size ten, twelve at most, and she had a true apple bottom.

"Wasn't he suspended?" Evan Malik said and then quickly covered her mouth."Oh, my apologies, I didn't mean to say that."

"He was suspended," the reporter said, following up on Evan's comment."Do you want to tell us how you feel about that?" he asked Milan.

"My husband is a great man." Milan smiled. "Sure, he hit a rough patch, but he's on his way back and will be better than ever."

"Thank you, Mrs. Starks, now on to you, Mrs. Malik," he said to Evan. "Is it true that you were the first to be cast for the show?"

Milan shifted her weight from one Christian Louboutin python pump to the other, praying the nausea she felt as she sized up Evan would go away. Evan stood five eleven, fabulously slender, a figure-eight shape, and skin the color of butterscotch. Her hair was cut in a short and spiky Halle Berry–inspired 'do with touches of honey blond that glimmered in the spotlights.

Milan hated that she and Evan had ended up in the same circle, because every time she saw Evan, heard Evan's voice, and was in her presence, Milan was forced to deal with the fact that Evan had won. Evan had ended up with the only man who made Milan feel true love was obtainable: Kendu. But since image was everything in this business, Milan planned to do her damnedest and pretend that they were all friends, even if the knife she had for Evan's back weighed down her Chloé clutch.

"Why of course, sweetie," Evan said. "Who wouldn't want to start with me?" She winked.

"It's been five minutes," Chaunci Morgan, Milan's neighbor and one of the four costars, whispered to Milan while maintaining a smile, "and already I'm sick of this bitch. Did she forget that she was a video ho?"

"Seems so," Milan whispered back.

"Excuse you." Jaise Williams, Evan's friend and their costar, turned toward Milan and then eyed Chaunci. "What did you just say?" she snapped.

"I said that she looks fabulous." Milan smiled at Evan. "She gives retired video hos, I mean vixens, a good name."

"Umm-hmm," Chaunci added, snapping her fingers in a Z motion. "A true fashionista. You better work it, girl."

"So, Mrs. Malik," the reporter said, "tell the world who you are and what it means to be on the show."

Evan paused. The microphone pointed toward her and the spotlights shining in her face caused her to draw a blank. There was no way she could say, "*Millionaire Wives Club* is a last-ditch effort to save my life, something to keep me busy and silence the self-destructive thoughts running through my mind." And she definitely couldn't say, "I may be married to Kendu Malik, linebacker for the New York Giants, but it's an unending struggle holding on to the motherfucker."

"Mrs. Malik," the reporter interrupted her thoughts, "is everything okay? Do you want to fill us in?"

Evan blinked and shot him a Barbie-doll smile. "I am a beautiful wife"—she arched her eyebrows—"an outstanding mother, and I have the talent and the foresight to seize the moment. And being on the show will allow all women to see what it takes to be me."

"And what exactly does that mean?" the reporter probed.

"What she means," Chaunci mumbled to Milan, "is that she thinks us peons are pissed that we didn't hit the same groupies party that she did."

Milan tried not to laugh, but then couldn't hold it in any longer, and when she looked at Chaunci they both cracked up, neither one of them stopping until they noticed everyone standing around them was silent.

"Oh," the producer, Bridget, said to them, batting her eyes, "don't stop on the boom mic's accord. For ratings' sake, carry on."

Milan was embarrassed; the last thing she wanted was for her and Chaunci to be seen as the troublemaking pair. "I'ma, ummm"—Milan pointed to the bar—"go and have a drink."

"I'll join you," Chaunci said, as Bridget motioned for the camera guy, Carl, to follow them.

Once they were at the bar and had ordered their drinks, Carl tapped Chaunci on the shoulder. Both she and Milan turned around. "When I cut the camera on, tell us what happened over there. Why'd you say those things?"

He turned the camera on and pointed it at them. "Evan works my nerves," Chaunci said, popping her lips. "I've known her for three days, since we met at the studio, and already she's been in my life too long." She shot Milan a high five. "And believe me, as editor in chief of *Nubian Diva* magazine everyone knows that I'm too classy to lose my cool, but trust me, I will not hesitate to tap dat ass." She pointed toward Evan.

"But since this is a nice place," Milan interrupted as she sipped her drink, "we're not gon' tear it up."

"So we're just going to sit here." Chaunci crossed her legs.

"And enjoy our evening," Milan added.

"Thanks, ladies." Carl smiled and turned away.

Jaise stared at the *E! News* reporter, wondering how she should introduce herself to the world. Should she tell people the made-for-TV parts of her life story or should she lower the boom, let 'em know the truth, and maybe, just maybe, some sanity-teetering superwoman somewhere would understand that this single-mother-doing-her-thing bullshit was overrated?

She stood next to Evan and her eyes shifted from the people mingling across the room to the reporter standing before them. Her open-toed pencil heels were aching her feet, and she wondered why she had committed to doing reality TV, especially when her postdivorce resolution was no drama. Yet here she was drowning in it. All because she and Evan had sworn that cable's *Millionaire Wives Club* was the new bling they needed to rock.

It was public knowledge that Jaise had married and divorced ex–heavyweight champion Lawrence Williams, but she wondered if anyone knew how much she had suffered in silence during their marriage. She'd been slapped, punched, kicked, and humiliated, almost daily, by her ex. And if people didn't know it, would revealing it make hers a story of empowerment or weakness?

Then again, maybe she would look like a shero if she revealed how she had walked out on Lawrence by placing a sedative in his nightly shot of Hennessey, waited for him to drift to sleep, grabbed her son, and then escaped to a battered woman's shelter.

But she had been married to him for seven years and never once publicly complained. There was no way she could now admit before the world that a man with money had clouded her judgment. And since some shit was better left unsaid, Jaise stood there, waited for Evan to finish, and when the reporter turned to her she had her intro down pat.

"Mrs. Williams," the reporter said, "can you tell us a little about yourself? We hear that you're superwoman. A single mom, the owner of the online Shabby Chic antique business—you seem to be doing it all."

"Superwoman," Jaise responded, laughing, "is a myth." She flung her emerald-and-rhodium-draped wrist. "But I am handling money and power quite well." She chuckled a bit. "I'm just so excited to be in the company of some remarkable women."

Once Jaise was done the reporter shook the ladies' hands

and said, "Good interview, ladies. Now I need to go and speak to your costars."

As he turned away Jaise let out a sigh of relief. She sat down at one of the tables and lit a cigarette, and Evan sat across from her. As Jaise eased her feet from her four-inch heels, she said, "I hope I can survive this shit." She looked at Evan and took a pull. "I keep thinking and rethinking what to say and what not to say." She let out the smoke. "I swear somebody is going to think I'm crazy."

"Girl," Evan said, as she watched Milan and Chaunci laugh and converse at the bar, "just be yourself."

"Be myself?" Jaise smirked. "Yeah, right."

"No seriously, I mean, hell, I have no problems being me. I meant what I said to the reporter."

"Well, I'm not that put together. I'm stressed and sometimes I feel beat down. And you know that's too real for TV."

"It's *reality TV,*" Evan insisted. "Speak to the camera as if you were talking to me."

Jaise laughed. "Okay, I'ma relax this bill collector's voice, put on my Brooklyn-mami twang, and say, 'I'm so goddamn tired of faking the funk. The truth is my sixteen-year-old son needs a man to call daddy and, hell, I do too.' "

Evan laughed, but her eyes were on Milan. She couldn't help but wonder what Milan had that she didn't. Why had Kendu chosen Milan for his best friend and why was Milan able to touch places and parts of Kendu that he wouldn't dare let Evan into? Kendu's rejection of her had steadily become Evan's obsession.

"What are you thinking about?" Jaise asked Evan once she realized she'd lost her attention. Jaise followed Evan's gaze to Chaunci and Milan. "Fuck them."

"That's it!" Bridget unexpectedly walked over to their table and said, "That's the spirit. Fuck them, and just so you know, they just finished calling you two a buncha rats' asses."

"What?" Jaise said, slipping her shoes back on. "They don't even know me."

"And from the sound of it," Bridget said, "they don't want to."

"Let's go and straighten this out." Jaise looked at Evan as she rose from her chair.

"Sit down," Evan warned Jaise. "I wouldn't give those low-budget bitches the satisfaction."

"Low-budget"—Bridget grabbed a napkin and a pen and scribbled down what Evan had just said—"bitch-es."

"I thought most producers didn't get involved with the cast," Evan snapped.

Bridget, who resembled a redheaded Heidi Klum, smiled and tossed her red hair over her shoulders. "Meet the new and improved way to produce."

"Anyway," Evan said, looking back at Jaise, "we have more going for us than to argue with a pair of half-dollar hos."

"So what makes you different from all the other women?" the *E! News* reporter asked Chaunci.

Chaunci did her best to hold a steady smile and act sober considering she and Milan had had one too many shots of Patrón and glasses of white wine. Milan smiled sweetly, knowing that if her friend said even one word it was sure to be slurred.

"Well," Chaunci attempted to speak in a steady tone, although her being tipsy was evident, "what makes me different is that I have my own, and all the rest of these women are uppity skeezers on the stroll." She turned to Milan: "No offense." Turning back toward the reporter she continued, "I'm not upset with them, though, not one bit. What woman wouldn't want to marry well?"

"But then they'd have to worry about groupies," Milan managed to add without slurring.

"Any advice about that?" the reporter asked.

Chaunci laughed. "Certainly, I have some advice. As soon as some groupie comes shakin' it around your man, bust a cap in her ass and then put one in him. Shit, I can't say he won't cheat, but make sure he's a handicap motherfucker doin' it. All right." She and Milan exchanged high fives again.

"So what do you think people will learn from the show?" the reporter asked Chaunci.

"That when these Joneses come down"—she sipped her drink with one hand and pointed her index finger with the other—"it's gon' be a motherfucker."

"And there you have it." The *E! News* reporter turned to face the camera. "I present to you the ladies of *Millionaire Wives Club.* Stay tuned!"